AN EMBITTERED
WITCH

WITCH KIN CHRONICLES, BOOK 6

E M GRAHAM

An Embittered Witch

Copyright © 2023 by E M Graham

Ebook ISBN 9781990667053

Print ISBN: 9781990667213

CHAPTER 1

Jet-lagged from the overnight to Edinburgh via London, I was crooked and cranky, the carry-on dragging behind me like a stone. I was ready to scream at the doddering pace of the passengers sleepwalking their way up the ramp while my stomach growled an order for coffee and food. The welcome scent of coffee brewing and the sugary hint of flaky pastry lured me to dodge and weave my way forward. When I finally saw the small coffee bar outside the Arrivals gate, my stomach churned, but not in a good way.

Margaret was perched at a small table in the Starbucks.

I awkwardly rolled my carry-on over to her table and paused, waiting. She didn't look at me, just sniffed as she stuck that patrician nose in the air as if waiting for an apology. Anyone watching us would have no problem seeing who had been responsible for the breakdown in the relationship between Margaret and myself.

As it turned out, someone was watching. With the Kin, of course, someone was always spying.

'There you are, finally,' she said, as if I was late for a pre-arranged meeting.

'Margaret.'

She sat there with her latte on the laminate table top before her, looking out of place in the modern plastic surroundings. A flick of her gloved hand indicated I should take a seat across from her. Her mid-calf tweed skirt and jacket flawlessly matched her tall brown equestrian boots and the draped shawl edged with fur. She tossed her long red hair back over her shoulder. She was nailing the 'forties vamp look that day.

A picture of the cartoon figure Jessica Rabbit came to mind, and I giggled, I couldn't help it. Lack of sleep does that, takes out all the filters in my head.

She drew herself up, offended, and spit the words out. 'This is your last chance. You need to come away, walk away from the Kin. Today.'

'Really, Margaret? I thought you'd already given me my last chance. Six months ago, wasn't it?'

Seeing her in an airport of all places, it was disconcerting. Margaret Forsythe had no need of clumsy mechanical transport, for she could transport herself across the globe with little more effort than a flick of an eye. She still hadn't shared how that was possible, and I'd long since given up hope that she would ever show me. After all, I'd chosen to remain with the Kin, to build my life here and follow my ambitions on the narrow Kin path instead of becoming a drifter, outside the law. Like her. I hadn't thought she would ever forgive me for that decision. Yet oddly enough, here she was.

I slumped into the seat across from her.

Rather than answer my question, she stared across at me, sipping from the frothy drink. The deep red of her lipstick didn't stain the rim of her paper cup.

I waited.

'You're your own worst enemy,' she finally declared.

Again I waited, merely raising my eyebrows while wishing I'd had the presence of mind to get my own coffee before confronting her. She would have waited, for the script was already written in her head. Cue entrance of Dara, and action.

But I refused to say my lines and play in her drama. Yes, I knew how to push her buttons.

'It's all going to go to hell.' She glared at me as if it was my fault. 'If you don't act.'

'What? What's the matter now?' I placed my elbows on the table and rubbed at my temples.

She held on to the table edge with both hands as she leaned forward.

'The situation has changed. Drastically.'

'Margaret, whatever bee is presently buzzing round inside your bonnet, it'll have to wait. I'm on my way to the Outer Hebrides to celebrate Hogmanay with Hugh and his family. Can we revisit this, whatever it is, in the New Year?'

She ignored my plea. 'As you well know, Cate's been delving into music.'

I shook my head. My mind must really have been fuzzy because her words weren't making sense. 'Yeah, she's been off on some course somewhere for the past few months. Music, was it? That's good. Peaceful. She hasn't been bothering me.'

The little black stud Cate had placed in my ear hadn't itched at all in the past few months. Hope had sprouted a hesitant tendril in me - hope that my father's ex-wife had forgotten about her cat-and-mouse games with me.

Margaret leaned forward to hiss her next words at me. 'With her new powers that she stole from the ley lines? You really believe anything about that witch is harmless? Peaceful, even?'

'What's the big deal? How does this impact me? Or more to the point, I should ask how it affects you, because I don't think you give two damns about me.'

'It affects me, because she will use you to get at me,' she said. 'Don't you see that?'

'Cate doesn't care about you, Margaret!' I pushed myself away from the table as I stood up, not an easy or graceful feat as the seat was fused to the table and it involved a bit of a squirm. 'She has everything she wants, and now she's finding other ways to amuse herself. Let's not draw attention to ourselves.'

I'd learned early on to fly under the radar of Cate's wrathful glare.

Margaret shook her head resolutely. I stared at her through my puffy, sleep deprived eyes. All I wanted was a nice quiet life, working my way up through the Kin on my own merits in order to achieve the lifestyle and recognition I'd always craved. Although Cate had already interfered with that.

'What's that in your ear?' Her sharp eyes missed nothing, even the tiny black adamantite earring. It wasn't like it was flashy or shiny in the light. No, the matte ebony of it sucked in light like a black hole.

I'd tried to remove it, but the front and back were fused together. The only way to rid myself of it would be to rip my ear off and that wasn't going to happen.

She stood up and rounded the table in a flash, brushing my hair aside so she could examine it. I shook her off.

'It's too late.' Her whispered rush of words and the furrow between her fine brow was the closest I'd ever seen to panic in Margaret. 'Come with me. Now. I can remove it for you.'

'Leave me alone.' I turned away from her, feeling the heat of shame coloring my face. It was my own fault, I'd allowed Cate to manipulate me into this. At her beck and call, a hostage to her, really. Yes, I knew things about her she didn't want known, but whose version would the Kin believe? Dara Martin de Teilhard, the renegade half-witch, or Cate, the Huxor, the matriarch of one of the wealthiest Kin families in the New World?

'It's no use,' I said to Margaret wearily.

Her large green eyes stared at me for a moment longer, then with a huff she suddenly spun on her heel, heading toward the nearest door. It happened to lead to the Gents. Again, Margaret was running away from me again, but this time without even a 'so long' or a nasty word.

From the corner of my eye, I could see many heads turned to watch her exit. Mostly men, openly gawking in admiration at the loveliness that was Margaret Forsythe in her long boots of the supplest leather and her polished face. But there was one man, I noted, one man whose eyes narrowed in recognition. He started as if to run after her.

Kin. Of course they were watching.

'Wait, Margaret!' Was I asking her to wait, to take me with her, or perhaps to wait, to more fully explain what the hell she'd been on about. No matter. By the time I'd pushed the swinging door open to the men's toilet, she was gone. Literally disappeared.

The Kin spy arrived at the door right after me. He was a youngish man, a Scots Kin I guessed, unmistakably aristocratic with his sweep of blond hair and freckles splattered across that long nose. He had a familiar look about him, though I couldn't say if I'd ever seen him before. But then again, the aristocratic Kin families were so inbred after countless generations of intermarrying that they all looked alike. He pushed past me into the Gents.

Pushing each cubicle door open so hard they banged against the stalls, he searched the washroom. The clanging echoed off the cold white tiled walls.

'Fuck.' The look he shot me was pure venom. 'She's gone.'

'What did you expect?' I leaned against the nearest sink and crossed my arms. Damned Kin spy.

'Not for her to disappear into thin air.' His eyes burned bright blue, startling in their vividness. 'What did you say to her to make her leave?'

That was rich, coming from a Kin spook. 'What makes you think it was me? Maybe she saw you and didn't like the look of you.' Him with his haughty nose and public school accent overlaid with a bit of Scots burr and chock full of privilege. The same stock Margaret came from, but she had forsworn all of it. Except for the trust fund, of course.

'Where did she go?'

'If I knew,' I sneered. 'I certainly wouldn't tell you.' On that note, I pushed myself away from the sink and left the room.

Margaret was gone, and there was nothing more I could do about it. I had no way to contact her. I could continue on my journey in peace, finally get that coffee and look for my flight to Stornoway. I took my time, fully aware that the Kin witch was trailing close behind me. He wasn't very good at his spy job.

I dawdled as I passed along the small shops within the airport, and for spite, spent an inordinate amount of time inside the lingerie store. I pretended to examine the fine silks (I balked at the prices for such tiny bits of froth and lace) but all the while I kept my eyes on him as he lingered against a half wall divider.

Who had directed him to follow me? Cate? The Covenanters, who still would not accept my meteoric rise through the Kin ranks?

My so-called overnight success with the Kin. The achievement of all my dreams. Hollow and false, leaving me with a bitter taste in my mouth, for none of it was from my efforts. I hadn't earned a bit of it.

It didn't matter, whoever he was or whoever had sent him. I wouldn't have trusted me either.

I waited as the airline personnel examined my passport and boarding card, and without realizing, heaved a sigh. The gate loomed ahead, the gate to whisk me away to the luxury of Hugh and his family's estate.

My run-in with Margaret had left me disgruntled, unsettled, reminding me of the fraying edges in the fabric of my perfect life.

CHAPTER 2

Hugh's family estate was an actual castle, with a turret and all. The window seat of the round tower looked out upon the lands which would be mine at some point, after our marriage. The moors and fields with the gray ocean beyond, and the wind. Oh my Christ, the constant wind at the tip of this island at the edge of the world. It never let up.

The Duchess was preparing for the New Year's party in this freezing pile of stones. The only warmth to be found was if you practically stood inside the gigantic fireplace with the burning Yule log.

It was so different here from the Winter Solstice and the quiet Christmas with Mom and Edna and Mark, and of course Jon, my father. That had been cozy with my loved ones all around, the smell of Mom's gingerbread baking, the fresh cut tree all hung with decorations I'd cherished all my life. The finishing touch was the velvet patchwork stockings hanging on the mantle for everyone.

But now, my presence had been requested to celebrate New Year's at Hugh's family estate. I still couldn't pronounce the name of it, let alone spell it. In Scotland, Hogmanay was the big seasonal celebration, and it was an honor for me to attend. Hugh had explained the history behind it, the Covenanters' influence and their dour refusal to embrace generosity of spirit or anything that smacked of happiness. At least that was my take on it, but then again, I had reason to bear a grudge against that crowd of joyless bastards.

Speaking of which, I hadn't spotted the tail assigned to me on the flight to Stornoway.

I made myself ready for that evening's party. The noisy thrum of private helicopters had vibrated through the panes of glass in the windows all afternoon, delivering guests from the neighboring islands for the celebration. Despite the chill from the stone walls, Hugh's mother had made the castle welcoming, and the Victorian wing of the medieval castle was all decked out for the big Hogmanay ball. Huge logs burned in the oversized fireplaces in the public rooms, while pine boughs imported from Norway decorated every door jamb. There was even a Christmas tree tucked away in a small corner. When I first saw it, my thought was that they'd placed it there in my honor so that I wouldn't feel homesick.

I lingered by that small pine tree, the perfectly shaped triangle from a commercial farm somewhere in England no doubt. I brushed the long soft needles with my fingers. The only decorations were a series of opalescent crystal balls ranging in size from as small as my thumb to larger than a teacup. Each one was so delicate it floated in the merest draft. My slight movement set them all vibrating against the needles, and I listened closely to hear their music, barely discernable in the growing hum from the merrymaking in the next room.

Each perfect ball rang with its own pure tone, faint as it was. I lightly touched each one in turn, listening carefully. All were like crystal notes to my ear, but one stood out. Yes, that small one near the top, it hummed with a note that reached into my heart, resounding like a memory forgotten. What were these tiny creations? Who had crafted such perfection?

'Do you like the tree? I thought a little bit of home would be a nice touch for you.'

The tiny black stud in my ear tingled. I recognized her signature scent of lilies and spice wafting in the air. My hand dropped from the crystal spheres and I slowly turned to face my father's ex-wife, the witch who was sponsoring and aiding my ambitious climb within the Kin.

'Cate!' I shrank back a little.

'So pale, Dara, are you not feeling well?'

The blood gone from my face now pounded through my head as my vision narrowed to her face. The one good thing about leaving home was leaving her behind for good. Or so I had thought.

'What are you doing here?' I hissed under the sound of sound of the violins and laughter. Cate's presence on this remote island could not be a good omen.

Arching an eyebrow as if surprised at my uncivilized tone, she replied, 'Celebrating Hogmanay, of course. Like yourself. I had to be in Edinburgh anyway, so I thought, why not nip out to the Sabiston estate to join you for the party?' Her lips curled up in a smile as she added, 'It's a small, small world, isn't it?

Cate extended one bloodred nail to touch the sphere I'd just handled. A whisper of its pure tone sounded again, but differently under her caress, as if it had dropped a half-note, tainted and wrong somehow. 'Aren't these so precious? I had them crafted in a tiny shop in Venice. Each ornament is calibrated to the inner vibrational sounds of a member of the household. The perfect gift for the magical family who has everything. I see you found yours.' She laughed, that cut-glass tinkle that scraped up my spine.

'How is that even possible?'

'Come, let us sit and catch up,' she directed me, ignoring my question. She led us to an oak pew set into the shadow of the grand stairway. 'I hear good things about your progress.'

Resistance was futile. There was no need to tell her anything, as she already knew everything I'd been doing during the past months. I sat in the corner of the ancient bench and stiffly sipped from my champagne flute. The pew had been removed from a Catholic church four hundred or more years ago during the Scourge. The tall back and sides boxed us in, and the heavy carvings cut into my flesh. This pew had never been intended for comfort or ease.

Cate carried on as if we were having a conversation. 'I have been traveling a lot.' Her raven hair glowed in the candlelight that reached us. 'Indulging myself, I must admit, in my studies.'

I tore my gaze away from the crystal spheres on the pine tree and turned my head to her.

'Music,' she declared. 'The power of music and magic. Ever given any thought to that?'

11

I shook my head mutely. Margaret had been worried because Cate was studying music. But it hadn't been piano lessons in her grand living room. Cate had been studying the magical properties of music. A cold chill crept up my spine which had nothing to do with the drafts in this ancient hall.

'Music hath charms to soothe a savage breast,' she quoted. 'And more, I am discovering.'

I felt her eyes turn on me.

'Yes, I've immersed myself in a deep study on the subject, in Italy and Morocco,' she continued. 'Do you know that for everyone, there is a single chord which resonates within our beings? Just like fingerprints, each is unique.'

I stared across the hall to the great mirror which hung opposite. It showed the two of us sitting side by side, perfectly centered, like a portrait within a frame of gilded and fancifully carved wood. The looking glass was old, the edges blackened with the oxidation of time and humidity, lending a dreamlike air to the reflection.

My midnight blue dress echoed my eyes, last summer's tan still evident on my bare arms. It was my only formal gown, the very one I'd worn last June when Cate first approached me. She, in contrast, wore a rich ivory velvet that skimmed her body like ice. With her black hair and eyes, the only relief of color was the splash of red on her lips and nails. I watched as she smiled and leaned her head toward mine.

'The specific chord for each person can also be used to tear a person inside and cause them to spiral to the depths within,' she whispered.

She noticed my attention in the mirror. Her eyes met mine within the silvered depths and her face slowly smiled. 'Mirror, mirror on the wall,' she whispered. 'Who's the greatest witch of all?'

A shiver rippled through my body as I looked into my own eyes. I saw my ambition, all the dreams I'd reached for in my innocence before Cate had taken me under her wing. In that ancient glass, I could see how hollow those desires were, and the price I'd paid for them.

Margaret had been right. Cate had been studying music. Music and magic. But what did this mean? I stiffened against the ice that crept up my spine.

I didn't even notice her leave, for she'd lent no warmth in that drafty hallway.

·····•·•····

'There you are.' Hugh's deep voice brought me back to the world. Sounded like he'd made a head start into the Hogmanay whisky already. He had taken pains to point out to me that it was 'whisky' here in the Outer Hebrides of Scotland, not 'whiskey'. 'Come on, Mum's anxious to introduce you around to the neighbors. It's not every day she gets to show off her new daughter-to-be, and a hero to boot.'

Hero. Dara Martin (de Teilhard), brightest new star in the Kin. I'd come a long way since being the despised half-blood witch in their midst. Feted and even sought after, everyone wanted to know me since I'd saved the ley lines back home last June. They still talked about how I had reached in and woven the strands together again after the Dark Elves had attacked. They didn't know the truth behind the matter, and I wasn't about to tell them.

My hand reached up of its own accord to finger the tiny black stud in my ear, always hidden beneath my hair.

It itched my skin still, like a hive buried deep, but I'd gotten used to the discomfort.

I gave one last glance at Cate's present to his parents, the small Christmas tree with its crystal spheres still shimmering with vibration. The beauty of their sound rang discordant to me now. They were gorgeous, yes, and flashy with their opalescent sheen, but hollow inside. Just like my meteoric rise through the Kin, just like my so-called achievements.

'Hey.' I wrenched my gaze and thoughts back to my fiancé and stood up. I reached for his hand, taking in a deep breath while I did so. His warmth surrounded me. 'Stay close, alright?'

'You have no reason at all to feel nervous,' he whispered. His warm eyes with the glints of gold deep within bathed me in their love and impetuously, he took me in his arms for a hug. 'And the Duke is requesting a dance with you.'

Hugh cut a fine figure in his traditional costume, the wool tartan kilt with a closely fitted black velvet jacket showing off his fine build. With my dark blue frock, we made a handsome pair, except that I still hadn't quite mastered the trick of walking in high heels. But he kept me in his firm grasp, not allowing me to falter as we made our way to the top of the shallow stairway leading down to the ballroom to where his parents waited.

I squeezed his hand in mine, my sweat already greasing the grip. My heart pounded so fast and my knees wobbled so that if not for Hugh's body keeping me upright, I would have swayed. Crowds always jarred my last nerve because the few times I'd been the center of attention were always disastrous.

As we entered the grand room, the Duke harrumphed and hit his crystal glass with the blade of a small ceremonial dagger he'd removed from his wool stocking. The crowd hushed.

'Smile,' Hugh spoke out of the side of his mouth as he nudged me. I must have pasted a passable grimace on my face, for he winked back at me.

The Duke commanded attention. A handsome man, of course, slightly grayed at the temples like an older version of Hugh himself. The overall thickening of his belly, shoulders and neck gave a preview as to how Hugh would look at his age. His mother was blonde and fine featured, an ageless beauty in her long black skirt, white silk blouse and tartan sash. The candlelight from the crystal chandeliers was kind to her, catching the healthy flush to her cheeks that came from a life lived running the Home Farm.

'It's a very special occasion,' Hugh's father said. 'I have the honor of introducing you to Dara, whose fame precedes her.' He paused as the crowd cheered and clapped.

'As you have no doubt heard, this young lady is lauded a heroine in her own land. Her talents and steadfast refusal to allow destruction to the ley lines, even at the risk of her own life, saved the day for the Avalon Kin.'

My blood pounded in my temples now, I could hear the whoosh of it forcing through the veins in my head, and my cheeks flared warmly. Dear Jesus, when would I hear the end of this? If they only knew the truth of what had happened, knew of Cate's treachery, but I couldn't say a word. I forced the smile to stay on my face. My jaw hurt with the effort.

'And I might add, we may have a special announcement coming soon?' The Duke twisted his head to smile at me, his eyebrows arched suggestively. The man had hit the whisky hard too, that was not healthy outdoor living rosiness in his cheeks but the flush of alcohol in an overheated room. He was enjoying himself.

Don't, I silently beseeched him. *Don't bring up the fucking ring.* Hugh and I had talked about marriage, yes, but there was nothing definitive and certainly not for a long time. I didn't want to be forced to accept that heavy, ugly engagement ring here, for to refuse it in front of all their friends and neighbors would have been the height of rudeness.

The Duke turned back to the crowd, and flashed a wink of his eye at them. 'A verra' special announcement,' he continued, but Hugh stepped in to save us both.

'Which will happen all in good time,' he interrupted, the large grin on his face disarming any offense. 'For now, let us drink a toast to Dara and, oh yes, the woman who helped her in the mission.'

He lifted his glass as I followed his eye to the crowd below us.

Cate. Her raven locks gleamed in the candlelight, her pale sharp cheekbones standing out in contrast to the gleaming ruddy faces around her.

She smiled, deftly orchestrating the illusion of a modest blush at this attention, casting shy glances all around as she made her way up the stairs, the train of her ivory gown trailing behind. Cate took Hugh's other arm. It was a good thing he stood between us. It was tempting to push her back down the stairs or...

Hugh felt my tenseness and moved his arm to embrace me, still holding my hand so I was locked within my own grasp like a straitjacket.

'Really.' Cate's voice was low pitched voice but still managed to project to every corner of the hall. 'Thank you, yet it was not my doing, but Dara's. I could only stand behind her and encourage her work. Her immense power and stamina are the reason I sponsored her within the Kin. This young witch will go far under my guidance, for the benefit of all.'

I lifted my glass in a toast like everyone else and tossed the drink down my throat. I was going to need more than this one dram of whisky to get me through the next few hours.

······

The three of us lingered on the staircase after the Duke and Duchess descended into the room to begin the dancing. The orchestra started up again and the room came alive in a whirl of kilts and tartans waltzing through the candlelit night. The whisky and champagne flowed freely now.

'So glad you could make it out here to the island,' Hugh said to Cate. I stayed silent, refusing to even look at her. I knew her for what she was, a treacherous, manipulative viper.

With one arched brow, she purred her words. 'I think someone is not so delighted.'

My jaw clenched as I turned on her, ready to spew my anger, but Hugh spoke before I got a chance.

'Nonsense,' he said, smiling warmly at Cate. 'Dara's a little overwhelmed with the night, that's all. Of course, we're all delighted to see you here. What could be more perfect?'

My back stiffened. I would have a little talk with Hugh later, a small conversation about him not speaking for me or putting words in my mouth, about him not patronizing me...

Cate picked up on my body language even if Hugh was blind. 'And perhaps I'm here to make sure they don't corral you into accepting that behemoth anchor of a ring,' she murmured to us both. 'Not before it's time, anyway.'

The laugh which followed was directed at Hugh, to let him know she was jesting, of course. Her white teeth flashed in the light.

He roared with laughter. 'Yes, Dara, we really dodged that bullet.' He grabbed my hand again. 'Come, our presence is required on the dance floor.'

The night passed in a swirl of dancing and drinking, and I saw no more of Cate after that. It was no use talking to Hugh about her either, at least not till he sobered up the next day. The Scots really took their Hogmanay celebrations seriously.

CHAPTER 3

The next morning after a hearty breakfast, and after most of the guests had melted away, the family donned stout boots and waterproof coats to set out for the obligatory New Year's Day trudge across the moors. I assumed that Cate would have left on the first copter out, anxious to return to the civilization of her Edinburgh hotel.

What was the real reason she'd come to the island? Surely not just to deliver the tree with the extraordinary crystal spheres? More likely, it was a show of her power, deceiving every other witch within the Kin. No one knew the power-hungry Cate like I had the misfortune to know.

Not even my father, Jon, who had been married to her for all those years, knew the depths of her schemes and machinations.

There was little here in the Outer Hebrides that could be of interest to Cate. Except Scarp. And the Crystal Charm Stone. My feet slowed in their rubber boots.

Surely not even Cate would dare to steal more power right under the noses of the Elders on that magical island.

But who would be occupying Scarp over the holiday season to protect the Stone from theft? No one. Not even a shepherd.

She wouldn't, would she? I shivered, and it wasn't just from the damp wind curling around my wet jeans. Then I jerked to a stop. Of course she would. Cate would be that greedy, that power-hungry.

Cate had proven herself to be ambitious beyond measure, even if no one else was aware of her treachery. And I... I couldn't say a thing.

'Why was she really here?' I had to raise my voice against the wind. As I turned my head toward Hugh's, a rogue splatter of rain hit me full on.

'Who?' He had stopped with me, as our arms were linked.

'Cate.' The rain dripped down my face and down inside the neck of my wool sweater.

'Well, she said, didn't she?' He looked up the sheep path to where the rest of the party was quickly charging through the muck, eager to have the mandatory walk over. Hugh's face was pale, paler than I'd ever seen it, possibly tinged with green. Late nights and copious amounts of whisky didn't agree with him, but fortunately Hogmanay only came once a year. 'She was in Edinburgh, and didn't want to spend New Year's alone. What is more natural than for her to join us here?'

He turned back to the path. The caps of the other walkers were disappearing over the top of the last hillock. I allowed myself to be tugged along.

'I don't think she's left yet,' he observed, leaning down closer to my ear. 'The Edinburgh helicopter couldn't make it because of the weather. She may have to stay over again. I can't see her taking the ferry.'

My lips clammed shut. Still here and no signs of her leaving tonight. How perfect for her. But if she had plans involving the Charm Stone, she'd better forget them, for I wasn't going to let her out of my sight.

....

When our bedraggled band of hillwalkers returned to the manor, Cate was ensconced in the small drawing room off the main hallway, the one furnished in pale blue silk. Sipping the excellent coffee and snuggled warmly in her white angora sweater, she gave a mock shiver when she saw us.

'I think you're all mad, but I applaud your healthy habits,' she called through the open doorway and laughed, that hated tinkling sound like breaking glass. 'I was thinking of taking a leisurely drive along the shore, to do a bit of sight-seeing. Anyone care to join me? But I suppose you're all too done in.'

'I'll go,' I replied immediately as I removed the dripping raincoat. It wasn't mine, just something I'd found within the depths of the great closet on the main floor. It smelled of ancient dogs and peat fires, and I was glad to get its heavy weight off my shoulders.

'How perfect,' Cate purred in response. 'I wanted to have a small chat with you.'

'Where were you planning to visit?' Forcing a cheeriness to my voice, I confronted her.

She cocked her head to one side, pausing to think.

'Scarp?' The word burst out of me and I glared at her.

'Good Lord, no,' Hugh's mother murmured. 'There's not enough daylight to get there and back, and –'

'You'll never get through the mountain pass, not today,' Lord Sabiston interjected. 'How about a tour of the town? Stornoway has a lovely harbor, and you can walk by the river, perhaps spot the otters.'

'Or the Bridge to Nowhere,' Hugh added with enthusiasm. 'That's not too far, and we can make it back by luncheon. It's one of the quirks of the island, can't be missed.'

'Well then, we must not miss it,' Cate replied graciously, sweeping her smile around to all as if delighted by the proposal. I stared at her, my eyes narrowed. What was she up to?

In the end, five of us set off in the large touring automobile. Hugh drove, with Cate as the guest of honor in the passenger seat. Huh. I was considered family now and relegated to the huge backseat. A very frail octogenarian aunt sat on one side of Lady Sabiston, with me on the other. As we set off, Hugh pointed out each passing attraction on the road, speaking loudly for the benefit of the ancient ears behind him.

The rain and wind were falling off, yet the sky remained leaden and dull. Through the windows, the landscape all around us was a smear of green and gray on this first day of the New Year. Even the ocean took on those somber hues.

We eventually bumped our way down a graveled road, the tires splashing through deep puddles. The aunt was busy explaining to his mother about a very intricate knitting stitch she had learned from the Queen Mum, back in the day. There was little to see outside, and the whole expedition seemed kind of pointless.

At last Hugh drew to a stop in a layby on the empty lane. 'There's the bridge, up ahead.' His voice had lost its vigor by now, and his eyes were bleary. The refreshment of the chilly walk had worn off, and the lack of sleep and overindulgence of the previous evening were catching up with him. 'It was built to connect the north side of the island to Stornoway, but the money ran out, and well...'

The finished concrete bridge gracefully spanned the gorge below with nine graceful arches showing man's taming of nature in the midst of this wild glen. Yet the structure merely led to a narrow track on the other side of the ravine. The road ended abruptly. Only Cate and I opted to walk the few paces to the bridge, for the aunt was feeling the chill and the damp in her bones.

We set off, keeping an arm's length apart.

'To answer your question,' Cate said softly as we picked our way over the pools of water still on the road. 'I'm really here to pass on some delightful news to you.'

I slid my eyes over to her. 'Really?' My voice was flat. 'You came all this way to tell me something you could have said on the phone, or in an email. You don't have a more nefarious scheme up your sleeve? Say, plans with the Crystal Charm Stone?'

She laughed, her good humor restored. 'Silly. I have no need of that. You helped me gain far, far more power by opening the ley lines for me.' She stopped to take a deep breath of the fresh air. It was damp still, with the sweetness of the rotting winter vegetation.

'Why would I need Scarp when I have this?' She held out her hand. On her gloved palm lay the tiniest black pebble.

'Right. Adamantite. You're the Huxor, so you control the magic metal sources back home. You're saying you have enough power? But that doesn't explain why you drank from the ley line.'

We were far enough away from the automobile that it was safe to talk without fear of being overheard.

'I'm still looking for an heir who is worthy,' she said softly. 'Take this in your hand. Tell me what you feel from it.'

'I don't want to be mixed up with your business. Done that before and you burned me.'

'Nevertheless. Please indulge me. Let's see. Remove your mitten and hold it, just for a moment.'

I took a deep breath to shove down my hatred and distrust of this woman. The piece of metal looked harmless enough. The smell of magic was on it of course, how could it not be? I picked it up. It tingled against my skin, letting its power be known, but other than that, I got nothing from it. What was her game now?

'See if you can fly with it in your hand,' she urged. 'I want to know what effect it can have.'

'Why don't you experiment with yourself?'

'I have, but as you say, I'm the Huxor. It will do anything I want it to. Except ... I can't fly. Yet.'

'Powerful as you've made yourself, you still can't do that?' I glanced back at the car. The people inside were obscured through the fogged windows. Perhaps I could do just a little hover and no one would see, maybe just a foot off the ground, just enough to show my superiority to this witch. My nemesis.

And I did. A smile curled my lip, lording it over her. I rose from the ground until I was eye-level with her, then another couple of inches for good measure. I let myself down gently, and passed the adamantite back to her. She closed her fist over it with a tight smile.

'It didn't have any effect at all.' There was a jeering note in my voice, a small victory over this witch who could bring my world crashing down any time she chose. I turned my back on her and continued with our jaunt.

We reached the bridge and walked along its span with the water racing and burbling far below.

'So, the good news.' She placed her white gloved hand on my jean jacket sleeve. 'You're to be assigned to the China delegation.'

She must have felt the jolt that raced through me. A flush of excitement, and then the deadening realization that this had only come about because of Cate's influence. 'There! See, all your dreams are coming true. You're working with the Kin, and traveling. Everything your heart desires.'

'And all thanks to you.' My words came out as flat as the feeling in my chest.

'Thank you for the acknowledgment.' She dipped her head, preening in yet another victory over me.

Rolling my eyes, I sighed. 'Let me guess. You're on the delegation team too.'

'Of course,' she replied sweetly.

'If it's all the same to you, I think I'll pass.' I hardened my eyes as I stared off into the distant moors.

'Don't be ridiculous.' Her voice was now sharp, severe. 'I need you by my side. I like to keep a close eye on you.'

I shook her hand off my arm, and turned to the other side of the bridge to watch the stream tumble down, flowing toward the beach. If only it was that easy to get away from Cate. I'd join the water gladly.

'Come now, I'm not a villain,' she called to my back. 'I'm your sponsor. We will do great things together.'

The anger that had been churning in my gut burst out. I whirled around. 'I don't want to work with you, don't you get it? I don't want these accolades and honors. It's all tainted and false. You set me up. You *stole* your power!'

'And you believe you didn't do the same?' Her voice knifed into mine and she laughed, seeing her thrust hit its target.

'It wasn't like that... Willem made me...' My rage faltered at the lie. I had chosen my actions. Unwittingly, to be sure, not knowing the consequences.

'We're two of a kind, Dara,' she snapped, ignoring my feeble protest. 'Whether you like it or not. We've both enhanced our powers in an unnatural way. Both of us have grasped the cup of life by its handles, determined to drink our fill.'

What could I say? She was right. The rain began again, just a small drizzle, more like a mist solidifying on my skin than a downpour, yet the sinking feeling in the pit of my stomach was colder than any weather Scotland could throw at me.

'You'll see. Great events are about to happen.' Turning her face up to the dark clouds, she smiled. 'I urge you to stay by my side.'

My own ambition, coupled with my ignorance had got me where I was. And in the eyes of the Kin, I was nothing without Cate's support. Was it really worth it?

'And if I don't? I could just tell everyone everything. Meg knows, don't forget. Margaret Forsythe was there. She saw everything.'

As soon as the words were out of my mouth, my eyes closed, wishing I could take it back. I regretted my outburst. I shouldn't have spoken, shouldn't have held Margaret's name out like a threat. But what could Cate do against her? She was surely the most powerful of witches in the world.

Cate didn't reply, merely narrowed her eyes at me across the bridge. 'Yes.' The words oozed out of her like pus from a deep wound. 'Yes, there's always Margaret.'

She turned back to the waiting automobile. Not another word passed between us.

....

The Hogmanay celebrations lasted almost seven days, that holiday week when no one knew what day it actually was. Each afternoon and evening was spent in a flurry of visiting, eating, and lots of whisky. Those endless drams of single malts and late nights were balanced out by the long dreary hikes in the rain. Every. Single. Morning. I'd be happy if I never saw another moor or glen in my life.

And then back to Edinburgh to recover from the holiday. The rest of January, there was little to do, but Hugh explained that the Kin work came in fits and bursts, either feast or famine.

I made the most of this downtime. I'd moved into Hugh's basement apartment, or garden flat as he preferred to call it, and busied myself transforming the former bachelor pad into a home. Mom and I spent hours on video calls as we discussed paint colors and sofas.

Despite the disdain I had for Cate's role in it, the thrill of receiving my first official letter assigning me to the

China delegation was awesome. I almost wore the words off the page as I read the thick linen paper over again and again. I dove into researching the purpose of the trip, which involved a lot of Chinese history.

We, the whole delegation, were going in order to assist the Chinese re-establish their magic. The Mandarin Kin had once ruled that land using the Emperors and Empresses as their puppets. It had been a regime of corruption and terror for the most part, even though some of the world's most beautiful works of art had been created over those dark years.

But within the past century or so, the political pendulum had swung hard. Normals had risen and reclaimed their rights, banishing first the Emperor and the court, and then the real powers behind the throne. All witches, even half-bloods, had been persecuted to the point that few would admit to having magic these days. The present governing body was only now acknowledging the need for practitioners of the craft, and its desire was to create an atmosphere of atonement. Magicians, witches and even sorcerers were being encouraged to come out of hiding, although from the sounds of it none of them really trusted this initiative. Or perhaps they'd all fled the country years ago. No one was sure.

The Kin Britannica and the EUROs and brother organizations from all over the world were coming to their assistance. And I was going too. Finally, I had a chance to see the world.

The bonus was there was no word from Cate at all. Hugh mentioned she was off traveling again.

'Where has she gone?' After our final conversation on the Bridge to Nowhere, I worried that she'd gone off in search of Margaret.

'God knows,' Hugh replied absently as he scanned the Kin Chronicle, one of the oldest and long-lasting newspapers in the country. It wasn't sold on newsstands, and it held no advertisements. It appeared through the mail slot at precisely 4:05 AM every single morning, even on Sundays and bank holidays.

I turned back to the kitchen window, looking at the beautiful but tiny courtyard. The frost glittered on the slate patio, while the large earthen pots held nothing but frozen dirt.

'Look at that,' he said. 'I wonder whatever this could be?' He took a sip of coffee, then his finger pointed to an article.

'Mmm?' I'd been lost in thought. 'What's that?'

'An interesting firsthand article.' Hugh chewed at his bottom lip. The *Chronicle* wasn't like modern day newspapers. Much of its content was sent in by witches throughout the world, and the editor's only job was to pick and choose what might hold interest for the readership. 'Sent in from Nairobi. It claims that the Great Zande has fallen asleep.'

'Seriously, Hugh?' I tore myself away from thoughts of what my backyard in Canada must have looked like right then, with a quilt of quiet snow settled over everything. For all I'd bitched about having to shovel the stuff from the driveway, snow had its good points. It covered up all the dead detritus from fall, making everything crisp and clean. I looked at him over my mug. 'Who or what is the Great Zande? A volcano? A dragon?'

'No!' His face screwed up in disgust at my ignorance. 'Zande is perhaps the mightiest sorcerer to have ever lived. No one knows his exact age. Another of his claims to fame is that he had never needed to sleep. Yet, when his aides went to get him to officiate at a ceremony, they found him fast asleep in his hotel room, and he hasn't woken since.'

'And that constitutes news in the *Chronicle*?' I rolled my eyes. 'On a more interesting note, Mom sent over three shades of gray for the living room.' I scrolled through my phone, then held it out to him.

He flipped the page to continue his story. 'The Chinese Kin are very worried about the portents and implications of this event. I wonder how this will impact the delegation?'

'Which of these grays do you like better?'

He wrenched his attention from the newspaper to look at the swatch photos. 'What exactly am I looking at?'

'This one – *Gray Dove*, or *Slight Linen*. I think *Iced* is just too green, wouldn't you say?'

'Yes?' He rustled the newspaper in his hand as if itching to get back at it. 'Is that the right answer?'

'Are you color blind, or do you simply not care about the home you live in?'

'Apparently so,' he said, settling back into the news of the witch world. He was not much help with the decorating.

CHAPTER 4

O ur peaceful domestic interlude came to an abrupt end one day with hardly any notice.

'We have to meet at Edinburgh Castle tomorrow,' Hugh announced as he came in from his run that evening. His hair was curled with sweat. 'Preparations for the trip to China.'

I laid down the paint roller and stretched my shoulders. I'd tried, but found out the hard way that house painting could not be achieved by magic. It required the old-fashioned slog of physical labour and the expert flick of the wrist to control the flow of paint. Hugh had offered to hire a painter to do the work, but this project had helped to fill the long dark days of January.

With the painting almost finished, this was great timing. 'When do we go?'

'That won't be for a while. First, we need the briefings, and to have the roles assigned.'

Oh well. At least it was something. The grayness of Edinburgh was starting to get to me. It was also dawning on me that I should have chosen a more cheerful color for the walls of the flat, something less reminiscent of the rain and mist outside. *Iced*, with its slight greenish tinge, might have been the better choice after all.

··········

We set off walking through Edinburgh New Town in the dawn's early half-light, in that early morning moment when the sun momentarily peeked out between cloud layers and gave hope for a sunny bright day. Off on my first real assignment for the Kin, I even skipped along the road leading up to the castle.

Of course, Cate would also be present, but I figured I could pretty much avoid her. I was under no illusions as to my importance on this trip. With my low seniority, I fully expected to be acting as a Gofer – running after coffees and photocopies. And there probably wouldn't even be much magic involved at all. That didn't bother me a bit. I'd finally be traveling and seeing the world. I held out my arms and twirled once. The world was my oyster.

We entered a part of Edinburgh Castle I'd never been in before, into a large boardroom specifically set up for the organization of the China delegation. It was a windowless room, lit only by old-fashioned fluorescent strip lights, and the walls were that peculiar institutional green popular in the last century. The only furnishings were a single desk on the slightly raised stage at the front of the room, a microphone standing next to it, and a few fold-up chairs laid out in loose lines in the center. Posters and maps and spreadsheets hung all around the walls.

It was crowded with bodies, full of Kin I hadn't yet met, far more people than there were chairs to sit them in. Of course, there would be witches from all over Europe coming with us on this trip.

And there was Cate. My stomach tightened as I watched her hobnobbing at the front of the room by the desk. Hugh made a beeline for her and the other bigwigs, while I turned in the opposite direction. The less I had to do with that treacherous witch, the better.

And - oh. Talk about witches I wanted nothing to do with. The spy from the airport was there, lounging against a far wall like he wasn't really a part of the larger group. He placed his long legs and arms awkwardly, as if not sure what to do with them. Just as I narrowed my eyes at him, he glanced round toward me and gave a start in recognition, those bright blue eyes momentarily opening to their fullest.

He left his perch and slowly weaved his way through the crowded room, heading in my direction.

I immediately retreated, moving toward the back of the room, trying to disappear into the crowd. When I glanced back, I saw that my ruse hadn't fooled him, and he had already begun to cut through the middle of the room.

Who was this guy? He couldn't be anyone very important if he wasn't crowding round the Very Important Witches at the front of the convention room. A mere spook, a lowly foot-runner for the Kin, despite the aristocratic nose.

His blond hair was cut unfashionably short, not in a buzz cut or with interesting designs shaved in, but as if he'd been going to the same barber since childhood, and neither of them were influenced by fashion. And unlike most of the other men in the room, his clothes looked like he'd bought them off the rack. They didn't fit properly, just as he didn't fit in with this crowd.

I hurriedly retraced my footsteps to the main door, but my exit came to an abrupt halt. The man following me became a distant memory when I saw who was entering the room. Win Chen, in all her imperial glory.

Win stepped smartly into the large room in black high heels, her face glamoured to smooth perfection and her dark hair shiny and lustrous, and longer than it had been when she was a student. She looked proud as punch to be included with the delegation, her being a young witch fresh out of Scarp, and she held her head as high as she could. A studied pause when she walked inside the door, looked confidently around, making sure everyone saw her.

Win. Had it only been a year or less since I'd last seen her on Scarp? Hard to believe, so much had happened since then.

The last thing I needed was that bitch while I was trying to deal with Cate, too. The memories of her and Oliver, and the other two, with their blatant prejudice against half-bloods, mocking my lack of magical knowledge and training, still rankled. Not to mention her insane competitive streak. This witch had no qualms doing anything to ensure success, whether it was using of her own magic and considerable talents, or yanking others down so she could step on their heads in her scramble to the top.

I stared at her smug face and my fingers curled into fists. Her and her Dragon Magic. She'd been so proud, so haughty, that I'd truly felt cowed, belittled in the face of such confidence when I first arrived on Scarp.

Perhaps Win felt that vibe emanating from me, for her face swung sharply round and our eyes met in that split second. Those dark eyes flashed wide in recognition before she dropped her gaze. Almost as quickly I turned my back, both pretending we hadn't seen the other. When I peeked over my shoulder again, she sat hunched over in one of the chairs, her hair curtaining her face as she furiously studied her phone, refusing to lift her eyes.

Something inside me relented at the sight. Perhaps Win, my fellow student on Scarp, hadn't been *so* awful after all. Not as personally obnoxious as say, Pauline Cromwell, the Covenanter's daughter. Win had been nasty to everyone. It was part of her competitive nature. She'd made no secret of the fact.

And she was no longer part of the pack. She was alone here, that much I could see. While I, I had Hugh.

I considered the situation. After all, it looked like she would be going to China, like me. We were now on the same footing and I could afford to be magnanimous. I could even be the bigger witch and be nice to her.

As a gesture of good will, I poured her a coffee and sauntered over to her lonely corner. Her shoulders tensed even more as she sensed my approach.

'Hey, Win.'

Her chin jutted up and she glared at me. 'What do you want?'

Just the sound of her well-educated, snooty English accent caused the spite to hackle the back of my neck again. Ah, frig it. She was just another privileged rich Kin kid. I didn't have to be nice to her, but what the hell.

'I have a coffee for you,' I said. 'Looks like it's going to be a long morning.' With my free hand, I pulled up a nearby chair and settled myself in.

She glared at the paper cup before accepting it, then she sniffed it.

'It's not poisoned.'

'You never know.' Win pointedly looked toward the center of the room, as if intent on ignoring me.

She wasn't going to get away with that kind of crap. Again.

'So looks like we're both in the delegation,' I casually observed, spreading my legs and arms out like a guy would, claiming as much space as I could. 'It's going to be interesting.'

She drew her knees in even more, smoothing the fabric of her skirt. 'I can't imagine why they're allowing you on board. If anything will upset the mission, it'll be your doing. You have the worst track record of anyone. That's what I heard.'

'Ah,' I replied, feeling the barb. I forced a light note in my voice. 'So people are still talking about me. The perils of Fame. But you, Win, I haven't heard a word about you. What have you been up to? Been keeping a low profile, huh?'

Funny how I instinctively knew which buttons to push. This was almost as satisfying as sparring with Sasha, my half-sister. And the passive-aggressive biting was way more entertaining when I came from a confident place like I was in right then. Yes, Win might be competitive, but I was more than a match for her sniping.

'I've been honing my Dragon Magic and brushing up on my language skills,' she said acidly, without turning to look my way. 'Preparing for this. I knew this delegation was coming, and I was determined to be included.'

'Languages?' That threw me for a loop. Win was all about her magic arts. Languages – anyone could learn them. Even I had a smattering of French and German from my misspent university years.

'Mandarin. Cantonese. Bayingolin. And Tibetan.' She bit off each word as she listed them. 'We are going to Asia, after all. I wish to be as useful as I can be. I have positioned myself so they will need me in the heart of the Discussions. That is the proper way to advance in this organization. Not stealing magic and bungling and being mixed up with shady sorcerers.'

Ouch.

'I have no doubt you'll be with the Huxor's group,' Win carried on proudly. 'As you have fooled her into becoming your sponsor. As such, you will be working with land claims.' She gave a sniff as she looked down her perfect nose, showing her disdain. 'She's going after the adamantite rights. If you'd had any foresight, you would have learned Mandarin at least. I don't see how you'll be much help at all.'

I gathered together what feeble pride I could muster.

'Actually, I'm pretty sure I'll be assigned to Hugh's group,' I told her, matching the loftiness of her tone. I nodded toward the front of the room where my fiancé stood in discussion with all the other honchos.

'You think so, eh?' She sneered, just as Johanna approached the microphone and a loud feedback squawk filled the space.

Dammit, she'd gotten the last word in.

The next hour was filled with a lot of bla-bla from those on the podium. The welcome statement, the statement of intent for the mission, the introduction of the key players. It was dead boring, and I was starving by this time. I stood up quietly and sneaked over to the entrance to see if the caterers had set up anything yet in the lobby for the morning break. This was Edinburgh, after all, and the Scots understood the importance of butter and pastries. I intended to get first pick at the goodies.

I glanced round before darting out the door. The blond spook was nowhere to be seen.

As I wandered by the long tables set out with refreshments, I frowned. There were no buttery pastries here, only the standard packets of shortbread and biscuits, individually wrapped in cellophane. Nothing to get excited about. I shoved a handful into my hoodie front before realizing there was no way I'd be able to eat them in the main room. It would be like unwrapping a candy in church, the noise would draw every eye in the room to me. I hastily opened one shortbread packet, shoved the contents in my mouth and, trying to munch as quietly as possible, went to slip back into the room unnoticed.

And there he was, just to the left of the doorjamb, partially hidden behind a large potted plant.

'Wait, I need to speak with you.' His voice was urgent.

'Well, I *don't* need to speak with you,' I informed him through my mouthful of biscuit even as I arrogantly flicked my hair back.

He ignored my efforts to quell him. 'You're friends with Margaret Forsythe,' he whispered, laying his hand on my arm.

I looked at that intrusive hand like it was a nasty big spider. He coughed and let go of me, but didn't move away.

I washed down the shortbread with my coffee before I spoke.

'I may have had run-ins with that witch, in the past,' I loftily informed him. 'But if you know the lady at all, you'll realize that doesn't necessarily make us friends.'

'I need to get in touch with her.'

'You and the rest of the Kin,' I snarked. He was persistent, I'd give him that, even if he was piss-poor at his job. Did he really think I couldn't see through him? 'Good luck with that.'

'I know you're not like the rest of them,' he said, flicking his head toward the room full of witches.

I drank another sip of coffee to hide my amazement at his nerve. Who did he think he was fooling?

'Oh, well done,' I remarked to him dryly. 'Pretending you're not one of them, and that your job isn't to ferret out Margaret's whereabouts, eh?'

I shook my head, lifting one eyebrow. 'Sorry, they'll have to look for another route to get to her,' I continued as I pushed past him to enter the room. 'In case you hadn't noticed at the airport, she didn't leave me her business card or address. So I'm afraid you're out of luck.'

The speeches came to a close, and people began milling around the room, looking at the lists which had just been posted in large fonts. There was a lot of buzz and chatter.

I spotted Win standing in front of one of the boards and headed directly over. I wasn't finished with that witch yet.

'What's happening?' I asked around the mush of crumbs in my mouth. I washed them down with the last of my coffee and wiped my mouth with my sleeve.

She turned to me, and if looks could kill, I'd be a goner. Daggers flew from her flint-black eyes and her face screwed up with rage.

'You!' Win shook so hard she could hardly spit out the word. 'You...' Squeezing her eyes shut as if holding in a scream, she stormed off toward the entrance.

Her extreme upset must have something to do with the assignments. I jerked closer, scanning the list for any mention of her name, or mine. My mouth fell open when I found them, realizing why she'd been so furious.

On the bright side, Win wasn't assigned to the inner circle, but that was the only good news. Hugh was, of course, but I wasn't either.

Dammit. My name was listed under Cate's division, together with Win's. Not only was I going to have to work under Cate, but I would have to endure Win constantly trying to outdo me, every step of the way. How annoying. How exhausting.

I swallowed the bitter lump which rose in my throat.

Not only that, but it looked like a really boring assignment. How could I get excited about mining and distribution rights? There was no magic involved in that.

CHAPTER 5

Cate gathered her tiny group at The Witchery restaurant. We were so few in number that the three of us didn't even merit a room, just the corner table at the back with an intricately carved wooden lattice screen for privacy. The white linen tablecloth glowed in the soft light cast by a single overhead fixture, and the silverware glinted like old money. At least we were being treated to a three-course lunch.

Win and I sat as far away from each other as we could, considering there were only three place settings. We had nothing to say to each other as we waited for Cate.

'Well, this is a happy group, isn't it?' Cate remarked drily as she took her seat and looked at both of us in turn. 'Cheer up, it's not the end of the world. I think you'll both be grateful for the opportunities I'm offering you.'

A waiter quietly poured us glasses of white wine without first asking us our preferences, and another laid a bowl of soup in front of each of us. It was a cream soup with bits of carrot visible in its thickness, and the smell was divinely hot and garlicky. The accompanying bread must have been fresh out of the oven, small rectangles of sourdough. My mouth watered and my belly rumbled, but Win's haughty expression showed she wasn't impressed.

'With all due respect, I feel my talents will be wasted with this assignment.' She punctuated her words by crossing her arms over her chest. 'I must object and request another posting.'

Cate's finely etched brows rose, intrigued by this declaration and not showing the slightest offence. She tore her bread into quarters, then buttered one piece. I took that as a sign it was okay to begin, so I immediately put spoon to bowl and started shoveling it in. I only dripped a bit on my hoody.

'And furthermore.' Win pointedly stared first at me and then Cate.

'What?' I asked. 'Finish your thought.' I used the linen napkin to wipe the creamy mess off my front, dabbing very delicately, or so I thought.

'She doesn't even have basic table manners! How can you subject me to this? We will be a laughing stock at the negotiations. No one will ever take me seriously again after this.' Win was so upset tears sprang to her eyes and she hit the table with both fists.

I wanted to reach over and smack her one, I was so embarrassed. What was she on about, table manners? I hadn't spit on my napkin to wet it first. Was I supposed to tuck the stupid thing in like a bib? We were eating soup for God's sake, and soup dripped.

The older witch merely smiled, and reached over to pat Win's hand. 'Things are not as dire as you believe them to be,' she said softly. She flicked a smile at me, including me. 'Table manners are easily acquired, and I think you will be quite surprised to learn the true nature of our mission.'

Cate refused to say more on the matter except, 'Business will be discussed over coffee.' Instead, she showed me by example the correct way to lift the soup spoon away from me, lightly touching the silver against the far side of the bowl to capture any rogue spills.

It worked, I was surprised to find, although it felt counter-intuitive to move the spoon away from myself instead of hunching over the bowl to prevent the inevitable drops.

I was still narked at Win for pointing out my ignorance, though. And I despised Cate just as a matter of course. But the food was too good to waste, and for the rest of the meal I waited to see how they approached the dining intricacies and followed suit, using the right forks and even to the point of laying my silverware at a prescribed angle on the plate when finished. I would never, ever allow myself to be embarrassed by Win again.

'Now then. To business.' The final dessert plate had been removed and coffee poured into the exquisite tiny cups. Cate leaned forward.

'As I was saying, the true nature of our small delegation. Yes, officially we are in charge of determining the mining rights of China's adamantite, and advising on the best, most ecologically sustainable methods of extraction.' She laughed and looked at us, as if expecting us to share the joke.

'Ridiculous really,' she murmured. 'Such a flimsy excuse when these discussions could easily be held over a Zoom meeting.'

Cate smiled again at us both, knowing she had our full attention now. Even Win's frown had disappeared.

'You have, of course, heard the terrible news about Zande the Great. He lies still in his hotel bed in Nairobi, apparently asleep.' She shook her head sadly. 'It's simply unnatural, for him. His claim to fame is that his magic is so strong, he has no need for the recuperative powers of sleep. Obviously, he's under a curse from a worker of magic, but who? Who is powerful enough to cause such a thing? What witch or sorcerer has the means?'

She shook her head again, but then all pretense dropped from her face, looking seriously at both of us in turn. 'Beneath the façade of mining rights, our actual mission in China is to find out what has really happened in this case.'

Neither of us had expected her to drop this bomb. The three of us were to be part of a real investigation, a magic one, and an undercover operation to boot. My heart beat fast. Never mind that I would have to work alongside Win. I could deal with that later.

And never mind Cate, either. Perhaps this was an opportunity to actually show my skills and prowess for real.

'But,' Win started, giving me a quick glance.

'But why China, you ask,' Cate said, nodding her acknowledgement. 'Why Asia, when the Great Zande sleeps in Africa? That, my dear fledglings, that is where you come in. We need to find the source of this enchantment, for he is most certainly under a spell. A spell so intricate, so devious, that the finest magical minds can't decipher it.'

Win's lips were a perfect 'O' as she listened to Cate's words. Her mind was far away, no doubt picturing how she would solve it.

'But,' I had to interject. 'If they can't decipher it, how do you know it's a spell?'

'I know firsthand. While I was on my recent travels to Zanzibar, I was requested to confer, being in the neighborhood, so to speak.' Cate sat straighter and lifted her chin. 'There is no fingerprint to the magic.'

Her eyes narrowed. I couldn't allow my face to show the shock flashing through my mind. *Cate had been in Africa.*

'I have my suspicions, of course,' she continued, after a pause. She glanced between the two of us. 'And this is why I specifically requested both of you for my team. Win, we need you because of your language skills. I fear we are up against a mighty foe.'

Win nodded eagerly and squared her shoulders, practically preening.

'Dara, you also are invaluable to this mission,' Cate said softly, her dark eyes luminous in the overhead light. 'For you are perhaps the only witch in this world who knows the culprit. You will help us find her.'

She caught the dawning comprehension, and she smiled. 'Yes, we need to find Margaret Forsythe and stop her before she strikes again.'

Margaret. No, this was all wrong. And Cate had been in Africa when the Great Zande had been cursed? Oh, no. That could not be a coincidence.

Margaret would not have had anything to do with a sleeping spell placed over some ancient sorcerer in Africa. It was a ridiculous, ludicrous accusation. Meg would have no reason to be there. She liked beaches and sunshine to warm her bones. Considering the discussion we'd had on the Bridge to Nowhere, this whole thing stank.

'That's preposterous, and you know it!' No way was I letting her do this.

Cate merely cocked her head in my direction, inviting me to explain myself.

'Meg... Margaret Forsythe would never do such a thing, casting spells like that. For what purpose, except to wreak havoc?' I shook my head. 'What reason would she have to do that? That's – that's just crazy talk.'

My eyes darted back and forth between the two of them. Win's mouth was a thin line of disapproval that I would dare speak in such a manner to Cate, yet her eyes reflected the never-ending calculations inside her head.

'Is it?'

'Of course it is, Cate.' I leaned back, and consciously adopted a more reasonable, calm tone. 'You don't know Margaret. I do, a bit at least. And the last thing she would ever do is cast spells on other magic workers.'

'And why is that?' Cate's tone remained cool, civil even, interested in what I had to say.

'Because she doesn't care! She doesn't give a damn about the Kin or their politics or anyone.'

'Doesn't care? Or is she, in fact, holding a deep grudge against the Kin? One perhaps nurtured during her im-prisonment, the long years underground. I would cer-tainly be perturbed if they'd done it to me. Perhaps you misinterpret her disdain for all things Kin. A witch of her power surely would never stand for such treatment. No more than you or I would.'

I shook my head stubbornly. I couldn't let her cast false aspersions on Margaret. The Scottish witch had many faults – I'd witnessed more than a few – and she could hold a grudge with the best of them, but Margaret had no quarrel with the Great Zande, not that I was aware of.

'And what if I tell you she had been in the area all that time? Since leaving Tomnahurich, excepting of course her visits to you.'

'She's not in Africa! She's on a beach somewhere.' Admittedly, my geographic knowledge of Asia was somewhat sketchy, but I knew that the first would be on the coast of the Indian Ocean while the other was inland. Wasn't it? I ignored the fact that distance was irrelevant for Margaret, conveniently dismissing how quickly she'd come to me when I was half a world away. 'The only thing her confinement in that damp dungeon left her with, was an overwhelming need to soak up the heat of the sun.'

Although, that wasn't all of it. Those long years underground with nothing better to do than think had also given Margaret a wisdom that surpassed the petty political machinations of the Kin. And that was the real reason I was almost one hundred percent sure that Margaret could have nothing to do with the Great Zande's long nap.

But of course with Meg, there was always that one percent of uncertainty.

'Besides, she doesn't believe in spells,' I added, somewhat belatedly. I looked up from the table to meet Cate's gaze.

'And she's a good friend of yours?' she asked softly. 'Seen much of her lately?'

'Well, no,' I began, then hesitated.

Had news of our airport meeting reached Cate's ears? Her eyes told me nothing. Perhaps it hadn't been her who'd put the spook on my trail. Perhaps that had been the work of the Covenanters. I had no way of knowing for sure.

Cate wouldn't have used such a poor specimen to do her dirty work, though. I thought back to the spy's ill-fitting clothes and unfashionable hair cut. No, she would never have hired him.

But even if he worked for Cromwell and the Covenanters, surely some word of the meeting would have reached Cate, if only to pass on the glee of Margaret's terrible anger when she left me so abruptly.

Cate knew full well that when we'd last seen Lady Margaret Forsythe back home in Newfoundland, the Scottish witch had left in a flurry and a snit because she believed I had tricked her into opening the ley seams to allow Cate to soak in the energy.

Margaret was honorable, and that was precisely why I believed she would never have bothered to commit this crime. But I couldn't say all that aloud, not with Win present. My hand reached up to the little adamantite stud hidden beneath my hair. I couldn't say a word.

'She's no friend to the Kin, and you know it,' Cate drawled.

Win had been watching us both during this exchange, her narrowed eyes going back and forth as we lobbed the weight of suspicion. At last she spoke up.

'In the light of all this new information concerning our mission, I for one am thrilled to be included on this assignment, Cate,' she said, sitting herself up even straighter in her chair.

I started, taken aback by her interruption. This was hardly the moment for brown-nosing and competing. We were having a serious discussion about false accusations.

Win's dark eyes glittered at me across the table's expanse of white linen. Her competitive spirit was fired up and ready to go. 'We will find the hag Auld Meg and bring her back to justice. At least, I will. Doesn't sound like Dara's truly on board.'

Cate's slight nod of approval was just too much for me to stomach. 'But you have no evidence that it's Margaret who did this,' I blurted. 'You have a spell that no one can figure out. Does it have her scent on it? Is it actually a curse, or was it natural causes? Did you have doctors examine him?'

I stared at both of them wildly. 'And what does China have to do with it? Do you believe Meg is there?'

'No,' Cate replied. 'I have no reason to think she's in China.'

'Then why?'

She smiled like a cat who had discovered the butter dish. 'We're going to China in order to find the one witch who can help us undo the curse.'

Cate laughed delightedly, that hated tinkle. 'We're on a quest to find Li Minh.'

Dead silence greeted her announcement. Li Minh. Rumored to be among the most powerful witches ever. If she in fact existed and wasn't the Chinese equivalent of an Arthurian legend. She hadn't been seen this century, as far as I knew. If she was still alive, her whereabouts were a closely guarded secret.

And how this mythological witch came into so much power? Well, this was the stuff of legends indeed.

Win finally drew a loud gasp as if on a delayed timer. 'Li Minh?' Her tone was reverent. 'But she's just a story. Does this witch exist? How do you know?'

'I don't,' Cate said slowly. 'But I have sources...' She shook her head, the long raven black hair shining in the dim light. She looked at each of us in turn. 'So? Are we a team? You accept this assignment?'

'I'm in,' Win gushed. Her face shone as the thrill of the chase set her blood to race. It was a no-lose scenario for her. No matter which way it turned out, Win would achieve greatness, or at least haul herself one rung up the ladder. If we found the legendary figure, well, that would make Win a legend herself. On the other hand, if we lost and found that she did not in fact exist and never had, we would be known as the team of witches who dared to try.

Cate looked expectantly at me. I absolutely had to say yes. And it had nothing to do with all those hollow ambitions I'd once held to become a hero within the Kin. Meg had nothing to do with any of this. She was being vilified, and I now understood the real reason Cate wanted the other witch gone.

After all, we were the only ones who had been present that night last June. Cate didn't like loose ends. If I didn't accept this assignment, then Cate would make sure I was right up there next to Meg in the bonfire. I had to be involved in this investigation, if only to save my own skin. I would help to clear Meg's name, or at least to find some way to warn her. Though I owed her nothing at all.

I looked up at Cate and slowly nodded. The back of my neck tightened. Cate might be setting me up for a bigger fail than even my suspicious mind could imagine, yet, I had no choice.

CHAPTER 6

W e were free for the rest of the day. Hugh wasn't, which was just as well, for he wouldn't approve of my plans.

The first stop was to discuss this situation with someone who knew Margaret. The only other living witch who knew her well, in fact. The Venerable Nachtan, who else? True, he was the one who had somehow laid a curse on her, keeping her confined in the dungeon with her chronicle all those years ago. But there was more to that story than either of them were telling.

I'd seen the way he'd looked at her at Tomnahurich, his was a true love, possibly unrequited, but none the less powerful for all that. Even after all those years and the shit that had gone down between them, there were still feelings lurking in his old gray heart.

She had spoken disparagingly of him, yet at the same time there'd been an underlying tinge of affection in her words. I would get her to tell me the whole history between them, some day. If we ever met on good terms again.

I climbed the familiar dark stone steps to his tower, in no need of the faint light from the sconces to guide me. By now I knew every stone under my feet, every uneven surface and every dip worn from centuries of boots treading up and down their length. I knew exactly where I needed to stop and catch my breath, too.

I hesitated outside Mrs. Battersea's door, then decided against checking in with her. She was the keeper of VN, his personal organizer, and would only discourage my unexpected visit. I needed not just to see the Venerable Nachtan. I needed the element of surprise in order to get the most information from him. What I was looking for, I didn't even know. He wouldn't be in touch with Meg these days, he wouldn't know how to reach her. He wouldn't be able to tell me what she'd been up to, where she'd been over the past year since I'd freed her from his prison.

But I knew he would be on her side.

The door to his chamber did not open when I pushed on it. I tried the handle again, but it was locked tight.

I stood back in confusion. That door had always opened easily enough to my touch. Did he have it spelled or something to avoid unwelcome visitors? Did the door act on some kind of magical 'Invitation Only' access? No matter how much I thumped and yelled, it remained shut with no sign of the VN. Crap. I turned and made my way back to Mrs. Battersea's office door.

She looked up at me when I entered. She was dressed in warm navy today, the suit the exact same cut as ever, and her eyeglasses matching the blue. Mrs. Battersea was terrifyingly efficient and no nonsense, which made

her extreme fondness and reverence for the smelly, can-
tankerous old witch all the more puzzling.

'Dara?'

I guessed the tower's stone walls were so thick she
hadn't heard me banging and hollering upstairs.

'You don't have an appointment with Him today, surely.' There was concern in her eyes.

I shook my head. 'No, but I really wanted to talk with,
ah, Him. He's not answering the door. Do you know
when he, ah He'll be free?'

Pursing her lips, she shook her head. 'Ooh Dara, I'm
afraid He's not here. He's taken Himself off.'

'What, left the tower?'

'Yes, he's gone home for a rest.'

I waited a moment, but she was going to make me
squeeze it out of her. I had to play on her sympathies.

'That's not like him. Is everything okay with Him?'

Mrs. Battersea looked down off to the desk on her left.
'He did appear a little peaked, said he needed some time
away. To regroup. That he was... tired.' This last came out
as a whisper. Her eyes were round behind the spectacle
frames.

The Venerable Nachtan was never a picture of rosy
health, not with his pipe smoking and never getting
out for exercise in the fresh air. He'd been gray since
I met him, his hair and beard and skin all the same
not-quite-glowing shade. Much like *Iced*, now I came to
think of it. But he had been that way for several decades,
as far as I understood.

'Oh.' I didn't know what to do next, I'd been pinning
my hopes on the old witch. I needed him, because I
couldn't think who else to turn to. 'Any idea when he'll
be back?'

She shook her head. 'That's just it.' She leaned closer and spoke in a whisper. 'I've had no word from Him, and it's been two days.'

Even as I watched, the tiniest tear trickled from the inside corner of her right eye. I might have missed it if I hadn't been searching her face closely. This was serious. The unflappable Mrs. Battersea brought to tears? Something was very wrong with VN. 'What's going on with Him?'

She sniffed, then bravely drew herself together. 'In all the years I've worked here, this is unprecedented.' She shook her head. 'Of course, he leaves the tower all the time, it's not that. He's discovered Starbucks, and he'll go out for his pint on a Friday night. Once a year, he likes to go to his little cottage in the country. But that's in the summer, Dara. It's winter now, it's cold there. I doubt he has any form of heating, and as I said, I haven't heard from him. I keep sending out the carrier pigeons with messages, but the poor things just return, unable to fulfill their missions.'

Carrier pigeons, in this age of email and cell phones? I shook my head. This was not the time to get into a discussion about stepping into the twenty-first century.

Mrs. Battersea began to straighten papers and files on her desk that were already perfectly aligned, a sure sign of the stress she was feeling. I took a deep breath.

'Okay,' I said, more to myself. I needed to find Nachtan, and by doing this I could also put Mrs. Battersea's mind to rest. We had several days off before we needed to leave for China. 'Do you want me to go check on him?'

It was like the sun came out on that bleak Edinburgh day, her smile lit her face from end to end. 'Oh, would you, Dara? He's always so independent, but if you wouldn't mind nipping out to his country home, I'd be ever so grateful.'

'Out in the country?' I hesitated because, well, I knew my area of Edinburgh city pretty well and its public transport system, but anything outside of it was sure to mean long distances driving on the wrong side of the road, and not being able to read the map while doing so. Sure, having a driver's license was handy now, but it brought along with it all kinds of new worries I'd never thought to worry about before.

'I don't suppose he has a phone nearby, or any other means to get in touch?'

'No, no.' She dismissed the idea, already turned away to search one in one of the large filing cabinet drawers. She pulled out several large folded papers. 'That's why we use the pigeons. He finds their cooing more soothing than electronic instruments. He always says, 'Mrs. B, if a message doesn't fit onto a pigeon's leg, then the writer is sadly lacking skill with words." She smiled modestly. 'He would never, of course, have that complaint about me.'

She laid the folders out on her desk.

'Here's the map of the area,' she said. 'I'll just mark the location of his home.' She looked up before making the X with her red pen, an unexpected look of apology on her face. 'I'm afraid it's not actually *on* a road or lane. You'll have to do a bit of a hike, from what I understand.

'Now, this is the road map of Scotland,' she continued, then she pointed to a spot way over past Inverness, north of the loch. There didn't appear to be any marked towns or villages nearby. She was back to her usual efficient self now. 'You'll want to make your way up to Inverness, and once through there, find the A82. Don't cross the bridge over the Beauly Firth, you'll have gone too far. D'ye see?'

She waited for my nod of confirmation as I followed her finger on the paper. 'You'll tootle along the north shore of Loch Ness.' She looked up at me sternly. 'That's a left turning, that is.

She tapped the map after marking the turnoff point, then brought out an ordinance survey map of the area. 'It's fairly simple, just follow this road past Abreachan. Take a right turn there, you'll pass over three wee streams, then you take the road on the left. It'll not be paved. Ye park the car there and follow the path through the woods on foot, you should be able to find it no problem.' She looked up at me and beamed again.

'Here's the map of the forest,' she said, passing me yet another folded paper brochure. 'It's not hard going, I believe.'

'That's a long drive,' I said, looking at the three maps in front of me. 'It'll take a couple of hours to get there. And a long hike when I eventually arrive.'

She had the grace to look a little discomfited. 'Yes, a three-hour drive actually,' she agreed. 'Perhaps you're better off waiting until morning.'

'And you're sure he's there?'

Mrs. Battersea gave a quick, definite nod at that. 'Oh yes, that's where He said he was going, and He is a witch of His word.'

The maps were placed in an accordion folder which she handed to me forthwith. 'I'll arrange for a Kin car loan,' she finished with a flourish. 'You're abiding with young Sabiston these days? It will be waiting at your door at six thirty AM, along with a picnic hamper to tide you over.'

I studied the maps as I walked back to the flat in New Town. Dear God, it was a long drive, there and back in one day. That was if I didn't get lost or break a leg hiking up to Nachtan's cottage on the way. But there was no choice, was there? I had to speak with Nachtan.

....

Hugh stirred and yawned as I hauled myself out of bed and measured the coffee scoops. It was still so dark out that the glass door leading to the court-yard showed only a mirror image of me in the small kitchen, my hair still unbrushed. I had explained to Hugh that I was taking this free day to drive around the coast a bit, to sightsee, maybe drop up to Inverness.

He'd thought it very odd, frankly quite out of char-acter for me, and said so.

'We'll have lots of time to do this together in the summer, when the weather's nicer,' he pointed out. 'And I thought you were nervous, driving here?'

I shrugged, my back to him. 'I have to get used to driving on the wrong side of the road some time,' I said. 'Better out in the country when there's not much traffic around, right?'

'And Inverness.' He stopped. It looked like he was biting his lip to prevent the rest of his thought coming out.

'No, I'm not going anywhere near Tomnahurich,' I told him firmly, and his shoulders relaxed a little.

'That's good,' he murmured. 'Johanna's still trying to get back on the Fae's good side after all that to-do last spring.'

I stared at myself in the reflection of the garden door. I hadn't told him the truth, that I was terrified to set off on this journey. It wasn't just the driving. I'd Googled the distance. Mrs. Battersea was correct, as she inevitably was. An estimated three hours driving from Edinburgh to Inverness, and that wasn't counting the time I needed to budget getting lost on small back lanes and then hiking to the cottage. It was going to be a long day, and with the shortness of the January days here, I might not even return before dark.

The physical car trip wasn't what scared me. Something deep inside me, in my chest or my heart or where ever these things hide, it was breathing a hint that this journey would unlock a portal that once opened, could never be undone.

I hesitated at the doorway. I didn't need more crap in my life. I didn't have to do this, make this journey. I could just let Margaret defend herself from the accusations. She wasn't anything to me, was she?

Except that Mrs. Battersea was now counting on me, and one could never disappoint that good lady.

'Call if you run into any difficulties, then,' he murmured casually as he kissed me good-bye. He was still sleep-warm and cozy and I clung to that comfort for a long moment. 'There's always Kin around to give you a hand. Although they're mostly Covenanters up that way, still...'

I sure hoped there would be no need of calling on Elder Cromwell. I checked again that my phone was fully charged and that I had enough food to last in case I got lost on the moors overnight, and I set out the front door. There was the Kin car waiting, as promised, with the keys tucked into the ignition. Thank God it was a small one.

It was actually tiny, and a convertible to boot.

Hugh poked his head out the front door to look up to the car on the street, and gave a whistle. He managed to look impressed and a little put out at the same time. 'The Mercedes SLC! How did you manage to snag that one? You must have good connections, Dara. They don't loan that one out to just anyone.'

'Must have been the last one on the lot,' I murmured before he could ask any probing questions about my connections. I smiled and blew a kiss as I jumped into the vehicle, and I juddered, stop-starting all the way down the street until I figured out the touchy clutch pedal.

And I was off on my reluctant adventure, off into the still-pitch dark of the early morning on these unknown roads.

CHAPTER 7

I t was closer to seven o'clock when I left the city, and the sun wouldn't fully rise until half-past eight. That drive through the dark on unknown roads was among the most disconcerting of experiences I'd ever had. I'd recently acquired my driver's license, but that was in Canada, where we drove on the right side of the road. I had to force myself to stay on the correct side of the Scottish roads by chanting 'stay left, stay left' the whole time as I left Edinburgh, but that wasn't so awful. Getting to the main highway was the worst. I had no idea where I was going, just aimed the car and tried to ignore all the busier, impatient cars passing me.

My only savior was the GPS which Mrs. Battersea had thoughtfully caused to have pre-programmed for me. It helped me navigate out of the city and onto the A9 without too many hair-raising incidents. I knew once I navigated through Inverness I would soon turn off onto the A82 which promised to be quieter, with a reduced speed limit. And so I made my way along the north shore of Loch Ness, the home of the legendary monster, and happily could report no sightings of her.

It did my heart good to be so close to water again, even if it wasn't the saltiness of the ocean that I was used to back home. I rolled down my window to let that brisk air bathe my face. Despite the time of year, it wasn't that cold out, not like back home, although the North Sea wind did have a good bite to it at times.

On the long trip up to Loch Ness, I gave some thought to what I needed from the Venerable Nachtan, what he might tell me that could clear Meg's name with the Kin. Despite their suspicions, I knew in my heart of hearts that Margaret Forsythe had nothing to do with the curse laid upon Zande. How could she? More to the point, *why* would she?

She was quick-tempered, yes, and a touch narcissistic. But she didn't even bear a grudge against the Kin or Nachtan as far as I could see, although you'd expect her to be annoyed at the lot of them for casting her into a dungeon for the full span of a century. I would certainly be narked, if they'd done it to me.

Margaret was too busy enjoying her newfound freedom and her trust fund and the joys of twenty-first century living to be harbouring plans of revenge. Wasn't she?

Although she hadn't been happy when she'd startled me at the airport.

I bit my lip as I pondered, staring out across the lake. The January sun was harsh in its brilliance, yet still low in the sky, causing the opposite shoreline to be hidden in shadows. The morning mist still lingered over the water so that it all merged into indistinct gradients of gray.

Last year, Margaret had wanted me to join her. She'd argued her best against me continuing with my career in the Kin, even calling Nachtan rude names.

Nachtan was the only other person living today who knew Margaret. She'd hinted that they had been very involved in the past, that he had been her magical tutor hired by an indulgent father at a time when women weren't allowed to practice real magic. In a misguided effort to prove to the Kin that women could be strong, too, she'd actually lifted the Crystal Charm Stone from its resting place in the broch on Scarp to bring to Edinburgh, to fling her accomplishment in the faces of the dour male Kin witches.

She hadn't been trying to steal it, like they claimed. She swore the curse laid on her by Nachtan was an act of revenge by a spurned lover.

That was how she'd gained her terrific power all those years ago, from such close contact with the Stone. And also how the Venerable Nachtan had gained his, bringing the Stone back to its hiding place, and lauded as a hero.

Still, he knew her as no one else did, and with him by my side he would soon set Cate and the rest of the Kin straight on the ridiculous idea that Margaret Forsythe was out creating havoc in the world. She didn't even bother with spells, and had no reason to exact revenge on some unknown African sorcerer. What nonsense.

I hoped Nachtan had had enough rest, because he was going to return to the city with me whether he wanted to or not. This matter had to be cleared up before we left for China. I packed away the remnants of my sandwich, took a last swig of cold coffee, and set back on the road to the right turn off, along the deep valley winding up through the hills.

The car park was easy enough to find, even though there weren't any vehicles there at this time of year. In fact I hadn't seen a living soul for the past half an hour. Mrs. Battersea's map of the forest had my route marked in pen, and I prayed she had it right. I set off into the woods.

The trail began fairly pleasantly, passing by trees on one side, fallow meadows on the other with glimpses of the lake far below. It was only when it turned to enter the canopy of forest that I shuddered nervously.

It was dark under the pines, and quiet too, not even a bird singing or a crow's raucous scolding. I slipped along the path like an intruder into the waiting silence. At the stream, the map showed I should veer off the main path here and follow the water's course, but the route was little more than a rabbit trail.

How could there be a house at the end of this? Houses needed roads, or at least driveways, or even sturdy walkways to carry groceries along to avoid clambering over the rocks and risk falling into the bubbling stream so close by. More to the point, how had the Venerable Nachtan, that ancient witch, physically managed this? I could only hope and pray that Mrs. Battersea's map was accurate. I comforted myself with the realization that at least I wouldn't get lost in the wilderness, for I would only need to follow the brook back to Loch Ness if I couldn't find Nachtan's abode.

I'd almost passed it before I realized the tiny trail had ended.

It wasn't really a house at all, unless one was a Hobbit. I blinked, and I blinked again, making sure that what appeared to be a rough door actually was that and not a mirage of nature. It looked like a portal right into the hillside, but then my eyes adjusted and I saw that what I'd taken to be the granite and moss of the landscape was actually an ancient stone wall, all overgrown by the dampness of the water which ran directly by its side. There were no right angles or straight lines in the design. The entire structure appeared to have grown organically out of the peaty soil and the bedrock.

This had to be his 'country home'. It reminded me more of the shepherd's hut on Scarp where Willem had hidden. I took a deep breath and knocked gently on the ancient wooden door. Weathered and silver, it looked like it might crumble beneath my touch.

There was no welcoming answer. The door opened a crack at my slight touch, and I had to apply pressure to push my way through. I stepped inside and allowed my eyes to adjust to the darkness within.

It wasn't as dark as I'd expected, even though no chinks of light came through the well-crafted stone walls. The space was rounded, with wooden rafters. There were no material comforts here, no softness of a quilt, say, or a tablecloth over the solid plank table. Only roughhewn furniture sat there, and a blackened hearth with a huge chimney lay across the room. I made my way toward it.

The coals held no vestige of warmth, no lingering heat in the ashes. This meant the fire had not been tended for the past few days. How strange, for it was chilly and damp here in the structure. It could only mean that Nachtan wasn't present anymore. He must have left, gone on somewhere else, without letting Mrs. Battersea know.

That definitely felt wrong.

Had I missed him on my journey? Had he passed me by even as I was creeping north through the dawn? Dammit, a wasted journey. I stood up and looked about me with frustration, and it was then that I realized there was a second source of light in the space, apart from the open doorway. It came from a break in the stone wall to the far side of the fireplace.

Was this a two-room bothy, then? How luxurious.

I made it across the room in two steps. I had to duck my head beneath the unplaned wood of the jamb, for the opening into the second room was low. There was a window before me, or at least a break in the solid stone wall. Greenish light filtered through the pines behind the bothy. Still no sound of birdsong, though, only the susurration of wind through the pines and the quiet murmur of the stream flowing down the hillside.

But there, at last was the Venerable Nachtan. I breathed out a sigh of relief I hadn't even realized I was holding. Asleep on his bed with his hands by his side, palms up. With the grayish-green dim light through the pines in this shadowy room, his peaceful countenance reminded me of a painting, Ophelia floating in her watery grave, his long hair flowing out and his beard neatly combed in his front. His chest rose and fell with the slightest of movements.

'God, for a second there, I thought you were dead,' I said, my voice sounding too loud in this quiet space. When that didn't rouse him, I strode over and tapped him on the shoulder. 'Yo, VN, time to get up. I brought coffee and croissants, chocolate ones, your favorite.'

Still nothing. 'Nachtan, this is not a joke.' Not that the old witch had ever showed the slightest inclination for humour, not around me. 'You need to wake up!'

Panic edged my voice. I checked again that he really was breathing, that it hadn't been a trick of the light. Yes, and there was the faintest pulse threading through his veins as I held my fingers on his wrist. I dropped his cool hand and shook him harder, so hard that it was impossible for him not to open his eyes to object at my rough treatment of him.

Yet still not a gig from the old geezer.

'Oh, shit.'

My mind immediately leaped to the tale of Zande the Great. Zande who had no need for sleep but who couldn't be woken. Had Nachtan been cursed also?

CHAPTER 8

I had to run down the path by the stream a fair bit, out of the trees, before I could get any signal for the cell phone. Hugh didn't answer my call – he must be in one of those endless meetings still. I stood, helpless for a moment, running through my mind who I could call.

I didn't have Mrs. Battersea's number on me, and I didn't have time to make it back to the car to see if she had included it in her papers. I had no pigeon to send off with a message. There was actually no one else to call except Cate.

I brought up her name on my contacts and hesitated. Was I panicking over nothing? Perhaps he was merely in a deep slumber... But I knew the difference. I hadn't noticed the whiff of any lingering magic in the bothy, but on the other hand, I hadn't been looking for it.

No choice. I needed to call someone in the Kin, and the sooner the better.

Cate was silent as the words tumbled out. 'Where exactly is this place?'

'The north side of Loch Ness. Mrs. Battersea will have the coordinates.'

'Right. Please don't go back into the bothy, don't disturb anything. I need you to wait by the entrance to the path. There'll be a contingent sent out from Inverness immediately, and you'll need to guide them.'

She crisply hung up the phone, leaving me by the burbling brook, not another soul in sight.

If it was Meg who had done this terrible deed – and that was a huge IF because I didn't believe it for a minute, then I had to go back and find evidence for myself. I knew Margaret Forsythe's style, and I knew the imprint of her magic. If there was any hint of her in this evil deed, I had to ascertain it for myself. I checked the time on my phone. The Kin would take at least half an hour to arrive from Inverness. I had time to check the bothy, despite Cate's dire instructions not to re-enter the space.

I ran back up the rabbit trail to Nachtan's house of slumber. I sniffed all around Nachtan's recumbent body, and squinted at the light, then closed my eyes and opened my mind's sensors, but I got nothing. Both rooms were clean, not a whiff of Meg's magic, or of any other witch's, for that matter. Almost as if the place had been wiped surgically clean, it was devoid of anything but the smell of a fusty old witch. I hovered over the sleeping ancient once again.

'Wake up,' I shouted suddenly, as if I could take the curse off guard, but of course it was useless. I turned away, and my foot hit something, a piece of debris under his rough cot. It rolled away. And continued rolling along the packed earth of the room, in a way that nothing in the natural world could sustain. I got down on my knees in the dirt, lifting his blanket, and I saw a dim glint in the dark shadows at the far end, by the stone wall. My arm wasn't long enough. I had to lower my whole body to the ground and gently kick under the cot with my foot until the object rolled out again.

It came to rest by my boot. I slowly bent and picked it up, holding it to the light of the window.

A dark mirrored glass orb. I saw my own face peering back at me like through a fish lens, nose unnaturally large, with my blue eyes squinting on either side. I blew on it, tried to shake off the dust, then polished it on the front of my hoody.

I'd seen something like this object before. It was spherical, but not perfect in its roundness, like a hand-made glass Christmas ornament. Much like the crystal spheres on the tree Cate had brought for Hogmanay.

Yet different. Darker. The surface wasn't exactly like a silvered mirror, it had a dark overtone to it, leaving everything in the reflected background full of shadows. I sniffed it again with my mind's nose. Yes, it belonged to Nachtan, or at least he had handled it, but what was the sphere's purpose? The old witch had brought little else with him, except his pipe laid on the stone of the window ledge, and his staff leaning in the corner.

A mechanical sound interrupted my thoughts. It had been growing on the edges of my consciousness for the past minute or two, and with a start, I recognized it as the sound of the large Kin helicopter. Of course, there was one stationed in Inverness. How could I have forgotten? The Kin would be here shortly. Cromwell would have no need to drive the twisty roads along the lake to reach this spot.

My instructions had been to stay out of the bothy, to await the Kin by the path. I shoved the ornament safely into my satchel and ran out again, down the path, and reached the last meadow just as the large bird was settling down.

The Kin had sent a contingent of Elders. I was glad to see they took this seriously. Cromwell, of course, there was no chance of avoiding that one. He was dressed in a business suit, the first time I'd ever seen him out of his dour black robe. With his hair styled straight across his forehead, almost in a bowl cut, and the brown tweed of his suit tucked into his galoshes, he looked more like a figure from an old British comedy series than an Elder. In fact, I didn't recognize him till he scowled at me.

The other male witches were half-familiar to me. I'd seen them around Edinburgh and Scarp, but they all knew me, wearing mirror images of Cromwell's grimness on their own faces, and wellies on their feet.

The last one to exit the machine took me totally by surprise.

Cate. What the hell? How did she get here? She'd said she'd had business out of town, but I'd had no idea she was in the area. Yet it made an awful sense.

Hers was the one face that didn't appear to hate me on sight, but that didn't make me happy to see her.

She quickly swept across the grass to me in tall rubber boots, the really expensive kind that come with their own special wool socks. She wasn't dressed up to the nines as was her norm, but in the casual chic of blue jeans and hand-knit Nordic sweater. Her fringed suede coat was no longer the height of fashion, yet she wore it with panache.

'Where is he?' she asked tersely, while looking at the wilderness all around, for all the world as if she'd never been there before. She headed toward the main path, the only obvious one, but I put my hand on her arm to stop her.

'Over this way,' I said and led the group to the almost invisible route I'd taken before, the one that twisted between the gorse bushes and pines along the stream as the chopper's rotors slowed to a stop.

'You didn't touch anything?' Cromwell barked.

'No,' I assured him, a little exasperated. 'Except the door to get in. And I shook him, to try to get him to wake up.'

We reached the bothy, and I stepped aside to let them in.

They all remained clustered outside, eying the door and me with suspicion.

'What were you doing here?' One witch asked.

'How did you know to come to this spot?' The questions were coming at me fast and furious.

'I had to...' Dear God, I hadn't thought of that. I had no cover story to explain my presence here, couldn't tell them I'd hiked all this way to get Nachtan to help clear Margaret Forsythe's name.

'He invited me up for tea,' I blurted out, grasping on to the first thing I could think of. 'He wanted me to see his country place. We've grown very close, you know, over the past year.'

As soon as I'd said the words, I could have kicked myself. I couldn't come up with a more believable story? Like, me and the VN were best buds, and made a habit of hanging out together. Sure, we met at Starbuck's all the time.

It was a ridiculous explanation, especially as I had my doubts whether the VN even liked me. I hung my head, waiting for them to call me out on it. But to my astonishment, once they got over the initial disbelief of such an unlikely friendship, the Inverness Elders accepted the foibles of the Venerable Nachtan and made to enter the bothy.

Only Cate held back, staring at me with her dark eyes. Her brows were drawn together, just a little, and I couldn't read her face at all.

'Stay out here,' she commanded before ducking to enter into the dark hovel.

············

The five were in there a long time. I sat myself down on the nearest boulder, aimlessly watching the small stream burble its quick way down the hillside.

The sphere, I remembered with a start. I forgot to tell them about that glass object I'd found under Nachtan's cot. I opened my satchel and slowly withdrew it, holding it up to the weak rays of sunshine.

It fit in my hand like a billiard ball and it sparkled darkly, showing a reflection of me with the stone walls of the bothy barely discernable behind me. I closed my eyes for a brief moment and searched the orb but could sense nothing from it, except somehow it felt like Nachtan and not of the magic practitioner who'd put him under. I couldn't say exactly why I knew that, perhaps it was something about the warmth of the object even on this chill winter day, a warmth that had nothing to do with the material it was made of. If I sat still enough, I could almost hear the song of the glass, the vibration ringing through it.

The reflection of Cate appeared at the door to the bothy. Her eyes were on my back and she walked over to my rock without making a sound while I slipped the sphere into my satchel. I wanted more time to explore this metallic orb, to discover its secrets.

She looked at me with suspicion, then her eyes moved down to my bag. I held my breath, but she didn't say a word. Not right then.

Cate folded herself down on the rocks next to me and stretched out her legs which, even though they were encased in rubber boots, were lean and elegant.

'You know this doesn't look good,' she said in a low voice I could barely hear over the noise of the stream.

'Is it the same as Zande? The same kind of sleeping spell or curse or whatever it is?'

She looked down at me sideways from where she sat. 'It appears to be.'

'What does this mean? Is someone going around cursing all the most powerful witches? And who, who would do that? Who *could* do it?'

Nachtan was untouchable, surely. Hell, he was the *Venerable* Nachtan, the one so honored for his deeds and his own power and famous throughout the world of the Kin. Who, or what, could ever have gotten through his defences?

'Only a witch with great power himself, or herself, could pull this off,' she replied slowly. Her eyes were on the water. It shone gold from the stones beneath it in the winter sun. She flicked her head back to the bothy. 'They have suspicions. I will shield you and support you as best as I can, but be prepared for the questioning.'

'What?' I almost fell off my boulder, I turned round so fast. 'That's crazy. You're not saying they think *I* did this?'

'The Kin have to investigate all possible avenues,' she said. Her voice held no emotion. 'And you are here on the spot.'

'But I'm only here because I...' Then I shut my mouth again. Best not to go there. 'The coals from his fire were cold, nothing had been tended since at least before last night. I only got here today at noon. Last night I was with Hugh. You can ask him, they'll believe him because they know he wouldn't lie to the Kin even to save me!'

Her mouth was grim as she stared ahead, nodding in agreement.

'Besides,' I continued in a rush. 'How would I know what to do, how to cast a curse like this? They can't be seriously considering me as the culprit.'

She shrugged. 'You have managed to accomplish some amazing things in your brief career thus far,' she remarked drily.

I flashed her a dirty look. 'And Africa? How the hell do they think I managed to get out there and back without anyone knowing?'

With that, she took a deep breath in as if steeling herself. She turned her head on her elegant neck to look right into my eyes. 'It's your connection to Margaret Forsythe. They've come up with the theory that you're somehow working with her.'

She looked down at the stream again. 'And the worst part is,' she said slowly. 'If you look at it through the lens of Cromwell's utter dislike of you, their way of thinking and their beliefs, it actually all fits.'

'Cate!' I was too shocked for words almost, but not for long as I rushed to defend myself. 'You can't be serious, that's crazy talk, there's no way...'

She held up her hand, stopping my panicked flow. 'You know that, and I know that, but we have to convince *them*.' She jerked her chin at the stone hut behind us. The four male witches were only now emerging. Her voice became a fervent whisper. 'You're going to have to tell them everything you know about Margaret,' she said. 'And if you have any inkling as to where she's hiding these days, best spill it now. To save your own hide.'

As I let her words sink in, I could feel her gaze still on me, as if she were searching for something I was hiding from her.

And I realized from Cate's words that she had no idea of the airport incident, that unexpected meeting engineered by Margaret. So the spook hadn't been hired by her. But that left me with the burning question, who was he and why did he so urgently want to find Margaret Forsythe?

CHAPTER 9

We had to wait for an ambulance to arrive at the scene to bring Nachtan's slumbering body back to the safety of Inverness Castle. There was some consternation when the attendants realized they couldn't bring their wheeled stretcher up the path, and there was a further wait before the Emergency crew arrived with the burly team trained to rescue people from cliff tops and other dangerous spots. It was union rules apparently, and even the Kin couldn't overstep those boundaries.

We were finally allowed to take the helicopter back to the town. One of the Kin was given the pleasure of driving my Mercedes convertible back, and I took his place on the return flight.

My interrogation was held at the Castle, a place for which I held no fond memories. At least they didn't make me sit in the judgement chamber again, though. Instead we sat in the round room on the second story of the tower.

On the surface, it was a very civilized question and answer session, fuelled by endless cups of tea. When Johanna arrived, I had to reiterate everything I'd told the others.

'You say you have no idea where she might be now?' Her sharp nose remained trained on me like a bloodhound's, sniffing for the faintest whiff of falsehood or obfuscation.

'No, I never knew where she was,' I said yet again. Yes, I might be throwing Margaret under the bus, but really, what difference did it make to me? She had walked out in a snit because I chose to remain within the Kin. She hadn't factored my wishes and ambitions into her plan. I didn't owe her a thing. But I also didn't tell them about her appearance at Edinburgh airport. 'All I know is that she was dressed for the beach when I saw her in St. John's. She was drinking, I don't know, margaritas, I think, if that helps at all.'

I crossed my arms and wriggled my spine on the hard back of the wooden chair. I was getting mighty tired of all this.

'And how exactly did she travel both times?' Johanna wasn't letting anything go.

I shook my head, letting a small explosion of breath out through my lips. 'I have no idea,' I explained for the umpteenth time. 'She was far faster than the elves, that's all I know. She must have travelled thousands of miles in a very short time. Even if she'd been down in the Caribbean somewhere, that's a long way to go.'

'Flight, or some other means of transport?' The Master Elder appeared to be murmuring to herself. 'If only we had Nachtan to ask.' She tapped her fingers on the wooden table before beginning at me again.

'She didn't share this with you?'

I shook my head. 'No, she showed me how to physically fly, but I have no idea how she covered those great distances so quickly.'

'Flight, actual flight.' Johanna was lost in thought again. 'It's amazing. We will, of course, require you to write an explanation of this process so that we can replicate it. But that can wait for a later time.'

She took another breath. The room was silent, waiting for her to speak. 'And how did you call her to you? Explain again, please.'

The dragonfly brooch that had appeared in all its magic one morning on the balcony, the jewels glinting brightly in the sun, as colorful as Margaret herself. In times of need, if I touched it and called out, either for her or just to let my pain loose, she came. All this I told Johanna, and even as I spoke the words out loud, I realized how incredible this story must sound.

'And this brooch, is it still in your possession?'

All of this long afternoon, Cate had sat by my side, not uttering a word. But now she interrupted. Perhaps she didn't trust me still not to breathe a word about the events of that night last June in St. John's.

'Margaret removed it from Dara's jacket,' she said decisively. 'I saw this action myself.'

Johanna nodded, more accepting of Cate's word than of mine.

'And you've had no contact with this witch since?'

'None,' I lied firmly.

How much longer could this go for? After three cups of tea, my bladder was bursting, but no one dared interrupt Johanna until she was satisfied she'd picked every morsel of Margaret-related information out of my brain.

'Fine.' Johanna appeared to be relenting, but her brow was lined with worry. She stared round at the few of us in the room. 'We will have to send out a PANEC notification throughout all Kin-friendly countries to be on high alert for any sightings of this witch. She is not to be harmed, but we need to bring her in, with force if necessary, before she does any more damage.'

'We will, of course,' Cate inserted smoothly, 'Be doing all in our power to regain contact with her. While overseas.'

'I don't know if it's a good idea for Dara to be traveling at the moment.' Johanna made no secret about the fact she wanted to keep a close, very close, eye on me.

But really? My first chance to actually travel and see the world was being stymied, because of Margaret, of all witches. I couldn't for a minute believe she was responsible for these strange curses laid on the powerful witches of the world, not Margaret. She didn't care enough and she had no earthly or heavenly reason to do such a thing. Yet here we were, me being stuck in Edinburgh or worse, under the Covenanter's eyes in Inverness, all because they truly believed she was capable of such dark deeds.

'I think,' Cate spoke respectfully yet firmly. 'It's my opinion that Dara may be more successful in reaching out to Margaret Forsythe if she is removed from the Kin center. Margaret may be more inclined to be in touch. And who's to say where in the world she might be? There are beaches all over. I think, with a combined approach of Dara searching for her with whatever mind connection the two have, and Kin forces combing phone and credit card records, her trust fund activities and all that, we'll have more success. That's my thoughts.'

The room was silent as Johanna gave serious consideration to the idea, then she nodded decisively. 'Yes, I see your point, Cate. Alright, Dara will go with the delegation. And remain with you at all times.'

I closed my eyes, giving thanks to the universe or whatever that she didn't cancel my assignment. I was now more determined than ever to find Margaret, but not simply to save her from false accusations. At that moment, I was more concerned with saving my own butt.

But Cate wasn't done with me yet for the day. The two of us waited just inside the Castle's gate for the taxi which would bring me to the train station for my return to Edinburgh. I'd been inside enough that day, and now the evening was drawing in. I needed the fresh air.

'Did you remove anything from the bothy? Something you're withholding, not sharing with me?'

I turned to her, startled. So she hadn't missed that fact. She held her hand out.

I slowly opened the satchel and withdrew the orb.

'Interesting,' she said, her eyes avidly scouring it in the half light of the late afternoon. She took it from my hand and held it up to the streetlight. As I had done, she lightly sniffed it.

'Not a thing on it.' She sounded almost pleased with the result. 'What do you know about this?'

I shook my head and shifted my position on the hard boulder. 'Nothing. It was under his bed.'

'Alright.' She accepted my word and gently placed the glass into the deep pockets of her fringed jacket, I assumed for safe keeping. 'This... I'm afraid it's best if I keep it. And you don't need to share with the Kin. I think this might be pivotal in our investigation, and I do love a surprise.'

If I'd known what the origin of the ball really was, I'd have smashed it underfoot while I waited outside Nachtan's bothy, to let the stream carry the shards away. If I'd known then. But hindsight is everything, isn't it? I dumbly shook my head.

No, I wouldn't tell.

....

That is, I wouldn't tell anyone except Margaret. She needed to know what was going on, how her name was being bandied about as the guilty curser, and now my name as her associate was, too. This was not good at all.

Back in Edinburgh that evening, I walked down the Royal Mile, lost in thought. As far as I was concerned, the accusations against Margaret weren't my business. She could row her own boat up the stream as much as she wanted.

But when I was also facing their accusations, well, that changed things mightily. I needed her to come out of hiding to clear my name.

She'd been right in saying it was all going to hell. How had she known? I paused my steps, right there by St. Giles' Cathedral. This was too big a thought for me to pay attention to walking on the cobblestones at the same time. I leaned against the granite walls, for a new understanding threatened to overwhelm me and I needed them to lend me their solid support.

Was Margaret actually at the heart of these dastardly curses? Was she the instigator?

As Cate had pointed out, Margaret Forsythe had a good reason to hold a grudge against the Kin. Being locked away for a century would have upset the most stable of witches, surely. I bit my bottom lip and stared across the road at the tourists, still thronging Edinburgh even in early January.

Who's the most powerful witch of all? I remembered Cate's words as she looked at me in the old mirror. Power. Margaret was the most powerful witch of all There was no doubt in my mind. But still, it didn't make any sense. Yes, if she was going to curse any witch, it would be Nachtan of course, that would be tit-for-tat in her mind. But the Great Zande? Would Margaret have even heard of him, living in her little trust fund bubble, lazing on the beaches of the world?

A meeting with Margaret was needed. It had to be this evening. As I left the shelter of the stone walls, the wind picked up its bite. My feet kept on along the path I'd been following, down the Royal Mile, but it wasn't until I reached Holyrood Palace that I realized where I was heading.

Arthur's Seat. It was the closest holy place untainted by the Christian churches, high above the city of Edinburgh, a magical place for magic.

I brushed aside the memory of the last time I'd tried to work a spell up there, when I was attempting to find Mom in the Ice Kingdom. No, it hadn't worked, then. I'd just managed to call down a rainstorm on me and that jerk Terrance the goblin. But I also hadn't really understood what I was doing, back then.

The hill hadn't gotten any easier to climb, and the wind pushed against me every step of the way up there on the high ground. The last time I'd come up here, back when the energy of the Crystal Charm Stone was still pounding fresh in my veins, I'd practically bounced up the rabbit paths straight to the summit. The power in me had calmed down a lot since then, perhaps I'd learned to channel it appropriately or maybe it merely had found its level within me and my body had grown used to it. I rather missed the highs of it.

I took the road rather than the faint trails tonight. There was no moon to light my way.

Finally I reached the summit yet I had no idea what I was going to do, how I was going to call on Margaret from wherever she was. I would just have to wing it, reasoning to myself that surely to God, a witch of her strength, and a witch as powerful as me, we could somehow connect just by calling.

Taking a deep breath, I faced toward the east, and calmed my mind, letting only thoughts of Margaret in. Auld Meg underground in the Vaults, Lady Margaret Forsythe riding in her ancient Daimler, Margaret in her beachwear with the smell of margaritas on her like a perfume. I pictured her in all her various aspects, the few times I'd seen her. I summoned the feeling of her, her lightness of being, her snarkiness when I didn't agree with her.

Believe, I told myself. Believe that she is here next to me. Feel her aura, feel her magic print.

And there was something, a whirl in the wind, a presence not too far away. I could almost feel her by my side.

'Margaret?' I kept my eyes closed, the better to concentrate on that slight essence I felt wavering about. 'Margaret, please come. I need to speak with you. There's a matter which concerns both of us.'

I listened. Was that her laughter sounding, so faintly? It might be the wind humming through the power lines, far below at Holyrood Palace.

'Please, Margaret,' I said, still with my eyes clamped shut. 'What you were trying to tell me at the airport, I realize you were right. We need to discuss this. Now.'

I could almost feel the sunny warmth of her beach, smell the saltwater crystals in her hair, and I knew without a doubt she was listening. It was as if she was hovering over an old-fashioned message machine, hearing my pleas but not picking up the phone to speak.

'Goddammit Margaret! You were right, okay? Talk to me. Stop ignoring me. I know you have nothing to do with the curses on Zande and Nachtan. I believe this, but if you don't respond, I'll... I'll accept that Cate is right. I will work to clear my own name, and I don't care if I throw you under the bus while I'm at it. Speak to me now!'

And just like that, silence. The presence of Margaret had disappeared as if she'd pressed the reject button. Her absence in the wind around me was palpable.

I screamed out in frustration and raised my fists to the sky as the wind whipped my hair around my face. Then, I let go. Defeated. That was it then.

The lights of the harbor far below shone through the damp, each streetlight with its own tiny halo. Nothing moved down there. It was as dead as the connection to my former mentor.

'I don't think threatening her was the way to go.' A tall figure shifted in the wind and walked into my view. He huddled inside a trench coat inadequate for this winter wind, a scarf tightly knotted around his neck and a flat cap smushed down over his blond hair. His nose looked reddened with cold even in the faint light on the hill, and even as I watched, he withdrew a handkerchief from his pocket with which to wipe a drip.

The spook. No wonder she refused to connect with me. She must have known he was there.

'What the hell are you doing here?' I snarled at him, glad to find an outlet for my frustration. 'You scared her away. I almost had her!'

He shook his head. 'No, you scuppered it yourself,' he pointed out. His voice was surprisingly deep to come from such a thin frame. He had the aristocratic Kin accent though, that tone of privilege and confidence that made everything he said sound like a pronouncement of truth.

'You must know her well enough to realize that you took the wrong approach with her,' he added.

'What do *you* know of Margaret Forsythe?' I threw at him. My voice had dropped twenty degrees, not that I'd had any warmth towards him before. Yes, I'd failed to connect with her and that stung, never mind the possibility he might be right. I had chased Margaret away this time, as I had done all the other times. The sharp pain that rose up inside me had to be anger.

'Not a lot,' he said earnestly, shoving his hankie back into his pocket as he did so. 'That's why I've been following you - '

'You stupid Kin spy,' I broke across his voice. He didn't know anything about Margaret, and seriously, it was none of his business anyway. It was time for him to butt out. 'You don't even have the sense to stay undercover, do you?' I turned to go. I was tired and freezing, and so annoyed at life and this guy. I began quickly walking down the path.

He took long strides to catch up with me, managing to not even look like he was hurrying. 'While we're walking, I really think we should discuss the matter of Margaret. It's imperative I – '

'Imperative for you! Not for me. Not anymore.' I shoved my gloved hands deep into my winter jacket and picked up my pace, practically running downhill now.

'Stop interrupting me and listen for a moment, will you?'

I turned to him with the nastiest look on my face I could summon. 'No,' I barked. 'I will not listen to you. You are a pathetic specimen, a terrible spy. This is probably the only job you could get within the Kin. I suggest you quit, and find something you're better suited to. Something nice and mundane.'

I set my face back to the road ahead. We'd almost reached the bottom. 'But whatever you do, just stay away from me, and keep out of my hair,' I called back to him. 'You've seen for yourself that Margaret doesn't want to talk to me.'

It was only at that moment that I realized my face was damp. The wind had moisture in it, but the wet on my face was salt tears.

CHAPTER 10

I didn't see him over the next few days, so I figured I must have scared him off or discouraged him, or something. Then I completely forgot about him because it was time for the China trip. Hugh and Cate had left the previous day. I'd seen them both off on the large private Kin jet. I assumed it, or another like it, would be returning for the rest of us the next day.

I could hardly keep my excitement in, for finally I was going to travel in the style I wanted to become accustomed to. I'd travelled Business Class to Montreal with Mom last summer, but I had dreams that this experience would outshine even that luxury trip.

Yet I didn't forget my worries for Nachtan in his enchanted state, and I checked in with Mrs. Battersea the day we were scheduled to leave. He hadn't woken up from his Sleeping Beauty curse. Apparently he hadn't even stirred.

'Not a peep,' she said, shaking her head. She wore a plum colored suit today, but her spectacles frames were spring green. The two shades did not harmonize in any way. She was not herself at all today. 'Do you know they've sent him on to China already?'

'What? Why? But he's asleep.'

'Yes,' she agreed. 'He's being transported in a hospital bed. Cromwell wants to keep him close, for he believes they will find a way to undo the curse in Asia.'

I shook my head. The ways of the Kin were plenty strange.

'I need you to promise me, Dara, promise me you'll find whoever's responsible and make them remove this curse. He's not able to eat or drink, they've had to put in a feeding tube in order for Him to be nourished.'

She looked like she was about to cry.

'It's so very undignified for Him,' she continued. 'I fear He'll be painfully embarrassed when he comes out of it.'

I tried not to look too sceptical of her sentiment. When, if, he ever got free from this curse, the Venerable Nachtan would have more on his mind than the indignities suffered upon his physical form. He'd be pissed that any other witch got the better of him. Royally narked at the impudence, the gall, and this wrath would be a terrible thing to experience. I planned to stay very clear of him untill he had a chance to work it out of his system.

That's if we would be able to break the curse.

The thing that was puzzling me, along with the far greater minds of all the Kin, was how could this have come about? A spell to curse such great and powerful witches to sleep? I didn't know a lot, but Hugh had always said that spells weren't necessary, that mind power was the thing. So how was it possible that the great minds of Nachtan and Zande could be overpowered?

There had to be a way of circumventing their minds, their powers, whatever. At any rate, it wasn't my mystery to find out. I had to figure out how to get to Margaret and thereby save my own skin. The pride of the Kin was at stake, and as long as they could salvage that, they wouldn't care too much about collateral damage.

I left Mrs. Battersea to her fretting and ran down the stone steps of the tower. The limos were gathered in the courtyard below to take us all to Edinburgh Airport. Our bags had already been picked up early that morning. This was the only way to travel.

My carryon was exactly where I'd left it in the court-yard. The place was surrounded by soldiers, I'd known it would be safe enough and I couldn't bear to lug it all the way up the stairs and back.

In the stone paved area outside, individuals from the delegation milled loosely about, waiting. It was a big crowd. I looked for a familiar face, but couldn't see anyone.

How would all these bodies fit into the few limos parked in a row? I peeked into the nearest one. I'd never seen one of the luxury vehicles in real life before, just in movies. The inside was huge, so spacious with comfortable leather seats and plenty of leg room. I could imagine myself relaxing there, having a drink of cham-pagne (for surely there was a bar) and nattering on to my companions as we ignored the plebians watching us roll on by...

'Dara.'

The flat voice with the accent of privilege spoke near my ear, wrenching me from my daydreams.

'Come on, our ride is over there.' Win stuck a bright yellow card into my hand, then jerked her head around past the courtyard. With one last loving glance at the sleek black car, I followed her up the stone steps between buildings.

'Why do we have to come this far?' I asked as we emerged back into daylight. 'The cars are back there.'

She didn't answer me, but made a beeline straight for the closest of the two buses waiting nearby.

'Ah, no,' I said, refusing to take another step. 'That's not fair. Why can't they find room in the limos?'

'How important do you think you are?' Win muttered under her breath as she lifted her carry-on, preparing to go up the steps of the bus.

I followed her in. It was already half full, but Win didn't aim for the empty seats in the back, the obvious choice. Instead, she plonked herself down in the aisle seat of the first row, placing her carryon between her legs instead of finding room in the bin above and she nodded for me to take the one across from her. I found myself sitting next to a very large guy, Spanish perhaps, and it was with a show of great reluctance that he removed his briefcase from my chosen seat. He huffed when I hauled my own carryon into the non-existent space between my legs. My knee was forced to lean against the caramel corduroy of his pants, the fabric stretched tight around his thigh. He glared at me, but I had no choice. My other leg was stuck out into the aisle.

'Let's move to the back,' I whispered to her, then paused to let more people pass by. My seat companion shifted ever so slightly, taking even more of my allotted space. 'Quick, before all those seats are taken.'

She scowled over at me, but didn't say a word until the bus was filled and the engines started. The doors closed with a whump and the vehicle jerked into a roll through the service tunnel.

Then and only then did she lean over to whisper instructions to me.

'As soon as the bus stops, grab your bag and leave. We have to be the first ones off.'

I shifted uncomfortably, trying to reclaim some leg room.

'Can I ask why?' The bus was already stiflingly warm, with too many people using up the available oxygen. It would be about a half-hour ride to the airport. I looked longingly at the window, wondering if I could ask my seat-mate to open it.

Win looked at me as if she couldn't believe how stunned I truly was. 'So we get the best seats, of course. It's a long trip, and I don't want to be stuck by the bathrooms. We have to maneuver ourselves to be the closest to the Elders. I don't want to look like a loser.'

'It's a private jet, Win,' I said to her, not bothering to lower my voice. 'Haven't you ever watched movies? Those things are luxurious, and everyone has a great seat.'

She sneered at me again, holding herself tensely erect as the bus entered a roundabout at great speed. 'Really? And how many people travel on those jets of your imagination?'

Oh. I looked back at all the bodies on the bus, and thought of the other one, just as full. How many private jets would it take to transport so many people such a long distance?

'The Kin hired a commercial plane,' she continued, still in such a low voice that I had to strain to hear her over the rumble of the engine. She widened her eyes at me, mocking me as the understanding dawned. 'Yeah. These yellow passes don't entitle us to free champagne. We'll be stuck in Economy.

'So,' she continued. 'As soon as we stop, we need to be the first off the bus. Got it? Use your elbows if you have to.'

I nodded. 'But why be in such a hurry to get to Customs? We can't race through that.'

She shook her head impatiently. 'No Customs, the Kin have arranged to dispense with that formality. You just need to follow real close behind me all the way.

'Then we walk very fast – don't run! We can't look desperate. We walk quickly through the terminal to be the first to join the jet.'

She scowled down at the yellow pass in her hand. 'We need to sit in the first row, the very first. There are only two seats in that one, not three like the rest of the tourist class. If you make it there before me, choose the ones on the left. This is very important, and I'm counting on you.'

I was touched, in an odd sort of way, that she would be so concerned, and also that she wanted to include me. If anything, I would have thought our being paired together would have caused Win to try every trick in the book against me, to embarrass me and bring me down and, yes, make me appear to be the loser. 'Thanks, Win,' I took a moment to express my gratitude. 'I appreciate what you're doing for me.'

Her jaw dropped slightly. 'What do you mean? I'm not doing this for you. You're my partner, and I can't have you reflect badly on me.'

Of course. It had always been like that with Win. Everything was a competition. If I didn't keep up with her on this trip, she would make my life hell.

'Besides, I'm under strict orders by Cate not to let you out of my sight.' She scowled again, then tensed as the bus slowed to a stop. 'Get ready to move fast.'

CHAPTER 11

So now Win considered herself my keeper? I had no time to work up a grudge against this latest development from Cate, but I would have plenty to say later on. The moment the bus had drawn to a stop, Win was up and impatiently waiting at the front of the bus, her carry-on thrust before her. Anyone who valued their shins quickly got out of her way. She bounded down the steps like a rabbit before the hounds.

She didn't run, as she said, but she walked. Very fast. Win could have race-walked for England.

I traveled in her wake, carried forward in momentum by the vacuum left behind her, but I was still huffing by the time she turned away from the general commercial hub of the airport and through the doors of the General Aviation building. She must have planned the route out ahead of time, for she didn't pause for a second to check the signs. She knew exactly where we were headed.

As we approached the final glass doors leading to the outside, I glanced behind me. Our fellow passengers straggled behind us, unaware there was a race on. But the Spanish-looking guy who had so reluctantly given me space on the bus wasn't far off behind us. His shiny handmade shoes clicked on the polished concrete floors as he pounded along in a half-jog, his face set and grim.

Win paused at the glass door only long enough for the uniformed clerk to examine her passport and yellow boarding card. I'd forgotten to take out my identification and lost precious seconds as I searched through my bag, and Caramel Pants pushed me aside with his large belly, causing me to drop my ticket. It floated off in the breeze he made rushing through.

I quickly snatched it from the ground and darted back into line before someone else could push past me, and the two of us went neck to neck all the way to the airplane steps. He tried to use his gut again to gain an advantage, but I slipped around him and, by stretching my leg out, got to home base a split second before him.

And I took my time climbing the stairway, as there was no way he could push past me in that narrow space. I even paused to glance back and give him a sweet smile.

I was beginning to see the appeal of competition.

Win was already ensconced in the prized seats, the ones with only two chairs in the row and plenty of leg room.

'What took you so long?' she scolded me. 'That guy almost had you beat and then I would have had to sit next to him for the whole flight.'

She paused to scowl up at the man. He ignored us and proceeded to gracelessly dump his bag into the overhead container and throw himself into the window seat of the row across from us.

Once we were actually settled into our seats, Win prepared herself for the long flight. She removed a neck pillow, an eye mask and headphones from her bag, and shook the blanket provided out of its plastic bag. After she was nicely stuffed into this isolating cocoon, she totally ignored me for the next five hours.

On my one foray to the washroom, I saw that the plane wasn't quite full. There were plenty of empty seats. I had also been expecting a much larger airplane, but it wasn't the usual huge one with two aisles and center seating. I idly estimated the number of passengers in our class to be about one hundred. Still, it was a large delegation.

The toilet cubicle lights drew all the color out of my face. I washed my face and hands, then tried to pinch a healthy glow into my cheeks. It didn't work, so I gave up and just stuck my hair up in a scrunchy. Who was here to see me anyway? Might as well be comfortable.

I was just turning to leave the cramped space when the door opened. I jumped back in a fright – hadn't I locked it?

But I had no time to wonder about that because a tall thin body stuffed himself into the space with me and slammed the door shut again.

'What the hell?' He had his back to me, too close for me to see who it was. 'This bathroom is occupied, in case you hadn't noticed.'

He squirmed himself around to face me, but that left me looking at his white shirt. It was missing a button, and the collar was frayed around the edges. I looked up. Way up.

The spook. My blood began to boil. How dare he? And I let my indignation rip out of me.

The man had the audacity to lift his great ham of a hand and place it over my mouth. There was no room for me to struggle in this enclosed space, but I sure tried my best.

'I'm so sorry to do this,' he leaned down and whispered in my ear. 'But you left me no choice. I have to speak to you about Margaret Forsythe. Privately.'

He lifted his hand, and give him his due, he did look a little embarrassed. But he had no right to force himself into the toilet like this.

'How'd you get in here? That door was locked! There's no way you could have used magic.' Magic was forbidden to be used on airplanes by universal convention. To ensure adherence to this rule, adamantite magic blockers were also built into every modern aircraft. I never did understand the mechanics of it, but it was a safety issue.

'There's a little latch under the 'Lavatory' sign,' he whispered helpfully. 'It unlocks the door. Not many people know about that.'

'You still had no right to come in here!'

'You're absolutely correct, and I do apologize again. However, there was no other way to speak to you without being seen.' He straightened up and leaned back as far as he could as if to give me the personal space propriety demanded. 'I have tried.'

'I told you before, I have no idea where Margaret is! You can go back to your bosses and tell them that and stop following me. It's a waste of time. She comes when she wants and I have no way of calling her.' I stomped on his toes for good measure, as there was no other way I could fight back in this tiny space.

That didn't help matters, not at all. With a curse, his instinctive reaction was to hop on one foot and try to grab the injured member in his hand, but of course, there was no room for this maneuver. He ended up kneeing me in the gut with his gangly long leg and I hit the small of my back against the metal sink.

'Ouch!'

We were now an entangled mess of limbs. It was warm in the tiny space. I used both my hands to push him as far away as I could, which wasn't, of course, far at all.

'Let's call a truce.'

'Truce? Why don't we just get out of here? I promise, I'll talk to you. It's not like I can get away from you here on the plane, but I really have nothing to tell you that the Kin don't already know.'

'There's too many ears out there.' He squirmed around me and sat himself on the toilet. That was a bit better in that his action freed up some breathing space, but it left me forced to either stand between his gawky long legs or have him move his legs together in a very prissy manner. I kicked his shin to let him know which I preferred.

'Alright.' With a wince, he forced his knees together and twisted his hips. I leaned against the door and stared down at him. I crossed my arms, because I could, and because it helped me feel in control of this situation.

'I want answers first.'

He shrugged in acquiescence. His eyes were a really bright blue, even in the single light source which washed out everything else.

'Why are you on my tail?'

'I told you, I need to contact Margaret Forsythe.'

'I know that! But why? Who's your boss?'

'My boss?' He said the word like it was a ludicrous concept.

'Yeah. Which Kin are you working for? The Covenanters?'

It couldn't be Cate, after all, she had Win to keep an eye on me. Besides, neither Cate nor Johanna as the Grand Master of the Kin would set such a loser up to do the job of tailing me. The only other group I could think of was Cromwell and his gang. They were the logical choice.

He screwed up his face. 'Why on earth do you think I would have anything to do with the Covenanters?'

'So who, then? Who is looking for Margaret and why?'

'Me,' he said, his voice impatiently patient, as if he was speaking to a moron and knew he had to be nice. He spread out his hands in exasperation, but only succeeded in banging his wrist off the sink.

'I don't understand.'

'Then I suggest you give me a chance to explain.'

I thought about that for a moment, then gave him a short nod. 'Permission granted.'

He took a deep breath, as if wondering where to begin. 'I'm a lawyer, and I'm investigating Margaret's estate.'

I shook my head as if to clear out my ears. I couldn't believe what he was telling me. 'A lawyer?' My voice squeaked.

He nodded.

'But why all this sneaking around and ... and invading my privacy?'

'Keep your voice down! We can't let them know,' he hissed as he cocked his head to indicate the rest of the plane.

'If that's all you wanted, why didn't you just grab her at the airport?'

'I didn't realize it was her, then, did I? I was following you in the hopes you'd lead me to her. I never expected it to be that easy!' Despite his admonition to me, the timbre of his own voice rose.

I shook my head as if to clear it, then shifted my foot, forcing him to move also. 'And what's this about her Estate? She's not dead!'

'Of course she isn't. Otherwise, I wouldn't be looking to speak with her,' he replied. He was whispering again, yet he still had that speaking-to-an-imbecile note in his voice. 'There are certain matters pertaining to her estate which need to be cleaned up.'

'She has a trust fund.'

'Yes, a trust fund that was initiated a century ago, and legal matters have become more sophisticated since then.'

I stared at him hard. He'd missed a bit shaving, a patch right under his right jawbone. The man was thin, I could see the tendons in his neck, and his Adam's apple stuck out. But not in an unattractive way.

'So?'

'Her trust fund is vulnerable. It is imperative that I speak with her, to get her permission to tie up some loose ends before...'

'Before what?'

He glanced around us, as if there was room for anyone else to be hiding in the cubicle.

'Before the Kin get their hands on it,' he whispered.

'You're Kin,' I reminded him. He wouldn't be on this airplane if he wasn't, and besides, he couldn't hide the innate magic in those eyes.

'Sort of,' he mumbled, after a pause.

'How can you be *sort of* Kin? You either are, or you aren't.' Unless he was a half-blood like me, not brought up in the traditions. I cocked my head as I considered this. No, not with that face and bone structure. He was Kin through and through.

Although, he was a very shabbily dressed witch. And an emissary of the Kin wouldn't bother making up such a lack-luster story, their inborn arrogance wouldn't even think of it. I made the decision that he was harmless enough. Weird, but not a threat.

'Doesn't matter, anyway,' I told him, more kindly than I'd spoken before. 'Like I said, I have no way to get in touch with Margaret. So you're out of luck.'

He nodded, his shoulders slumped. 'I understand. She's a difficult one to get hold of,' he agreed. Then he straightened his back again as he looked up at me. 'Can I ask you, as a favor to Margaret, not to mention this to anyone?'

I nodded slowly. Whatever his reasons for seeking Margaret out, he was no threat to her, or to me. 'Good luck with it.'

I took that opportunity to slip out the door. It wasn't until I was back in my seat at the front of the plane that I realized I hadn't even asked him his name.

CHAPTER 12

Win didn't emerge from her cocoon again till we were somewhere over Russia. I had no idea what time zone we were in or even precisely the date anymore — were we traveling towards tomorrow or back to yesterday? Whichever way, we were headed into a winter's evening over the northern reaches of Siberia.

I had long since kicked off my boots and was sitting cross-legged in the seat. It was comfortable enough. Win was tucked into her corner by the shaded window. With the curtained wall in front and the tall seat backs behind us, we were isolated, in an intimate cave of darkness.

I watched the little plane on the screen in front of me make its steady way towards Asia until I became conscious that she had changed position.

'You're awake then.'

Her brown eyes were still sleep soft, and her usually tense, wiry body was relaxed, still in her warm nest. The only sound was that of the jet engines. Outside it was night. No one could hear our conversation.

'I never thought I'd say this, but kudos to you.'

Her mouth wasn't two feet from me, yet I still had to strain to hear her. I'd never expected to hear those words or that sentiment coming from Win.

'For what?'

'You're smarter than I realized.'

'Right, like you mean that.' I laughed cynically. 'It almost sounded like a compliment when you put it that way.'

'No, I'm serious.'

She had to be setting me up for something, but I wasn't going to give her an opening.

'You've never given me a chance to show you just how brilliant I am,' I replied airily, then couldn't help but add, 'You were too busy hating me because I was a half-blood back at Scarp.'

She shrugged in agreement. 'Didn't hate *you* as such,' she said. 'It was just that you were unexpected. I had the whole year planned out, and it was going very well. I'd researched all the others – Oliver, Fergianna, Pauline, and I knew I could outmaneuver the lot of them. I knew their strengths, their weaknesses. I knew who I could afford to dismiss and who I had to suck up to. But you...'

She broke off.

'Me?'

'You were thrown into the mix all of a sudden.'

'Thrown to the wolves, you mean,' I muttered.

'I had no time to troll you on social media because there was no connection on Scarp, not for the students,' she continued, ignoring my interruption. 'I was greatly annoyed at that disruption in my plans. I had to attack you, find your weak points, any way I could.'

I stared at her. Loud warning bells were ringing in my head, and I wondered where this confession was headed. Everything Win did, every human interaction she made, there was always a reason behind it. A plan, something to further the agenda of Win.

'So? What's your point in bringing all this up now?' I found I was still bracing my spine against the tall seat back.

'I just wanted to say kudos,' she repeated herself. Her voice wasn't reacting to the hostility in mine. She remained calm, almost sleepy in her tone. 'You've come so far in such a short time.'

She yawned and stretched her limbs, loosening the blanket which had been so tightly wrapped around her. 'I really believe you were as clueless as you presented when you first came to Scarp,' she continued. 'All of us thought you were putting on a big act, but you were actually for real.'

'And now? Why do you think I've come so far, as you put it?'

'It's obvious to me,' she said. 'But then again, I am a master gamer. You're playing Cate Huxor, you're using her to leapfrog right into the heart of the Kin.' In the darkness, I couldn't distinguish her pupils from the brown surrounding them. There was no judgement in her gaze, no shaming, just a lazy, late-night admiration.

I shook my head. If Win only knew the real truth... but there's no way I would share that. And I had to remain vigilant. This unexpected softness, this intimate setting, it was probably just a ploy to make me open up to Win, give her information she could use against me later.

'Win, I'm at the same level, professionally, as you,' I said, my voice cool. 'I don't see that as any kind of leapfrogging.'

She shook her head and looked down at her lap. 'I'm here on this delegation because of my languages, that's the only reason I was chosen over, say, Oliver. None of the other Kin can speak so many of the Chinese dialects, which is precisely why my parents started me learning them when I was three years old.'

Did she say *three years old*? I didn't think I could even remember back that far. No wonder the young witch was so competitive. It was bred into her bones. 'Shit. I didn't know.'

She gave a one-shouldered shrug. 'But I get the feeling that you have something on Cate. You're using that to get ahead, to push through the barriers that would normally be in your way.'

Instead of hating me for what she believed was an underhanded tactic to further myself, she admired me. Yes, she was right in that I did have something on Cate, but this information made me her hostage, not the other way round. And that was the only reason I was here on this trip.

....

As we flew into the untimely dawn, high above the clouds, the sun's brilliance was relentless in forcing us all to wake up and partake of breakfast. And coffee. There was never a better smell to cut through the stale air of the silver bullet which carried us across the land mass below. Coffee really was liquid gold sometimes.

I'd fully expected that Win would revert back to her former ways of cutthroat manipulation, of acting like everything was a competition which she had to win at all costs, and I hadn't been looking forward to dealing with this on a daily basis. But to my surprise, she remained (at least with me) friendly and almost open, treating me as an equal. It could only be because she honestly believed that I was as devious as herself.

Win respected me. Which meant I really couldn't disappoint her with the truth.

She grew as excited as a little kid on our approach to the huge Chinese city, yet I could also sense unease underlying her tension.

I looked past her out the window, and all I could see was a layer of gray, the sign of major pollutants in the atmosphere. She grew silent at the sight.

'You've been here before?' I asked her.

She gave a short nod, then wrenched her eyes away from the window. They were still soft and vulnerable from her awakening. 'My early years were spent here,' she said. 'And we went back every Chinese New Year to my grandparents' home. I still have very strong ties here.'

'Will you be seeing your relatives then, if you get a chance?'

'Oh yes,' she said emphatically. 'It's my duty, and besides...' Win grew silent.

'Besides?'

She thought for a moment. Beneath her cheek muscles, I could see her tongue playing over her teeth, as if she were debating her next move. She finished counting the pros and cons and gave a decisive nod.

The announcement for us to replace our seatbelts sounded right then, cutting through her words. I thought she said she had to visit a temple, but that wasn't reverence in her eyes. No, it was fear. Pure fear.

The old Win peeped out for a moment, pugnacious and daring me with her eyes not to breathe a word of her secret. The jet's engines changed in sound amid the noise of the landing gear engaging as we prepared for landing.

The plane jumped a little, a lot actually, as we entered unexpected turbulence on our descent. It was far too noisy to continue our conversation, and the moment was gone. Win put on her red wool coat, smoothing it down, and she turned back to the window. She said not another word on the matter, not until much later when she really had to call on my help.

·······

We were deposited at a huge, westernized hotel, one of the large chains with a good name. I paused after I got off the bus and looked up, way up. There was absolutely nothing about the building to suggest we were in China. We could have been in any city in the US or Canada.

Hugh was waiting for me in the chandelier lit lobby, as he had promised, but was passing the time in conversation with someone else. His eyes leaped to mine the moment we walked in through the revolving door. With a smile, he beckoned me over.

We hugged and even kissed, and I held him longer than I needed to. It was only at that moment that I realized how absolutely exhausted I was, discombobulated with not having slept a wink during the flight. My body was gearing down because I'd been awake for too long, yet the bright sun outside denied that it was time for bed. My mind was bleary, and it must have shown on my face.

'You'll have a bit of jet lag,' he said kindly, holding me at arm's length. 'You're not used to the long-haul traveling, and I don't think your flight was as comfortable as mine.'

'Oh,' he said, almost as an afterthought. 'Let me introduce you to Rob. He's managed to get himself included in the delegation. You can never have enough lawyers.' This last was said with a genial laugh as if everyone knew the difference to that statement.

So now I knew the name of the man who had accosted me in the toilet.

'Rob.' I held out my hand reluctantly. I made sure to narrow my eyes at him.

'Hullo again, Dara,' the lawyer said, smiling as if he didn't see my dirty look. He glanced over to Hugh. The two men were of a similar height. 'We met on the plane coming over.'

I dropped my hand as quickly as I could, covering the action up with a yawn. Rob nodded uncertainly, then made himself scarce.

Hugh gave me another small hug, then reached into his suit pocket. 'Here's the key to the room. You go on and do whatever you need to do, sleep, eat, relax. I'll check in later.' He gave me another peck and then left.

I felt a sharp gaze at the back of my neck. I turned my head to see Win was staring at me, her eyes unnaturally wide, and her own room key dangling in her hand. Within seconds, she was at my side, clutching my arm.

'That's Hugh Sabiston,' Win whispered furiously. 'Are you sleeping with him?'

I shook off the unsettled feelings which had risen from that encounter with Hugh and his so-called old friend. I didn't understand why the disparagement in Hugh's voice had bothered me. Rob was so clearly a loser.

'We're... close,' I said modestly. I didn't need to bring up the almost-engagement. That was none of her business.

'You really are something!' I looked up, taken aback at the vehemence of her words, but she was smiling. In fact, I'd never seen such a big grin on her face. 'You're working Cate, and him too? Girl, I'm impressed.'

'It's not like that...' I began to say, then gave up. Fine. If she wanted to believe I was as devious as her, that was cool. Her respect for me was increasing by the minute, and who could say no to that? If I didn't have to dodge the arrows and darts of Win's disdain, then our enforced time together would pass much easier. 'Yeah, smooth move, eh?'

She took my arm, and we walked toward the bank of gleaming elevators. 'And did I hear him say you're sharing his room? Seriously?'

I shrugged, a little self-conscious. What was the big deal in this day and age? 'Yeah. I can't see any problem with that, do you?'

She gave a twisted smile. 'No. Because it means I get a room for myself.'

'We were supposed to be roommates?' The idea was disconcerting. Barring Hugh (that was somehow different) I'd never shared a bedroom with anyone before except for Fergie, on Scarp. Although I'd grown fond of her and actually missed her snores when she left, I could never have said I got used to having another human being so close to me when I slept.

'Yeah, the Kin are pretty cheap when it comes to the new recruits like us.' She held her key up. 'Yes, I am so going to enjoy this.'

She pressed the button to call an elevator. We waited along the bank of gleaming brass doors.

'And -' She seemed to hesitate. 'That was Rob with him, right?'

'Apparently.'

'Strange to see him here,' she mused. 'I thought he'd given up working with the Kin.'

'Guess not.' I stood straighter and pulled my carry-on closer.

'He's an odd one,' she declared.

'Not that odd, surely.' I shrugged one shoulder and tried to laugh off my defense of the man.

'No, he's weird. He could have so much, but he rejected it all. Who would give up that?' I saw her shake her head in the mirrored wall, then she moved next to me, entering my personal space. 'You're going to introduce me to Hugh, right?'

I guess she considered me her friend now, insomuch as Win had ever had anyone she could label as that. She didn't bother to hide the avarice shining in her eyes.

'Yeah, I guess so.'

'Great,' she said. 'I'm so thrilled about this trip. It's going to open up so much opportunity for us.'

I watched her as she moved back to her own space in the elevator. Thrilled? Not an hour ago, something had frightened her beyond belief. Temple, she'd said. A visit to a temple.

Chapter 13

I'd tried to lie down, but despite feeling so out of sorts and wrongly placed in the day, I couldn't even relax. I'd made the mistake of having coffee sent to my room, and the caffeine kept me hyped up. Hugh would still be in his meetings, and I was bored in a nerve-jangled sort of way. Win wasn't my favorite person, but I didn't know anyone else here, so I texted to see what she was up to.

While I waited for her to answer, I looked through the Room Service menu, but nothing was appealing. The photos of the western food offered were faded, coloring the dishes in unappetizing shades of beige. I stared out the window of this high-rise hotel, looking down at the teeming city life below. The main road was crowded with small cars and trucks and bicycles and people on the sidewalks, so many people everywhere. Although the hotel itself could have been plunked down in any westernized city, the streets surrounding it had a surreal air of not being quite of this century. The inner city blocks that I could see were made up of small alleys and lanes crisscrossing each other. It was hard to tell how high the houses were, and from my angle, none of it made logical sense. Yet each individual in the throng below moved with purpose.

It was gray down there in the old parts of the city, no greenery, no color at all except for sparks of brilliance from the LED signs, but there had to be good street food down there. This was Beijing, after all. The hotel was in the heart of the old district. Now my mouth watered at the thought, and my stomach woke up. I had to explore it.

Checking my phone again for Win's non-existent reply, I decided to set out on my own. Crossing the front lobby, a man in the bright red hotel uniform stopped me with a smile and an American accent. 'You need a taxi?'

'No, thanks, I'm just going out for a walk.' I looked up to a flash of red sweeping by the tall glass windows of the street. That was Win's coat, it had to be. She looked to be in a hurry, and was walking with purpose. Curious, I made to run after her, but the man stayed in my way, blocking me into the corner by a large urn.

'I can get you a guide. You need to be careful where you go,' he cautioned. 'There are some bad areas, even this close to the hotel.'

'No, I'm just going to catch up with my friend,' I said, trying to squirm around him.

'The Hutongs, for example,' he continued. 'The local small neighborhoods. They are not good places for tourists, only the government sanctioned ones can be guaranteed to be safe. Those will be good and clean, with no bad elements. You can have a proper tourist experience.'

Win was already out of my sightline. No matter, if I ran, it would only take me a moment to find her.

'No,' I said, finally physically pushing the man out of my way. 'No, I have to go!'

I sped through the lobby, politely elbowing my way through the crowd of people registering at the desk and the piles of luggage everywhere.

When I finally pushed through the door and onto the street, I quickly glanced in both directions to see which route she was taking, but there was no sign of Win at first. Then a large bus pulled into the traffic and I spotted her up the road and across, her red coat disappearing around a corner down a side street.

'Win!' I yelled out, but there was no way she could have heard me from that distance, not with all the traffic noise. So I sped up again, darting through the stalled vehicles to get to the other side, almost getting run over by a moped which weaved its way through the jam, and I jogged along the gutter till I reached the corner she'd turned down.

I stared down the lane. It was a rabbit warren of people, endless people, but few vehicles here so not as dangerous. I glanced up at the street sign to note my surroundings in case I got lost, then laughed, for of course it was written in Chinese characters. I couldn't read it. A thrill ran through me. I was truly in a foreign country now.

It started out as an adventure, chasing Win through the labyrinth of back alleys and lanes. It was still fun at that point. I kept note of the turns in the off chance I didn't catch up with her as I proceeded down the crowded laneways. But I wasn't too worried. I could still see flashes of that bright red coat up ahead. I looked all around me as I hurried through the small street, wanting to take in the strangeness, to get a better sense of my surroundings.

The smell was most noticeable. Old cabbage and boiled vegetables and a peculiar tone of sulfur rising from the gutters. Unrecognizable spices mixed with diesel, and here and there a whiff of cleansing incense cut through the air.

The buildings were three, perhaps four stories tall, leaning towards the street like they were competing for the sunlight. People, bodies everywhere, paused at the vegetable stalls, sitting on the stoops, hanging out laundry far above my head, and each of them talking and calling out over the street racket.

It was sensory overload to my sleep deprived brain. A wave of dizziness threatened. The sounds and the smells were overwhelming. I leaned against a concrete house wall and waited for it to pass. I thought of retracing my steps, to get myself out of this din, but knew I was totally lost by now. Win would be my only way out.

Looking up, I caught a last splash of red turning yet another corner, through an arched gate, so I pushed myself off again and began to run in earnest, unmindful of the obstacles in my path, using my elbows where necessary to push through. And the voices all around me grew louder.

Suddenly it was as if I'd stepped into Alt, an unfamiliar Chinese alternate world filled with the most terrifying of beings, and I could only take in glimpses of the awfulness all around me. The air was smoky from incense and filled with loud discordant melodies, a misfit orchestra with no player on the same page. The racket grabbed at my brain and tore at me inside. Huge white painted faces loomed from the murk, their eyes rimmed with kohl, and wraiths shimmered in the air, faces painted with agony, darting towards my head like crows wanting to pluck out my eyes.

Was this what the man at the hotel had been trying to warn me about? The Hutongs of Alt Beijing?

I covered my head with my arms against these visions. They couldn't be real, but my movement was instinctive. A golden fearsome dragon reared up in front of me, blinding me with the smoke from his nostrils, and everywhere I turned there were more painted faces jeering at me, pushing me, pulling me down. Through the hot incense a figure loomed out. She could have been an Empress with her golden headdress inlaid with the deep jewel tones of cloisonné. Her face too was dead white, but her eyes sparked as she whispered to me, the sibilance cutting through the racket all around but the sound of the words not quite on this plane of existence.

I couldn't remove my eyes from hers, like burning coals they drew me in to their mystery, then she held out an object and I knew she was commanding me to take it. I reached out. The small object exactly fitted into the hollow of my hand, cool against my skin. It was a deep green circle, opaque, perhaps jade? I looked back up to her to question her, to ask why, but she was gone.

In her place was a cackling, toothless old woman, dressed in drab, jeering at me. 'Find Win,' she screeched, or I thought she did. Perhaps she was insulting me in Mandarin, I didn't know. She screeched again and laughed. Oh how that sound ripped through my head.

I wrenched myself around the last corner, through the narrow gate I was sure I'd spotted Win slip into. It led into a dark tunnel under the building, but there was brightness immediately up ahead.

At last I found the respite of peace. There were no people here in this courtyard, with tall concrete walls, but it was a dead end, with no sign of my friend or her red coat.

I slumped against the nearest wall, gasping for breath, willing my heart to slow down. As my vision cleared I became more aware of the utter silence surrounding me in this hidden courtyard. I hesitantly removed my hands from ears and listened. Not a human voice, no music, not even a bird call.

The space was, as I'd noted, an enclosed courtyard, an empty place with a rusted water pump in the center and only a single doorway breaking up the expanse of the lichen covered walls stretching high above my head. A tiny window sat to the left of the door, arched and covered with iron grillwork. Win was not here.

Nobody was here. A single drip from the pump sounded loudly against the cobbled ground. Water. The thought of the cool refreshing liquid filled my head, and I was seized with a desire to drink.

I hesitated. Had I slipped through into the Chinese version of Alt? It had felt that way, and if so, I should be cautious before imbibing anything here. It could be a Mandarin Fae land, and anything I ate or drank would bind me in horrible ways... But I didn't even know if Beijing had an Alt, and my thirst was overwhelming, so I took my chances. I worked the handle and after a moment, a gush of water rewarded me. I wet my finger in the flow and hesitantly tasted. It seemed good, not polluted, so I bent my head to drink directly from the tap. I drank till my thirst was quenched.

As I rehydrated and my senses returned to normal, it came to me that I must have stumbled into preparations for the Chinese New Year.

'For frig's sake,' I scolded myself. Of course that was it. The costumes, the masks, the fire-breathing dragon – it all made sense when I looked at it in that new light. I hadn't slipped into another dimension at all, I was just disoriented from low blood sugar and a lack of sleep.

Yet I still held that piece of stone in my hand. I inspected it closer. Perhaps an inch and a half wide, it was circular and flat in shape, with a crossbar on the diameter. The cool jade had the texture of glass against my skin, the deep green glowing, and I sensed a foreign magic about the thing. Why did she give it to me? What were the words she'd said? It was in Mandarin, or perhaps some other offshoot dialect. I cursed my basic ignorance.

For now, I placed the object in my jeans pocket for safety. I had to find Win.

Wiping my face with my sleeve, I looked around again. I knew Win had come into this courtyard. I could still see in my mind's eye that red coat disappearing through the very same gate I'd come through, so she had to have gone through the single door. I was reluctant to follow her, for this was no longer a simple matter of me casually catching up with her as she strode through the lanes. Knocking on that door would bring my actions uncomfortably close to stalking. I glanced back at the dark gateway from whence I'd come, the long narrow tunnel beneath the building, and I shivered. I wasn't quite ready to brave that show again, not yet. It was too soon.

But I couldn't just sit there, waiting for Win to re-emerge. That would just be weird.

So I summoned up all my courage and slowly approached the door, willing Win to come bouncing out before I had to knock. But she didn't. To stall, I checked my phone again. Perhaps she had replied to my texts.

But my phone was inexplicably dead. There'd been plenty of juice in it before I left the hotel. That didn't feel right, not at all.

And it proved beyond a doubt that I was in a Chinese version of Alt.

I felt the cold knot of fear rising again, not just the panic of finding myself in the middle of a foreign magic dimension, but the hard frozen nugget of justifiable terror. I banged on the door, shouting and calling Win's name, but there was no answer.

I stepped back, preparing to pull myself up to look through the tiny barred window, when the heavy plank door opened of its own volition. My mouth was suddenly parched again, I couldn't find the spit to swallow down my fear.

'Win?' My voice quavered in the deathly silence. 'Are you there, Win? Are you playing a game?'

No answer.

'Come off it Win, not funny,' I continued in the barest whisper. 'Okay, you fooled me. You got me.'

I heard a sigh from the open portal, like a long slow gust of wind, but there was no movement of air in this sheltered courtyard. There was nothing for it. I'd come this far, I had to enter.

Forcing one foot before the other, I ducked my head and entered the doorway. It was dark inside, and colder even than outside. I was in a corridor with stone walls and floors, yet my boots made no echo.

Looking about me, I nearly jumped out of my skin, for there before me, suddenly and with no noise of movement to announce her presence, stood a woman. She was dressed in old garb, a loose yellow robe with another flowing, paler garment beneath that. Her black hair was intricately braided into a hairpiece that stood up from the back of her head. The rest of her hair disappeared into a single braid behind her back. Her face was serene as she lightly bowed to me.

Oh, and I could see the individual stones of the wall behind her, faintly, but they were definitely visible. She also had no feet, her robe ending about six inches above the ground. So definitely, a ghost. Where the hell had Win led me?

But the spirit wasn't trying to spook me. Her smile was barely there, and the peace emanating from her was palpable, a solid presence. She turned to lead me down the long corridor which stretched before us.

In for a penny, in for a pound. One of Hugh's ridiculous sayings. What I wouldn't give to have him here by my side, but he never seemed to be around when the going got tough for me. I swallowed, and fervently hoped this spirit was bringing me to Win.

All the doors were closed along the hallway, all except one. She paused outside it. The door itself was unlike the others, not solid planks. Instead, it was round, a circle, and made of lattice. The wood was carved into a labyrinth pattern.

Through the spaces, I saw a figure kneeling before an altar. The candles on either side gave the only light, and in the golden glow they cast, I saw the red of Win's coat. She appeared to be praying. I felt rather awkward. I wanted nothing more than to run to her and make contact with a real human after the weird experiences I'd traversed through, but I couldn't interrupt her. It wouldn't be respectful.

I turned to my guiding wraith, but she had disappeared again, leaving only the dank chill of the stones.

It was only then I became aware of the low notes sounding through the room before me, a harmony of beautiful notes. I couldn't tell what kind of instrument created these – it could have been human voices, or wind instruments, or even a stringed mandolin. The notes were pure though, and so restful to my ears. I stayed where I was, just listening.

All of a sudden Win gave a sharp cry and arched her back, her hands thrown into the air. The incense, already smoky in the room, thickened and morphed and a dragon shape appeared before my eyes, all red and gold, with beady eyes and a terrifying visage. I cowered next to the open door, but the dragon wasn't concerned with me. It roared and darted toward Win, its summoner, but she remained kneeling before it, bravely holding her arms out.

And then, the dragon writhed and in the space between its fearsome legs and wings, a vision appeared. It was a room like none other I'd ever seen, the walls curving to meet the ceiling like a cave. Were they walls? Their texture was more like coral, the whitest coral, an organic structure which had seemingly grown from a marble floor.

But those walls looked alive. What I'd first taken to be coral-like protrusions were actual carvings of the heads of fantastic beasts. Dragons, lions, strange birds with terrifying beaks. In the wavering light of the single lantern on the table in the vision, their shadows breathed, a swarming mass where solid walls should be.

This room, or coral cave, was sparsely furnished with only a rough cot in the small space, the weathered wood frame holding a thin mattress, a blanket and, clearly, a body. I leaned in closer to see better. Her figure (for it was a woman) wore a simple pale robe, much like my ghostly usher. Yet this person was real, in as much as a vision could be solid. I peered closer without coming further into the room. She was beauty personified, not glamoured, but she had the loveliness of purity as if she was a holy being.

She made no movement, and neither did Win.

Suddenly another person stepped into view in this diorama, a tall figure, who stood over the rough bed and the seemingly lifeless body lying on it. My heart sank, for I knew that straight-backed posture, the graceful turn of the long neck, even before she showed her face. Her auburn hair glinted darkly in the faint light. Her modern pantsuit in the finest cream linen was a designer I'd never heard of, undoubtedly exclusive only to the very wealthiest of customers. The trust-funded aristocracy.

Margaret Forsythe. As if she felt my recognition, she whipped around to face us, her audience, and her eyes narrowed. She couldn't possibly see us, Win had created a vision with her dragon magic and although we could see the scene clearly, it was magically impossible for the looking glass to be reversed.

Wasn't it?

CHAPTER 14

A terrible rage convulsed Margaret's face and she pointed her finger directly at Win through the cloud of incense, still kneeling before the altar and the vision she had conjured.

'Kin,' she spit, her sibilant hiss reaching sounding through the altar room. 'Of course, the Kin.'

Though I couldn't see her face, I could tell Win was petrified, unable to stop the vision or Margaret's rage reaching through. I gasped involuntarily and tried to withdraw, but the movement caught the witch's eye.

'You.' The maddened glitter of her eyes caught me in their thrall, and it was my turn to stand unable to move, like a butterfly caught with a pin.

The wrath of Margaret was a fearsome thing. The hatred and anger in her gaze cut across the vision. I hadn't felt such terror since the first time I'd seen her as the hag deep underground in her cursed cell in the Edinburgh Vaults.

By fixing on me, she must have loosened her hold on Win, who was quick to act, clapping her hands defiantly. As her hands moved together a sound like a soft gong vibrated through the room, more felt than heard, and the dragon and the scene before us disappeared along with Margaret and the solitary figure on the bed, all dissipating back into the thick cloud of incense. The only sound was Win's heavy breathing, ragged gasps. She stood up slowly, as if it was an effort. She bowed to the altar, empty except for the two candles, then made to leave the room.

And only then could I breathe again.

Her shoulders slumped and a line of worry indented the center of her forehead. Her aspect was sorrowful, and her gaze was far away even as she made to leave the room. She looked totally wiped. The conjuring of this fearsome visage had exhausted her.

I recovered myself, removing the piece of jade from my pocket, ready to brandish it in front of her to explain my presence. I should have cleared my throat or something, given her a head's up that I was there, because she only looked up when she was almost upon me, and such a screech she gave, I swear it rang from the rafters for moments after.

'Jesus Christ Dara!'

'Didn't mean to scare you.'

'How the hell did *you* get *here*?' She emphasized both the person and the place in her question, as if my presence in this ghostly monastery was inconceivable to her.

'I, uh, I followed you.'

'What, like you just walked on through Lijiang Alley?' Utter disbelief was in her eyes and her tone. 'No way, that's impossible. You could never have made it through.' At these words, her face took on an expression of unadulterated fear, and she quickly checked behind me, to see who or what had accompanied me.

'But I'm here,' I said, simply, and even Win couldn't argue with that simple fact. She shook her head and began stomping away, down the corridor to the courtyard beyond. 'And a ghost brought me to the temple or whatever room that is.'

She gave another start. I saw her back tense up, but then she pushed on through.

'What is this place?' I called after her as I hurried to catch up. I didn't want to be left alone with a foreign ghost no matter how benevolent she might be. 'Is this Chinese Alt?'

We reached the lonely, quiet courtyard and trod the cobblestones directly to the pump. She worked the handle up and down till the water flowed in a steady stream, then scrubbed her hands and face. Drying herself on a cloth she removed from her bag, she turned back to me. Resignation was on her face.

'Not Alt, as such,' she said. 'Not like you know it, with the artificial veil kept in place by the Kin in North America.' She sighed, then sat heavily on the small wall of bricks surrounding the water station. 'It's very difficult to infiltrate the barrier,' she added. 'Which was why I was so surprised to see you.'

She remembered to be suspicious of me, and scowled. 'How did you do it, anyway? Who brought you through?'

I shook my head. 'I already told you, no one. I was following you.'

My hand ached, and I realized I was still tightly clutching the jade object. I opened my fist and held it out to her. The sharp outline of the circle remained in my palm. 'A woman told me to give you this.'

Win jumped back in fear at the sight of it. 'Who? Where did you get this?' She was fascinated, though, for she leaned forward to inspect it more closely.

'She was dressed really fancy, great big head dress, lots of red and gold in her robe,' I said. 'Out there in, what did you call it? Lijiang Alley, before I followed you through the tunnel.'

Her eyes were round as she stared at me, disbelief warring with the suspicion. 'The Empress? The Empress approached you and gave you this?'

I shrugged. 'She didn't introduce herself.'

'Oh, no.' Win's face dropped.

'Win, what the hell happened back there?' I flicked my head back towards the door. Lowering my body, I joined her on the ledge. 'Were you casting a spell or something? It looked like pretty powerful magic. Who was the woman on the bed?'

'No! I wasn't...' She played her tongue around her teeth as she thought, then looked at the jade piece in her hand again. She closed her fingers, making the object disappear from view, then looked back up to me with a new understanding in her eyes. She shoved her hand in her pocket. 'You. That angry witch was looking at you, wasn't she? You know her?'

I nodded mutely.

'Who is she?'

When I didn't answer her, she reached out with both hands and shook me by the shoulder. 'You know her, and she knows you! You better tell me, because this is serious shit. Do you understand?'

I wrenched myself out of her grasp and pushed her away as I stood up to face her head on. 'No, I don't understand! I don't get what's happening here, or what was going on there.' I flicked my head at the now closed door.

'Was it Margaret Forsythe?' Win asked, her voice pitched so low I almost couldn't hear her.

I hesitated, then nodded again. There was no use denying it. Whatever Margaret had been up to, well, it was her own lookout. Her renewed stream of anger at me hadn't done anything to endear her to me or ease the hurt she'd caused.

Win stood very still for a long moment before she spoke again in a soft voice. 'That changes everything, you realize.'

'I really don't understand. None of this.'

'No, how could you?' She tentatively held out the jade object again, lifting it to the weak winter sunlight. I saw the lights gleam deep within it. 'Okay. I guess I need to tell you things. Looks like we'll be working together.'

'You don't exactly sound thrilled at the prospect. And we already are working together, remember?'

She shook her head. 'No, I mean *really* working together.'

Her mysteriousness was starting to irritate me. 'Okay, so you said you needed to tell me things? Good, because I have a lot of questions.'

'I'm going to tell you.' She cut me off. 'But only because I don't have a choice. The demons let you through the Alley. And the Empress spoke to you.'

I nodded in agreement. Finally. But I wanted the whole story, right from the beginning. 'So, the ghost back there.' I jerked my head towards the now closed door into the building.

'She was a Buddhist nun,' Win said softly. 'Once upon a time. The magical pockets formed around the old nunneries. These were the only refuges. Nuns still guard them. Even the dead ones.'

After another long moment, Win continued. 'We'll speak of this later, when we're outside again, in private. I'll tell you everything, but you'll need to promise not to say a word.'

I looked all around us at the barren courtyard. 'This is pretty private.'

'No, oh no,' she demurred. 'Not safe enough here. We need to get back to the *ping fan*, the mundane dimensions.'

'If it's so dangerous here, can I ask why you needed to come?'

She sighed, and her eyes narrowed as if assessing my trustworthiness. I bristled a little. 'I have been given a very difficult task,' she said, her voice soft in the absolute quiet of the courtyard.

'By Cate?'

She nodded again. 'Yeah.' Something in her tone told me she wasn't as enchanted with the witch as she appeared to be when in her company. I tucked that little bit of intel away to digest later.

'I have to find Li Minh.'

'The witch? I knew that,' I said. 'Remember we discussed it at The Witchery? You seemed excited by the prospect.'

'Yeah.'

'I thought there was some doubt as to her existence,' I said slowly, trying to remember what I'd heard.

Win laughed. It was a bitter sound. 'Oh, she exists,' she said. 'The Great Betrayer. Wherever she was, whatever havoc she'd been creating lately, it is my job to find her and get her on our side, without being killed in the process. Margaret didn't tell you that.'

She looked up at me, her eyes haunted. 'The shit's getting real now, Dara. Li Minh exists. And I... we, just saw her. But she's been cursed by the sleeping spell too, or she will be. And as you saw, there is no doubt that Margaret Forsythe is to blame. Now we need to find out where Li Minh is, before Auld Meg finds us.'

CHAPTER 15

'Li Minh still exists, somewhere. And we have to find her before anyone else does, or she might not exist much longer,' Win continued. "There's a lot riding on her staying alive.'

I had so many questions for Win, I didn't know where to begin. Who or what was Li Minh? What had she done to earn that terrible title of The Great Betrayer? Where were we, anyway, at that moment?

And Margaret, what role did she play in all this? But I couldn't go there. Not yet. Because the vision had told me more than enough.

Win saw the questions in my eyes, and then turned her face toward the narrow slice of sky above our heads. As quickly as it had come out, the sun had disappeared again. The day had grown noticeably darker in the short time we'd been outside, although it should still be the middle of the day. Those were ominous clouds gathering far above us.

She shook her head. 'Not here. We need to get out of this place. Can't linger.'

We stood up and faced the dark tunnel, the only exit from this unnaturally quiet courtyard.

'In order to get back out through there alive, I need you to follow me closely,' Win said. Her voice was terse, and brooked no argument. 'Here, take my hand, don't let go no matter what. Only look at the ground in front of you. Even better, close your eyes and let me lead. Close your ears, too, if you can. It'll make your passage easier.'

She paused another moment, and added, 'Whatever you do, don't use any form of magic to try to defend yourself. It will only make them all real. There's no way you'll win against them, and I'm not going to stop to save you.'

So we approached the darkened gateway of arched stone. Through the other side, I could see daylight, a brighter grayness where shadows moved. I really didn't want to pass that way again, through the terrifying throng of bodies and noise and smoke and chaos.

'What exactly is out there?' I asked, holding back.

She tugged my hand impatiently. 'It's a pocket of supernatural, all squished together, concentrated into one space. I already told you this. The Buddhist nunneries were the only places to escape the scourges, and everything had to gather in their protection. I'll explain in more detail later. We need to go now. There's no time to answer all your questions.'

With that, she jumped into the tunnel at a run. I had no choice but to flail along behind her. I remembered too late to keep my eyes closed. A terrifying cat-like creature loomed outside the gate, its double row of teeth gnashing as its spiked tail twitched. It roared at the sight of us. Every instinct for survival in me wanted to keep my eyes on this awful creature and unleash something, ice bombs maybe, anything in order to scare it away and allow my escape. But I forced my head down and squeezed my eyelids together as instructed. The horrible being sure seemed real, I could feel the heat of its breath in my hair. I had to trust Win on this.

She led me quickly and surely down the cobbled stones of Lijiang Alley. I couldn't close my ears off, not when I was clutching her hand with both of mine to ensure we didn't get separated. The sounds came to us from all angles, the screaming, the firecracker blasts set off way too close to us. It was as if we were in a war zone. And worst of all was the discordancy, like a thousand untuned violins scraping inside my head.

We ran for ages, it seemed like. I didn't take into account the various twists and turns I'd taken to reach the courtyard, those calculations were long gone from my head. I could only set my trust in Win.

Finally, she slowed to a walking pace.

'We're safe now,' she said. 'We're out of Lijiang Alley.'

I opened my eyes again to see the normal hubbub of the hutong, the ancient neighborhood of homes all higgledy-piggledy, jostling each other, and the normal people in the street going about their daily business at a relaxed pace. No one spared me a glance, even with my blue eyes in the sea of brown. They were used to tourists wandering through these lanes.

In no time at all we'd reached the main street, and what a welcome assault on the senses it was with the automobile horns blaring, the crush of people and bikes, and the sweet smell of exhaust. It was as if we'd been transported through time and dumped back into the twenty-first century.

I was so happy to be in the familiar mundane world again, I almost hugged the newspaper vendor. I was that relieved to have made it safely through the madness.

Win didn't stop, though. She made a beeline for our hotel across the road, dodging the slow-moving traffic. I had to follow her very carefully, for those motorbikes could appear out of nowhere and they allowed nothing to get in their way.

She only paused to let me catch up when we were safely within the glass doors.

'We'll go up to my room,' she said in a whisper, and then spoke out in a more normal voice. 'Let's order some coffee and pastries from Room Service.'

In no time at all, the elevator had whisked us up to the room we would have shared, if it wasn't for Hugh's presence on the trip. It was smaller than the one he'd been granted, with two single beds and a couple of armchairs by the window, and it was situated on the fourth floor. The view overlooked the back of the hotel, the bins and rooftops and the air exhaust funnels, but the coffee was good.

We settled back in the armchairs, both of us sitting cross-legged. After gulping down her first cup, Win then placed her hands on her knees and closed her eyes as if in meditation.

'What are you doing?' I asked, watching her over my own mug, savoring the warmth in my still chilled hands.

She flicked her eyes open impatiently. 'What do you think?' she hissed. 'I'm placing a circle of white noise around us so no one will overhear what I'm going to say.'

'There's no one here, Win, just us two.'

'Westerners are so soft,' she said under her breath. I didn't point out that with her well-heeled, cut glass British accent, she was just as Western as I was. Her eyes narrowed as they glared at me, like I was to blame. 'You don't know what it's like to live in a regime. There's always someone listening, ready to turn you in. And for sure all the rooms are bugged by the Chinese Kin, not to mention the government. Don't you know anything?'

I let her do her thing. If it made her feel more secure, then perhaps finally she would answer the many questions running through my mind.

'Can I help create this dome of silence?'

She shot me a final glare before closing her eyes and commencing her work. She opened her small perfect mouth and emitted soft tones, like Om chants. The sounds were barely audible, but she was putting her whole being into them.

I could sense no change in the atmosphere around us. I looked out the window and up at the sky, where the clouds were still dark and thunderous looking. If we were at home, I would expect a heavy blanket of snow, but this was Beijing, a different country. I didn't know if they got much of the white stuff here. It had certainly turned cold enough, though. I snuggled into the oversize armchair a little deeper, the hot mug cradled in my hands.

Finally Win opened her eyes again, and sniffed the air. 'Okay, we're good.' She poured another brew for herself and sat back. Yet she remained silent.

'So? After all the dramatics, you going to tell me this big secret?'

'You need to take this seriously.' Her eyes narrowed and her chin jutted out.

'I am taking it seriously,' I bit back. 'What happened back there, down that alley? It was scary shit. I didn't want to end up in Chinese Alt, believe me. And what exactly was that place, anyway? You didn't really explain.'

'I told you, it's not Alt, not like the Kin's Alt, but a little cell of magick. The government calls it a cyst. All the magical beings and the supernaturals got squished into these pockets.'

'So there's more than one around the city? How did they form?'

She thought for a little while. 'How much do you know of Chinese history?'

'Ah,' I said, casting my mind back to dim recollections of World History and various movies I'd watched many years ago. 'Not a lot. There used to be dynasties of Emperors, but then the Europeans tried to infiltrate China, colonialism happened, and the people got sick of all of the excesses and overthrew the ruling class. A few times, if I'm not mistaken.'

She shook her head in disgust. 'Jesus. I'm really going to have to start at the beginning.'

Win hadn't turned on the lights in the room, despite the fact that the day was growing darker. She stared out the window into the grayness outside, collecting her thoughts. 'Before you understand any of what I'm going to tell you, or why I'm here in China, I have to give you the background of what really happened in history, not the bits and pieces of Mundane stories that you picked up from Hollywood.'

I sat back and uncrossed my legs, swinging them over the side of the chair. 'Okay. I'm listening.'

'Li Minh started the unrest, or at least, she played into it.'

'And she was...?'

'Is,' Win reminded me. She went on to give me a very short expurgated and concise history of modern China. 'It all began when Western civilization tried to make inroads into China. It weakened the political structure. And China threw off the mantle of the Emperors and Dynasties, the ones who were the ruling class and all of them were magical practitioners, much like the aristocracy in Britain. What began as a political counter-revolution from some upstart magicians eventually turned into full scale revolt from non-magicals. What you call Normals.'

'What did your Li Minh have to do with all this? Did she start all that?'

'She was a powerful practitioner of magick. Of course, she came from the ruling classes. She was the force behind the original revolution, what is known as the Boxer Rebellion. She didn't like westernization, or the influx of Christianity, and she also didn't like the excesses in the Emperor's Court. She said, rightly enough, that the whole system was rotten to its core.'

'So Li Minh is a revolutionary hero. Why is she known as the Great Betrayer?'

'No!' Win shook her head vehemently. 'Not a hero, not at all, at least to the Chinese Magickals. She was able to become such a powerful witch because, you know the old story, she was greedy and drank from the ley lines.'

I nodded. An old story indeed, and perhaps not so old. Look at Cate, but of course I couldn't say a word about her, even under Win's dome of silence.

'She abused her power to lead the Mundanes into rebellion, and in doing so, upset the balance of power and ever since the country has struggled, always a tug of war between the Magicks trying to regain what they'd lost, and the Mundanes who will not let that happen. She realized what she'd done, so she ran away and had never been seen since. At least, not officially. There were rumors, and that's what Cate needed me to research.

'So, to get back to your question about Lijiang Alley. Communism is a Mundane construct, and it absolutely abhors the idea of a magical elite, doesn't trust anything out of the normal run of things, even religion. All of the magic world was pushed away from the mainstream, squeezed into the interstitial parts of life, places like Lijiang.'

'And the nun ghost?'

She nodded impatiently. 'The Buddhist nuns refused to be subservient to the new governments and regimes or give up their spirituality, so the magick cells cluster around their temples.'

'And these nuns weren't imprisoned or, or killed for their disobedience?'

'How could they be? They refused to acknowledge the existence of the State as a higher power. The Communists, the Red Army, all these don't exist for the nuns. So they can't harm them.'

'But the nun was a ghost...'

She shrugged. 'They had sworn to protect the magick. I guess it was a very strong vow, lasting even through death.'

I found all that a little difficult to get my head around. However, I'd just passed through an alley of demons twice in one day and survived, so I let it go. 'And what were you doing in the temple? Were you casting a spell?'

'No, I was scrying. Looking for Li Minh.' She looked around the room nervously and whispered, even though her dome of silence must still have been in place. 'Not just Cate is looking for Li Minh. The delegations believe Li Minh is the only one who can lead this country back to a balance of power.' She sat back in her chair and folded her arms across her chest. The story was over.

All that secrecy for this bit of information? 'What's the big deal, then? Why did you have all the dramatics and omm-ming? You're looking to get in touch with this old witch, who did some bad things, saw the error of her ways, and now she's needed to bring her country back to a middle ground. So what?'

'It's not that easy!' She shot up in her chair. 'You don't understand. Li Minh is a touchy subject. The ruling party of China doesn't want her found, and the Magicks find her too embarrassing to accept back into the fold. She made them lose face. Some witches would rather kill her than just let go of the whole thing. I might get killed, even looking for her!'

'If it's so dangerous, why did you agree to do it?'

'Are you kidding? This is my ticket into the big leagues with the Kin!'

She sat back and added, in a more casual voice, 'Oh, and now that you saw the vision, your life is in danger too.'

'No way! I didn't ask to get mixed up in this!'

'But you did,' she pointed out. 'You purposefully followed me today into a magick cyst, you accepted the jade from the Empress – you're already up to your eyeballs in everything. Your life is at stake now, just like mine and Li Minh's.'

This was all crazy, and I told her so. I was present on this delegation only because Cate wanted to keep an eye on me. International espionage? Revolutionary insurgences? Death threats? No, I hadn't signed up for that.

Yet she was adamant. 'And what about Auld Meg? I'm afraid that she saw us both, even though it was a vision. I tell you, we need to keep this quiet.'

'Okay, okay,' I said finally. 'I accept what you're saying. It's all crazy, but okay. The thing is, you say no one can know about all this?'

She nodded emphatically.

'How about Cate? We going to tell her about the vision you had this afternoon?'

Win hesitated, and cast her eyes down. She hung her head for a moment, then looked up again at me and leaned forward as if to whisper.

We locked eyes, and I nodded slowly, imperceptibly. I thought, I really thought by this that Win understood that Cate was a baddie through and through. It was a relief to finally have someone who understood. The adamantite stud was itching in my ear, and I opened my mouth and was about to break down and confess my own experience with Cate, when we were interrupted by another's voice in the room.

'Yes, do tell Cate. Please.'

CHAPTER 16

Win and I both sat up as one, turning around to face our boss.

'Cate!' I pasted on a smile and grabbed for something to say, something to cover up what had just passed between Win and me. 'We were just talking about you.'

Yes,' she replied, her voice dry. 'I heard.'

I didn't dare risk a glance at Win, afraid I might reveal the guilt that lay between us.

'By the way, Win, in future, remember to put lock spells on the door,' she added. 'Not that it would keep me away, of course, but anyone with a master swipe card could have done the trick. You two were so wrapped up, you didn't even hear me enter. The white noise spell works both ways.'

She smiled genially. 'Always be vigilant.' Cate sat on the edge of the nearest bed, forcing us to swivel our armchairs toward her. 'So tell me all about your afternoon. Any luck with the scrying?'

Win nodded, then shook her head. 'We found Li Minh.' She darted a glance over at me. 'And Margaret Forsythe. Or at least a premonition of what will happen.'

Cate's eyes widened a fraction and she pounced on this like a cat. 'Do tell,' she purred, leaning forward from her perch on the bed.

'Looks like Margaret will get at Li Minh before us,' Win continued bitterly. 'Perhaps she already has.'

'We don't know that, just because she was there. It was the ghost of things to come, right? Not what has already happened.' I half-heartedly burst out, but it was a feeble defense of the indefensible. I immediately wished I had kept quiet.

Win merely rolled her eyes.

'So Margaret. Just as I thought.' Cate narrowed her eyes while she looked at me as if she was calculating my loyalty to her.

I nodded slowly. 'She was standing over Li Minh's body.'

'And where was this?' Cate asked sharply.

'I had a sense,' Win said slowly. 'It's like a.... like a cave, but it's not rough. More like an underground room, but the walls – I've never seen anything like this. As if they are made of small rocks all piled on top of each other. I saw Li Minh in the vision. She was alive and well enough, but sound asleep, just like the Great Zande and the Venerable Nachtan must be. I have no idea where she is.'

'An underground room, like a cellar?' Cate asked sharply. 'Was she being held captive?'

Win shook her head. 'No. But yes, but...' She looked over at me.

'Those rock walls weren't a natural formation,' I offered. 'Some of the pieces were carved, animal heads, dragons even. And the Chinese lions. They were pretty fearsome and alive looking, even though they were obviously carved from stone.'

'What kind of stone?' Cate sat very still, her whole body tense. 'Marble? That kind of white stone?'

Win and I looked at each other and nodded. 'Maybe?'

Cate stared out the window past us to where the skies had imperceptibly turned dark gray with a red streak for the sunset, her long red nails tapping against her thigh. 'A manmade structure of white marble rocks piled on each other, with carvings,' she mused aloud. Then a small smile began at the corners of her mouth, but that was as much as she permitted. 'Who would have thought?'

Her dark eyes were bright like a sparrow's as she turned back and looked at both of us. 'This is a very interesting turn of events. You're going to have to find her,' she said finally. 'Win, you now have Dara to help. Get to it. We need to find her, and fast.'

'From what Win says, finding Li Minh is stirring the pot, and is going to make a lot of people angry,' I pointed out. 'I didn't exactly sign up for this kind of danger.'

'Yes, you did,' Cate threw at me absently. 'Read the contract you signed. It's in the fine print.'

···········

'So. Margaret,' I said to Cate, once we'd left Win's room. I kept my voice low as we padded through the carpeted hallways.

141

'Yes,' Cate replied. 'We need to lure her here before she can lay the curse on Li Minh. There's a lot at stake here.'

'Luring...? You mean setting a trap for her?' My back was immediately up, although I understood the seriousness of the situation.

'How else are we going to stop her?' She pressed the button for the elevator. 'You realize, it's not just Li Minh, and the curses on Zande and Nachtan.'

The door opened silently. We stepped into the wood and mirrored space, Cate standing smack in the middle of the small floor. I moved over to the side.

'It's your future and life, too. Need I remind you?' The door slid closed.

She needn't. I was all too aware of the precariousness of my situation.

'I think she'll be keeping an eye on you, and that's how we can get to her.'

'I doubt it. She was pretty definite in her final good-bye that night by the Avalon Temple. You were there. You heard her.'

I didn't bring up the airport meeting. The less Cate knew, the better.

She smiled enigmatically. 'We'll see.'

Good luck, I thought to myself. Good luck if you want to use me as the carrot to bring Margaret Forsythe to you. The abruptness of her last departure still stung, even after all this time.

'You're wasting your time,' I said to Cate. I also didn't tell her about my failed attempt to contact Margaret in Edinburgh.

That small smile remained on her face as the elevator brought us up to the heights of the hotel.

The door opened silently to let me out. Cate was staying on a higher floor, higher even than Hugh's. She spoke her final words to me as I exited.

'Just figure out how to bring her here. And soon. The Kin still want to put the finger on you, and I'm the one holding them off, remember,' she said in the pause before the door glided shut again.

In other words, lure Margaret here or else.

·····•·•····

There was no way to find Meg. The witch had ignored my last plea for help, and I felt sure there was nothing I could do or say to convince her to come here to China, to meet with Cate.

As difficult as it was for me to accept, after the vision we'd witnessed in the Temple, it looked like Margaret was the culprit, the one who had cursed both Zande and Nachtan. And now, it was going to happen to that mysterious figure Li Minh too, unless I could find a way to prevent that. Which brought me right back to the issue of Margaret ignoring any pleas from me.

I entered the room to find Hugh waiting for me. He surrounded me with his warm arms and I collapsed into them.

'Where were you?' he asked, then he held me out to examine my face. 'You haven't rested, have you?'

I shook my head.

'You look ghastly. I'll order some room service and you can have a good quiet evening. An early night is needed, I think, judging by your appearance.'

I let him take charge. I had no energy or fight left in me.

My first night in China, you'd think we would have had a fine selection of local delicacies, but instead Hugh ordered some solid, very British stew with fresh bread and I was thankful for this comforting familiarity. The accompanying red wine went straight to my head, yet my sozzled mind wouldn't let go of the problem of how to conjure up the witch who wasn't talking to me. And it wasn't coming up with a solution.

Hugh was happy enough to carry on the one-sided conversation.

'Poor Rob,' he was saying when I finally tuned back into him. 'So strange to run into him again. Here, at a Kin delegation of all places.'

My ears perked up. 'But he's Kin, isn't he?' Although Rob himself hadn't been too sure of that in the bathroom cubicle of the airplane.

'He was, to begin with,' Hugh said as he buttered a slab of bread. He paused to take a bite, and mused as he chewed. 'At least, he went to prep school with us. That's where we met.'

He swished a sip of wine around his mouth and, once that was fully appreciated, took up the story again. 'Of course, he was never much of a witch, truth be told.'

'Not magic?'

'Oh, it wasn't that. He could hold his end with the best of us, but he never bothered with it much.' Hugh looked over to the floor to ceiling window which looked over the teeming city. The endless stream of car headlights winked through the night. 'He simply didn't have the competitive edge which was required, had no get-up-and-go, as the Americans say.

'It didn't come altogether as a surprise to learn he'd dropped out of the firm, at least the business end of things. I'd heard he'd foresworn the Kin, gone off on some Mundane kick or something. Not quite stable, is my guess. Like I said, he was never that good a witch, anyway.'

Right at that moment, I could sympathize with Rob for choosing to leave the Kin behind. In my sleep deprived state, with Cate's threat hanging over me, I would love nothing more than to be shot of the whole lot of them. With the exception of Hugh, I quickly told myself.

'He's a lawyer, of all things,' Hugh said with a laugh and a shake of his head. 'When I think what he's turned his back on, a man of his position, I shudder. The Kin is much better off without him.'

A lawyer. Rob had told me that. A lawyer, looking to discuss Margaret's trust fund with her.

And suddenly, my whole mood brightened, for I had the answer to my problem. It had been there right before me all along.

What did Margaret cherish, more than anything? Her new life of lazing on sunny beaches, which was only possible through the trust fund her father had set up for her all those years ago. I had no doubt that the new message I had to send her would elicit a response. With Rob's help, we'd get that witch.

Before she struck again.

....

I should have slept like a log that night to make up for the jetlag, but instead I found myself lying awake in a jangle of nerves, unable to stop the thoughts racing through my head. Beside me, Hugh slept like a man with a clear conscience.

Margaret was the one behind the curses laid on the great witches. Knowing Margaret as I did, it was hard for me to wrap my head around this fact. It made no sense, none of it. It just didn't feel right.

Yet, on the other hand, it all made logical sense. I could accept Cate's explanation that the witch must hold a terrible grudge against the Kin for locking her underground for more than a century. She had every right to be pissed at that, and for her to use her show of power against the most powerful magic practitioners of the globe, well, that was thumbing her nose at the whole of the Kin worldwide.

This was all very logical, in a warped sort of way.

But that logic didn't explain why the pit of my stomach fell every time I thought of it, every time I remembered the vision of Margaret standing over Li Minh's sleeping body, her face twisted in anger and her finger pointing directly at me. It was a terrifying sight, yet I kept going back to it, time and time again as if by doing so I could change the course of action.

I would try to contact her again, using Rob and his lawyerly worries as bait. The more I thought about this plan, the better I felt. Her trust fund was the only thing that mattered to her in her new life.

What I wasn't clear on was my own motivation in reaching out to her. Was I doing it to stop her wreaking her revenge on the magic world, or was I doing it just to save my own ass?

I lay on my back and stared at the reflected city light on the ceiling. It would have been easier if I could have discussed it with someone I trusted, but there was no one. Win was the closest thing I had to a peer, but her opinion wouldn't be unbiased. It would be too tied up with advancing her own position within the Kin.

Neither Mom nor Dad could give advice on this. It was way out of Dad's league, and Mom was still star-struck over the fact I was engaged to marry a Duke's heir.

Right, about that. Hugh. I sighed to myself, a deep one that came right from my core. I hadn't been very honest with myself lately. Or with him either. And perhaps him with me.

It was hard to put my finger on, but the cord of attachment which had connected us had frayed somehow. I used to love that he was so upright. I admired his steadfastness, his adherence to the rules, his dedication to his work and the Kin.

And now? Those things were the very sources of friction between us. When we spoke, sometimes I could hear his impatience toward me while I, too, was beginning to hate his refusal to look at the gray shades of life. The Kin was everything to him, and his work was how he defined himself. He couldn't even see Cate's evilness. To him, she appeared as a cohort, one equally as dedicated to the good work done by the alliance of magic practitioners.

And Cate. I sighed again and rolled away from Hugh. Through the window I could see the dark glowing of lights from below, from a city that never slept. It would make total sense to tell her my plans to contact Margaret through the ruse of the trust fund.

Because, really, what did I plan to do when I had Meg in my grasp? Lasso her with a rope, magicked or not? Then turn her over to the Kin, saying here you go, that's the culprit. It's all up to you to make her drop the curses now.

Even if it were possible for me to overpower her, that didn't guarantee the salvage of my reputation. She could easily point the finger at me, accuse me, and no one would know the difference.

Rob. My mind relaxed at the thought, and a small smile came to my face. He was strange. Nerdy. Rather gangly of body, as if he'd not yet come to terms with the growth spurt of his teens a decade past. How could I have ever mistaken him for a hireling of the Kin, him with his shabby clothing and messy hair?

And just as quickly, that smile was replaced by a frown. I was planning to use him to save my own butt. Pretending to do him a favor, yet only giving him enough to serve my own needs. Just like a frigging Kin would do.

Unless. Unless I didn't turn Margaret over to the Kin. If I simply used the occasion to beg her to lift the curses, make her see sense, then she could let Rob tighten up the trust fund rules and toddle off back to her sunsets and beaches and margaritas, with not a worry in the world. And that would be the end to the whole thing.

Right?

And I could like myself again.

CHAPTER 17

The actual work of the delegations turned out to be boring to the nth degree. Hugh was loving it, though, caught up in all the meetings and nuances and hammering out details like it was a big game. At breaks and mealtimes, when he remembered to come looking for me, he was full of the intrigues and gossip of the latest developments.

I didn't seek him out much, though. All of that really wasn't that interesting to me.

Cate, of course, was also caught up in the glamor of the politics, and often Win would accompany her because, well, Win loved it all too. For the week of the delegation and meetings, I was fairly free to go my own way, as my unofficial job was to make sure I lured Margaret in.

The sightseeing trips were another matter, and there were a few of them to relieve the dullness of business.

The second day of the conference, a trip to the Great Wall was scheduled, that huge structure stretching more than five hundred kilometers long. Cate insisted I travel on the luxurious bus with her so we could talk on the two-hour trip.

I had already introduced Hugh and Win, and he had enthusiastically taken her onboard as translator, so they were off on some other bus.

'Any luck yet?' Cate asked as she settled in again next to me. She had spent most of the ride so far making the rounds of the bus, her cream fur hat and coat highlighting her presence as the most elegant traveler onboard. Everyone's eyes were drawn to her. 'You still haven't told me how you plan to reach her.'

We could speak openly here, for the backs of the seats were high and the air conditioning system kept up a steady stream of white noise to prevent our words from carrying.

'No,' I replied. I stared out the window. 'Even if I could make contact with her, I need a good reason, something to draw her in and cause her to appear. Any thoughts?'

'I would think that's an easy one. She's being blamed for the curses and needs to clear her name.'

'But why would she bother with that? She doesn't care about her reputation, and if she's doing the cursing, well, it stands to reason she would want everyone to know it's her, right?'

'You don't sound fully convinced that she's the guilty party.'

I looked up. Was that a faint light of suspicion in her eyes? 'Well, we don't have proof, really,'

'The proof of Win's vision is enough for me,' she retorted. 'Unless there's something you're not telling me.'

'No, I don't know anything more than you do.'

'So you're not involved? Cromwell was pretty certain that you had a hand in it, being on the scene like that.' She was still holding this threat over my head. 'I need you to come up with something, and soon,' she continued urgently. 'Let me know. I'll have to rearrange my schedule to be present.'

'She won't come if she knows you're there!'

'Then you'd better not tell her.'

The bus pulled to a stop. I hadn't even realized we were getting close to our destination.

'Ah, the Great Wall of China,' Cate said, a smile now back on her face as she stood up and looked at the men sitting behind us. 'Now, Mr. Wong, I'm going to require you to escort me along the Wall and tell me all the fascinating history of the Badaling section.'

That left me free to wander along the huge structure myself, and I was good with this. I needed to find Rob.

·····•·····

I held back as Cate and the Chinese delegates entered the Mutianyu Station for the cable cars which would take them up to the Great Wall perched on the hilltops high above our heads. After a few minutes, I spotted her fur-wrapped elegance in one of the tiny cars, so I held out my blue VIP ticket and passed through the gate alone.

It was freezing cold out there, and I was glad of my parka and toque. The station was largely open to the air and not heated. The diesel-laden air snapped at my cheeks.

A ticket taker wearing industrial ear muffs ushered me into the loading zone using hand signals. The noise inside the structure was tremendous, coming at us from all sides in the space, the rumbling of engines and winches. The small cable cars bumped and ratcheted as they entered the structure, and the doors squealed every time they opened and shut.

As I waited for the next cable car, I anxiously looked around for Rob. I hadn't seen him since the previous day, and I could see no sign of him now. Perhaps the delegation kept him busy with legal matters, or maybe he had no interest in sight-seeing, which meant this whole day was a bust, getting me no closer to luring Margaret in.

There was no one else waiting for a car to the North Eight Tower, which suited me fine. I never liked to share enclosed spaces with strangers.

When I got into the cable car, however, he popped up behind me, jumping into the car just as the guard slammed the door closed. The collar of his trench coat was pulled right up by his ears, as if he really was the spy I had thought he was.

It was a tiny car, basic in its design with two seats each at the front and back facing each other. The walls were mostly windows, allowing for great panoramic views from all angles.

We stood there staring at each other for a moment, and he had just opened his mouth to speak when the guard banged her fist on the door, yelling something at us, and the car jerked into gear. He was thrown against me with the motion, causing both of us to fall against the seats.

'Dammit, I'm sorry,' he said after we untangled our limbs and were safely sitting across from each other. I moved my legs out of the reach of his feet to avoid further damage. He was too clumsy to trust, not when we were going high up in the air in a rocking car.

'Look,' he said, his voice very quiet and fervent as he leaned toward me. The blue of his eyes was as bright as the clear, cold sky. 'We need to discuss this. Don't run away again, please.'

'We're in an enclosed space,' I pointed out to him. 'Nowhere for me to run to.'

My complaisance caught him off guard.

'Oh, right then. Well.' He seemed at a loss as to what to say next, now that he had my attention.

'It's okay. We need to do this. We need to find Margaret.' We were coming out of the covered landing place and into the crisp air. It was a sunny day, and the snow below us was blindingly bright. I raised my eyes, and there I saw the first stone tower and the Wall stretching away on both sides of it, gleaming in the sunshine. I drew in a breath at the grandeur of the sight.

'Look at it,' I urged him. 'Behind you.'

Rob twisted in his seat and was also silent for a moment. The car was now silent except for the sound of wind in the wires.

The ground dropped away from us, and I turned my head to look out the back window. The village below was already tiny, the people were merely little figures going about their business in the miniature world.

'We're really here,' I whispered as my eyes came back to the structure rising high above our heads. The stone wall ranged along the top of the line of hills as far as I could see, more of it emerging the higher we travelled. 'The Great Wall of China.'

Our eyes met. His were shining as mine must have been. Up here in this airy space, away from the Kin and Cate, my spirit suddenly felt free. This was the first sunshine I'd seen for many a day, the smog and the grayness of Beijing had lifted and I was finally seeing this land in all its glory. As the car rose ever higher, I could now see the blanket of trees covering each slope under the mantle of snow. After the bustle and crowds of the city, the land stretched on for miles, seemingly uninhabited.

'So quiet,' I breathed. 'So still.'

It was peaceful, at least until the car reached the next pole and rattled over the attachment, shaking us like the turbulence of an airplane passing through a storm.

We looked at each other and laughed. Foolish, really, it wasn't that funny. Perhaps we were lightheaded with the lower levels of oxygen in the air, this high up.

Too soon we reached the top, another covered and noisy space, and we gladly escaped out to the air.

And there on the battlements of the wall, we could truly see the scope of this engineering marvel. I'd seen the photos, but the flat two-dimensions could never do this vista the justice it deserved. Off into the distance, as far as the eye could see, the stone and brick wall stretched along the mountain ridges, with guard stations built every few hundred feet. Despite the brightness of the day, mist hung between the furthest peaks until the far distance took on the appearance of an ancient painting, with each successive valley a deeper shade of mauve.

'Amazing.' It was such an inadequate word for sight before us.

'It's more than four thousand kilometers long,' Rob remarked.

As I looked to the east, I caught sight of Win's bright red coat amidst a group. That was not good. I needed to speak with Rob alone.

'Let's go this way.' I grabbed Rob's arm and headed west. The wind howled through the open windows of the sentry tower. Here, sheltered by the stone building, we were almost out of the constant, cutting breeze.

He shivered and huddled into his coat.

'So,' he said eventually. 'Margaret.'

I nodded. 'Yeah. We need to find her.'

'You're onboard with helping me, then?' His blue eyes searched mine behind my shades.

I turned away to face the vastness before us and nodded, then tightened my hood to shore up the cracks found by the wind.

'Why the change of heart?'

The stone wall beneath my gloves was cold and unyielding, yet worn smooth from the erosion of centuries of weather. What could I tell him?

I hated to lie to Rob, but how could I tell him that Margaret was guilty of such a heinous crime? Not only had she somehow laid curses on the greatest of the magic practitioners in the known world, but she had done so solely to payback her grudge against the Kin Britannica and to prove her own power. I still had a hard time believing it, even though I'd seen Win's vision with my own eyes.

Margaret's trust fund wasn't going to be much use to her where she was going if she was ever caught.

And she had to be caught. I had to clear my name, or I'd be going right there with her. To show the Kin I wasn't part of her scheme, I had to prove my allegiance by trapping her. Somehow.

Rob was still waiting for an answer.

'I need to speak with her,' I said finally, and I realized I'd made up my mind. 'I need to speak with her, without anyone else around. I have to find out...'

I had to find out the truth, even though I was pretty sure I knew it. The sun was fast disappearing behind the onrush of clouds moving south from the mountain ranges. They were heavily laden, unable to rise above the peaks.

'Also, I need to get her permission,' he reminded me. 'About making changes to her trust fund.'

'Yes.'

'When you say, without anyone else around, I take it you mean – ' He flicked his head back the way we'd come.

I nodded. The wind had picked up in the short time we'd been out here, and even the stone tower offered little protection from it.

'What's really happening?' Rob stepped away from me, taking the last of my shelter from the biting wind. Those clear eyes pierced me, his keen, lawyerly mind working. 'What are you keeping from me?'

We stared at each other, both frozen to the spot, me unable to answer, him unwilling to let it go. And it began to snow, the cold hard ice pellets whipping and stinging our faces, finding their way down the back of my neck.

A shout from the beyond the tower, someone calling my name.

'Hugh!' I stepped out from behind the stone, removing my now useless sunglasses as I did. Turning to Rob, I quickly said, 'Can we talk about this later? Privately? Meet me down in the hotel bar this evening.'

He nodded, then followed me as we joined the rest of the delegation.

....

Cate's eyes ran over Rob's disheveled figure and just as quickly dismissed him. Instead, she placed her arm on Hugh's and called out to me.

'Come, it's time to leave now.'

We all trouped back to the cable car station. Rob got lost in the crowd somewhere, and Cate maneuvered the four of us – herself, Hugh, me and Win into a single cab. She pulled me down to sit beside her, leaving the other two to sit facing the valley below.

They were excited and nattering on about the wonders of the Great Wall. both flushed with being out in the crisp air and their eyes sparkling, the snowflakes melting like sparkles on their hats.

Hugh noticed me looking at him and he stopped mid-sentence, as if reminded that he'd been neglecting me a bit during this trip. Win also shut her mouth and darted a glance at me before looking out the window to the mountain slope rushing up at us.

'Dara, what happened to you? You missed the whole tour,' Hugh said, leaning forward. 'You wandered off in the opposite direction. You couldn't have heard a word.'

I shrugged it off with a smile. 'I was just off exploring,' I replied. 'Getting away from the crowds.'

He didn't have a chance to dig deeper as Cate now spoke.

'This evening,' she began, and Hugh immediately turned to her.

'You won't mind if I borrow Win again?' he asked. 'She's turned out to be very useful with the talks. So much easier to work with a personal translator, and I think she's quite charmed old Ding Wo. He's coming round to our side.'

Win flushed with pride. 'Ah, you just have to know how to get round the men of my culture,' she said.

Cate wasn't happy about this. 'I'd rather thought you and Dara would help me double check the maps for tomorrow's presentation, Win.'

'They're all done.' Win frowned. 'You know I spent an hour on them early this morning. Everything is in order.'

We were nearing the station. Cate gave in, and did so gracefully. But as we made our way out of the station and back into the brisk winter, she grabbed my arm.

The pinching grip hurt a lot, even through my parka. 'Does it bother you?'

I shook my arm free, but she gave an impatient twitch of her head when she saw my incomprehension. I followed the direction of her meaningful look.

Hugh and Win were standing in a group, all of them chattering excitedly as Hugh exercised his considerable charm on an older Asian man, perhaps this was Ding Wo, and there smiles all around as Win cutely interjected with a quick translation.

'You mean them?' I looked closer. My boyfriend and Win were standing closer than was strictly necessary, but that didn't mean anything. The burgeoning friendship between them hadn't bothered me at all. At least, it hadn't until this moment. I felt a short stab of jealousy rise. Trust Cate to find the nasty side of any situation.

'No,' I said. I squashed that little niggling doubt down. Perhaps the Chinese had a different definition of personal space. They were both enjoying their assigned jobs, and it actually worked out great for me. I was free to meet with Rob this evening. 'No, Hugh and I are solid. What are you insinuating?'

'I know men,' she said. 'And if I were you, I'd want to nip this in the bud.

'Well, it's your life,' she continued, her voice low and dry, then she changed the subject. 'What are your plans for this evening?'

'I'm working on something. I have an idea about how to contact Margaret.'

'That's great,' she said smoothly, a smile plastered back on her face in case anyone was watching. 'You will keep me apprised of the situation?'

I nodded, then gave a sigh of relief as she turned to schmooze with some of the delegates.

I was off the hook. Free of Win this evening, and free to talk with Rob.

CHAPTER 18

At dinner that night, the usual small feast with more dishes than a person could do justice to, Cate nudged me with her elbow without saying a word. I looked up to see her pointedly watching Hugh and Win again, while pretending not to.

He was topping up her wine glass while she giggled and scolded him. Ding Ho was looking on fondly while trying to peek down the loose folds of silk covering Win's chest. I looked away. The whole thing was rather sickening, how the two of them were playing up to that old guy.

'I think it was a mistake to bring Win along,' she murmured. 'They are getting far too cozy.'

I shook my head. 'It's nothing. You know how the pair of them are so focused on work,' I said. I shifted uncomfortably in my seat and deliberately forced my eyes away.

Then couldn't help but look back again. I was right, surely? Hugh and I were practically engaged to be married for God's sake, I'd met his parents and everything. The duke had even strongly hinted to his friends and neighbors of the promise.

Here was just another reason to hate Cate, as if I didn't already have enough.

Hugh must have felt my burning stare. He glanced my way, started, then looked back with a smile even as he was shifting his body just a tad away from Win's. He gave a wink which seemed to teeter just an inch from embarrassment.

I pulled my lips into a semblance of a smile back at him.

Damn Cate for pointing that out. I was pissed at her. I'd never felt jealousy for a man before.

As I played with the noodles in my bowl (I wasn't having the best luck learning to use chopsticks) I explored this feeling. I expected it to be green and devouring, with a tinge of hate and resentment and arrows. Just like I'd felt towards Sasha, my half-sister, for so many years.

But as I probed deeper, I realized it was just surface hurt that I was feeling, almost like an insult which didn't quite have much sting to it. In fact, it felt like probing the hole where a tooth had been, back when I was a kid and losing my baby teeth. Grief at the passing of something which was such a part of me, yes, but a little excitement at the change, and almost relief that it had finally happened. I was ready to move on to larger things, to stronger teeth.

I shook myself out of it and pushed my wine glass away. No more of that, I was starting to sound crazy even to myself. I looked up to Hugh for reassurance. We smiled weakly at each other as we met across the span of the table.

'Margaret.' Cate's crisp voice cut through. 'What's happening on that front?'

I hedged a little, and she pushed on.

'I'm getting missives from Edinburgh,' she said, leaning closer to speak in a low voice. 'Cromwell's been in touch with his contingent, and they're making waves. He truly believes you're guilty with Margaret, and they're putting pressure on Johanna to recall you back to Scotland under armed guard. The Venerable Nachtan is a national icon, and cursing him was too much of a slap in the face. The Covenanters are looking for someone to string up, and if they can't have her, they'll settle for you. Johanna has other things on her plate right now, and she may just cave in to their demands.'

I swallowed and reached for my water glass, but my hand was shaking too much. I had to set it down again.

'So, Margaret,' Cate nudged.

'Okay,' I told her and turned to face her, keeping my voice as low as hers. 'There's this guy, Rob. Do you know him?'

She shook her head.

'He's a lawyer, somehow connected to the Kin. A bit of a goof, really. Hugh said he's not much of a magic practitioner. Anyway, he's looking for Margaret too, something to do with tying up loose ends with her trust fund.'

Cate nodded. 'And?'

'I can use him to find her, I think.' I laid out my plan, what I had of it. I would somehow call Margaret, with Rob's help, using the trust fund as an excuse. How I was going to call her, I wasn't sure, but she would respond to this.

Cate listened closely. 'A little weak, but better than nothing,' she said. 'I'll need to be present when you do this, in order to subdue her. But no need to tell him that.'

'How are you going to... subdue her?'

Cate smiled, a tight grimace of her lips, and she patted my hand. 'Don't you worry about that. I have it all in hand.'

....

Apart from the lights behind the bar and the spotlight on the singer, the room was lit only with stripes of LED lights along the walls, the colors changing in a rhythmic pulsing beat to the overly loud music. Purple. Pink. Red, green, blue then purple again, all neon in their intensity and only serving to highlight the unchanging shadows in the corners.

I hesitated at the doorway. Subterfuge didn't sit well with me, but I had no choice in this. I had to save my own butt. If the Covenanters could get Margaret, then Cate and Johanna together would convince them to leave me out of it. I straightened my shoulders and walked in.

I almost didn't see Rob, his long legs folded over each other as he waited at the end of the bar, an empty glass in front of him. I wondered how long he'd been waiting. He appeared hypnotized by the wailing woman on the small stage, her metallic dress shooting out rainbows of reflected colors like a human disco ball.

'Hey.'

His eyes slid toward me and he nodded, then moved his legs so I could take the stool next to him.

I shook my head. 'Not here. Let's go outside for a walk or something.'

He looked around the bar. There were very few people there, and none of them were from the Kin Britannica. 'What's wrong with here?'

'Too loud,' I replied. 'And the flashing lights give me a headache.'

He accepted this explanation and climbed off the plush stool. I waited till we'd exited the building and had gone past the hotel lobby windows before I paused. The half-melted snow underfoot was refreezing in lumps, making walking treacherous.

The street was as noisy as before, the flow of cars and even bicycles never ending, the press of people on the sidewalks pushing past us. The sharp wind whipped down the snow upon the hooded figures.

'Not the best evening for a walk,' he noted. 'Come on, let's get out of this crowd.'

He made as if to turn down one of the alleys but I stopped him with a shudder.

'No, don't,' I said, remembering what could lurk in those spaces, in the Hutong alleys. 'Here, let's go in here.'

I darted into the closest door that looked like a public place.

'A whisky bar,' Rob said with pleasure as we entered through the glass door. Directly ahead of us before the entrance into the bar itself, was a tall glassed-in display case. Tiny spotlights within shone on boxes that fancy whiskies came in, the labels indicating every famous and rare distillery in Scotland.

Inside, the discreetly lit bar stretched the whole length of the deep and narrow room. There were few customers at this early hour. We took a table at the back.

'And cocktails,' I noted, taking the large menu in hand.

A server appeared before us silently. His black suit blended into the shadows, but the crisp white shirt glowed in the blacklight coming from somewhere in the room. He smiled, and his teeth shone white too.

'I'll take the Macallan.' Rob told him, almost rubbing his hands in anticipation.

I glanced down at the drinks listed in Chinese figures with English translations below and my eye was caught by some of the ingredients. Metaxa with chocolate? Egg white? Herring?

'Eh, just a rum and coke for me,' I muttered, putting the card back on the table.

Rob looked askance. He was about to say something, but then he shrugged and shut his trap.

The waiter brought us our drinks. Rob sipped appreciatively, letting the taste linger on his tongue before he swallowed. Then he cleared his throat.

'So, Margaret. You've changed your mind?'

I nodded as I played the straw against the ice cubes. 'Yeah, I want to help you find her.'

'Why the secrecy?'

The glass jumped in my hand and I looked up into his hard gaze. Those blue eyes which were so bright against the snow along the Great Wall were gray like steel in this dim light.

'No secrecy,' I said, as if puzzled by his question. 'You said her trust fund is in danger, and I want to help her.'

'I said her trust fund contract needs to be tightened in order to protect it from abuse. There's no need for secrecy there, unless you have reason to believe someone or some organization might be looking to abuse it.'

'Well, you know, the Kin...' I shrugged. I took the straw out of my drink and laid it on the napkin, and then took a good long swallow from the glass for courage.

'Yes, I'm familiar with the Kin, but no, that doesn't tell me anything. Explain why you don't want the Kin to know of our meeting.'

Jesus. This guy must be a good lawyer. I wouldn't want to run against him in court. I had to give him something close to the truth, because I had a feeling those eyes would cut through any bullshit.

I drew a deep breath in as I thought, then let it out. 'Okay. I'll be up front with you. You've heard of the cursing of Zande and Nachtan?'

He nodded.

'The Kin suspect that she's behind them.'

He stared at me for a whole minute. That might not sound like a long time, but it was long enough to be very uncomfortable as the subject under scrutiny. This whole meeting was going wrong. I was supposed to be the one in charge here, using his bureaucratic need to tie up loose ends as a ruse to lure Margaret to justice and to stop her rampage of curses on the greatest witches of our time.

'And?' He prompted me to finish. He took another slow sip of his whisky and let it slide down his throat. He was in no hurry.

And he was forcing me to lie to him. I had to squirm out of this any way I could.

'Why are you so interested in helping Margaret, anyway?' I wasn't just dodging his question, I was genuinely interested. 'Does your law firm handle her trust?'

Rob set his glass down on the table. 'I'm not a member of a firm,' he said. 'You could say Margaret is a client of mine.'

'Either she is or she isn't. A client, I mean.'

He nodded in acknowledgement of my point, then lifted his eyes back up to mine. 'Fair enough. I manage her fund.'

Rob sat across the table, calmly waiting. It was my turn to answer his question now. I took another swallow of my rum and coke, and the ice cubes clinked against my teeth.

'The Kin think I'm mixed up with her and I have to clear my name.' I said it in a rush. It was a relief not to lie, even if that was only half the truth.

He pondered this statement. I could almost see him turning it over in his mind, looking for ramifications and possible scenarios. He took his time. I didn't dare say anything else.

But then he reached his decision. He took one last swallow of whisky to drain the glass, then shook his head.

'Then no. I respectfully decline your offer to help.' He stood up as if to go.

'Wait!' I couldn't believe he was bailing on me. It wasn't supposed to be this way. 'But maybe we can clear her name too and, and she won't come just for me because she's pissed at me. I need you there with your trust fund issues. That's the only thing that'll get her to show her face.'

He shook his head again as he put his arms through his trench coat, that thin inadequate covering from the cold outside. 'Sounds too much like a plan to capture her,' he observed as he pulled one glove onto his hand.

'But she's guilty!' I was standing up now in desperation. If I didn't have Rob, I had no plan to reach Margaret and clear my name. 'And, and wait.'

He paused before walking away.

'Her trust fund,' I said, hating myself even as I spoke the words. I thought of Rob's shoddy clothing. No man would dress that way if he had the means to buy proper bespoke clothing. 'It's not going to be much good to her when the Kin capture her. If the rules are so loose, well, you might be able to let some if it flow your way.'

His eyes widened as the meaning of my words sunk in. I had surprised myself too. The Kin ways were rubbing off on me. That was my only excuse.

He rubbed his chin with his gloved hand, and shook his head. 'You really don't get it, do you?'

I stared at him, willing him not to turn his back, not to leave me in the morass of my own self-hatred of that moment. Give me a chance to regain my self-respect, I silently begged him.

'I vowed years ago not to have anything to do with the Kin or organized magic,' he said. 'And I'm the heir to Lady Margaret's father's estate. I would no sooner steal from my own family than I would be mixed up any further with Kin like you.'

He looked down and pulled the other glove on. 'I thought you were different,' he continued softly, then looked back up at me. 'I really thought you weren't part of them. I was wrong.'

And with that, he left. Leaving me with the bill, I noted with the part of my brain that wasn't sinking in despair.

Oh, yes, he was definitely Margaret's kin.

CHAPTER 19

I nursed my grudge against that wretched excuse
for a lawyer, holding it close to my heart and re-
living every awful moment of that meeting. I fumed
to myself, having no other audience until much later
that evening when Hugh returned to our room.

'Still up?' He was sweaty and his hair had the kind
of dishevelment he only got when returning from a
run. He was wearing Lycra.

'Were you jogging in Beijing? In this weather?'

'No, we, uh, I was at the gym. The hotel gym,' he
said. 'Really feeling the lack of exercise, you know.
And all the feasting. I'm becoming a bit of a porker.
My suits won't be fitting me soon.'

He jovially pinched his flat belly, then busied himself removing his damp clothing as he prepared for a
shower. He hadn't yet met my eye.

'You said we.' My voice was flat. 'Who was *we*?'

'Ah,' he said, as if I'd said something brilliant. 'Yes, Win was there. We met there at the gym.' The bathroom door shut behind him and I soon heard the water running.

I turned off the bedside lamp and lay back against the pillows. So that's how it was. He and Win accidentally meeting at the gym? Getting all sweaty together. I closed my eyes and looked inside, trying to gauge how I felt.

First and foremost, I hated Cate for pointing out her suspicions about Hugh and Win. Well, I hated her for all sorts of reasons, but that one was standing out right at that moment. I probably wouldn't have given it a thought if she hadn't brought it up.

And Hugh. Had he tried to cover up the fact that he'd been with Win at the gym? They had been spending a lot of time together, but only over the past few days. I shook my head. Ridiculous.

Win wouldn't dare, would she? Pretending to be my friend so suddenly once she found out about me and Hugh. She was competitive, that girl. No, I couldn't even think about it all.

Because. I squeezed my eyes further shut as if to block out the thought which crept up, the thought I was really avoiding. Because I found myself not really bothered. Not as bothered as I should have been.

Because I was too busy hating myself. I saw Dara Martin De Teilhard again through Rob's eyes as if he'd been holding up a mirror, and I didn't like what that girl had become. Not a pretty sight.

I sighed and turned over to stare at the open curtains. The lights of Beijing were just a distant glow from our twenty-first floor room. Win thought I had everything. A sponsor in the Kin to help me up the ladder of ambition, a guy who was equally poised. We were going to be the power couple of the Kin. Yet all this was so false.

All my victories were hollow. All my success was brought about by Cate, my father's hated ex-wife. Cate, who was holding me hostage.

And now I had to find a way to entice Margaret into Cate's clutches in order to save this sorry ass of mine. Which might not even be worth saving, except that I was innocent of her crimes, and I was going to fight to save me anyway I could.

Hugh was in the shower for a long time. I lay there, listening to the water play off his body, and tried not to think about anything anymore.

When I heard him finally come back to the room and ready himself for bed, I stayed with my back to him and pretended to be asleep. He didn't try to wake me up.

In the last moments of drifting off, a realization dawned on me, one that strangely enough relaxed me enough to fall the last step. I'd been stung far more by Rob's dismissal of me than the possible affair between Hugh and Win.

··········

I had to change my plans. Rob wasn't on board to help me lure Margaret into the clutches of justice, and after last evening's meeting, I found I no longer had the heart in me for the hunt. His opinion of me had shaken me to the core, and I needed space and time to let that sink in.

Now that Cate was sure I'd been convinced to assist her with Margaret, Win was no longer assigned to dog my every footstep. She was free to help Hugh with translations. I had no idea how Cate was keeping herself busy during the days, and I had every intention to avoid her.

Sipping my morning coffee, I opened the sheers on the window and stared out, past the city with its never ending humanity and noise and volume, and I let my eyes rise up. Up past the bustle and smog, past the buildings, to the mountains beyond the city. Our hotel room faced to the west, not the north, so I didn't see any of the watch towers we'd visited the other day.

The mountains in this view were free of human structures, at least from this distance. They rose in their majestic ruggedness, even in the winter the dark green of fir trees was visible above the city skyline of towers. Solid in their peacefulness, they'd been there forever, watching empires rise and fall.

I was seized with a sudden longing to be surrounded by the wilderness in those hills. How far away were they? From up here, it looked like the main road ran straight toward them. Was there a bus, or could I take a taxi?

I had no jobs to occupy me with the delegation. No one really cared what I did or if I was present. I wasn't needed, I realized bitterly, to the Kin.

'I'm taking a sight-seeing day,' I said without turning around.

Hugh was behind me, I could see his reflection in the glass. 'There are lots of tours, and so much to see,' he agreed as he leaned forward in the mirror to knot his tie. 'Check at the front desk, they'll arrange something for you. We'll be going to the Forbidden City this evening, but there are the botanical Gardens and the huge museum.'

I had no desire to see the rest of the city. My experience with the Hutong had been all bad enough and I didn't want to risk another run-in with a Lijiang Alley kind of place.

At the front desk, I requested a map of the forested, western area of the city, a packed lunch, and a taxi. I was all set.

The cab ride was long, at least a half hour through the endless traffic of cars and bicycles and mopeds and trucks. How could so many people exist in one place? With my driver's limited English and my printed map of the area, I managed to convey to him my destination.

And then suddenly, we were there, at the foot of the mountain. It was a residential area, full of apartment buildings on small lanes, all nestled into the base of the rise. He stopped right at the end, where the mountain began, too steep for any architecture to perch on it. He pointed to a series of stone steps almost hidden in the trees, telling me in Chinese to take these.

It was a long way up, and I knew I couldn't even see the summit from where I stood. A hell of a higher climb than even Signal Hill back home. Well, this was it. No way to go but up.

I walked up those steps for an hour or more, the air growing more crisp and clean every time I paused for a breath. As I rose, I felt freer as if I was losing the chains I'd been adding to myself, weighing me down. The chains of ambition, forged by my own actions, from every choice I'd ever made, all of this fell off me as I walked and let my mind be free in the mountain air.

There were no other people here. No other footprints in the half-melted snow on these stone steps, amazing considering the throngs on the roads below. And when I reached the summit, or near enough, I found myself on a road, more of a laneway really, a lonely path that wound around the hills and trees, with hardly a house in sight.

Cars had passed by earlier, I could see from the tire marks in the freshly fallen snow which blanketed everything in a quilt of silence. But apart from these few signs of humanity, I was alone. Just me and the birds in the trees.

As I walked, I contemplated what a strange thing this was, my decision to arrive here. I'd had no destination aside from needing to be surrounded by wilderness. Besides packing a lunch, I'd had no preparation, hadn't even arranged for a ride home.

Yet, around the next bend, I found my destination.

The road hugged the base of the next rise of hills, and in a quiet corner, almost invisible in the snow, there was a tiny temple, or shrine. It was a simple structure, hardly bigger than a bus shelter. The roof was arched stone, and inside it held only an altar. The snow hadn't entered this enclosed space, and I could see the remains of candles and incense on it.

I looked up past the roadside shrine and saw ruins rising into the mountain above me, built right into the rock by the looks of them. Intrigued, I followed what must be the path, my footprints crunching through the pristine snow.

More steps, of course, but not many this time. The stone beneath the snow was old and worn, and I picked my way carefully. If I slipped and broke a leg, no one would ever find me here for I'd told no one of my plans. They led me into a ruined building, a shell with stone walls and wooden rafters. There was a holiness about this undisturbed site, a peace in the depths of the shadows,

I passed through an archway. Around a central court-yard there were simple rooms leading off, the doors long rotted away. Perhaps it had been a small nunnery at one time, but now was home only to birds and other wildlife.

I looked back the way I'd come. In the distance, I could see the smog of Beijing and tall buildings, far, far below from where I stood. There were no other foot-prints in the snow except my own, no signs of human life.

Yet I knew, right there, somehow, that I wasn't alone here.

I paused, and listened closely, but there weren't any sounds, not even the silence of a held breath. Yet I could feel eyes on me.

'Hello?' I called out, only realizing once the words were said how silly that was, for if there was anyone there they would speak some dialect of Chinese, cer-tainly not English. *'Nie how?'* I said in my uncertain Mandarin.

There was no answer. Had I inadvertently stumbled into another magic cell? I sent hesitant feelers all around me from my mind. God alone knew what could be lurk-ing here in this forgotten foreign territory. Lijiang Alley had been bad enough, and that had been smack dab in the middle of one of the most populated cities on earth.

My bet would be dragons. I looked again behind me at the silent stone ruins. Could I protect myself from the fire if I accidentally woke one up? I cast my mind back to the dragon I'd created from the clouds over Edinburgh, oh so long ago it now seemed. It had breathed smoke, or at least a close approximation of it, but its teeth had been nothing more that mist. I doubted whether iceballs would have any effect on a real dragon.

I slowly began a quiet creep back to the arched exit. If there'd been anything to hide behind, I would have run towards it. Instead, I was out in the open, and someone was watching me. Worst of all, there was a creeping feeling of familiarity, a sense of knowing whose eyes they were, as if I'd felt their gaze many a time.

I stopped in my tracks with this realization. Someone *was* watching me. Through magic. How rude.

'Hello?' My voice rang out, not tentative at all this time, because I was pissed and I wanted the watcher to know it. 'Cate, is that you?' There was no answer, just the squawking of birds in the tree. I looked to find what had disturbed them, but could see nothing.

It wasn't her. I couldn't sense the feeling of malevolence that accompanied her, that undertone of an axe waiting to fall on me. But if not her, who?

'Hugh?' My call was much more tentative this time, because he wouldn't do such a thing. It just wasn't a Hugh thing.

'Win.' My voice was flat. If that bitch was daring to play these kind of games with me...

A single, deep-throated chuckle rippled through the space between trees and ruined stone walls. I searched all around, my eyes caught by every shadow. Oh, yes, I knew that laugh.

'Margaret. Stop it right now. Show yourself.'

I listened carefully, but there was no answer, not even an echo of my own voice. 'Well, I know you can hear me, you coward. Listen up. I'm getting blamed for your deeds.'

Still no reply, but I had the feeling I'd caught her interest. 'That's right. The Kin know you've committed these curses on Zande and Nachtan. I don't know why you've done this, but you have to quit it right now! Undo those curses.'

I waited.

'I know you're guilty, because I saw you in Win's vision. I saw you leaving Li Minh asleep in her cave.' I knew I had her full attention now, I knew by the way the birds were now silent, and I knew through the warm breeze that was flowing through my hair.

'For the love of the goddess, don't do it, Margaret! Leave Li Minh alone, and let the others out from the spell.' My voice was desperate as I pleaded. 'You don't need to prove anything to the Kin. You have everything you want in your life.'

As a last ditch effort, I burst out, 'You want to screw over my life? Is this why you're doing it? Well, it's working. Your spiteful, hateful actions are ruining my life, taking away my future. If the Kin can't have you, they're going to go for me as their scapegoat. Do you get it?'

Still no reply, that bitch. I couldn't fight her in her own field, her knowledge of magic far outstripped my own. I scuffed the snow underfoot. 'Well then, fine. Be like that. But you know what?' I lifted my head and looked all around me. Not a bird sang, not even a branch waved in that balmy breeze that continued all around me. I loosened my scarf and took off my toque.

'You might as well turn yourself in, because they're going to get you in the end. How do I know this?'

I savored the silence, knowing she was hanging onto every word I said. And it was with a feeling of satisfied revenge that I continued. 'Your nephew Rob is looking for you. He says your trust fund has problems, that the rules and stipulations are primitive and it won't hold up to a court challenge, not these days. And the Kin are definitely going to grab it from you, you know that.'

I took a deep breath. 'And now that Cate and the Kin are aware that Rob is looking for you, they're going to keep the closest eye on him. Probably have his room bugged. The minute you show yourself to him, bam! They'll have you.

'How do you like that twist in the story, huh? Hoist by your own petard, as you would say.'

It felt good to unload all my frustrations and anger on her. That is, until it was spewed out and laid bare to the open air. Then it didn't feel so good anymore.

'You can't win this time, and it looks good on you,' I mumbled. I was still waiting for a response from her, but there was nothing. Nothing, except for the deep chill which suddenly settled in this dell. It formed on the stone walls in glittering frost, and bore right into my bones. It froze my eyelashes and burned my ears.

That was it. That was her only response. With my words to her, I'd burned any bridges I still had with Margaret, and that witch was pissed.

I replaced my hat and huddled into my parka and stumbled away. Back through the laneway and down the countless steps, back into the relative warmth of the city below. I walked along the main road until I could flag down a cab and somehow convey to him where I needed to go.

When I got back to the hotel, I realized only four hours had passed from start to finish. Despite the intense physical effort I'd put my body through, I wasn't the least bit hungry for lunch.

CHAPTER 20

J ust as well that I wasn't looking to eat, because Cate sniffed me out the moment I returned to the hotel. 'So?' She appeared at my side while I waited for the elevator. I said nothing until the brass sliding doors had closed behind us.

We stood side by side. I watched her in the mirror. She was staring down at me, her arms crossed with impatience.

What to tell her? She was going to be displeased with every single update, for I'd failed spectacularly on all fronts. There was no way we were going to lure Margaret anywhere near us. Not now that I'd warned her the Kin knew what she was doing, and that they planned to punish her for her deeds. Punished severely with her trust fund removed, even if they couldn't lay physical hands on her. I would be surprised if the Kin hadn't started that action already. Margaret might remain free, but she would have no money to finance her lavish lifestyle.

And I'd managed to scupper any chances of using Rob as bait to lure in Margaret. The lawyer had seen through my deception with his x-ray vision. Perhaps Margaret had probably already reached out to him to give her consent to tighten the rules.

Not that it would do her any good. The Kin Britannica controlled the banks and the laws of their country. They would do as they wished.

'Rob is out,' I told Cate. 'He doesn't trust the Kin.' I unzipped my parka and removed my toque. The tiny space was growing warm.

'You must have told him.' This wasn't in the form of a question.

I shook my head. The elevator doors opened onto my floor. I paused before stepping out, waiting for the shit storm.

But it never came. Cate merely laughed it off, too casually.

'Oh well,' she said, with a tiny smile dancing in her eyes. 'Looks like it'll be your head on the Covenanter's platter.'

'But Cate,' I said. I held my hand on the elevator door to keep it open as I tried unsuccessfully to quell the quick flush of anger that ran through me. I took a deep breath, forcing my voice to stay light and level like hers. I had to play the game. 'You'd vouch for me, though. Wouldn't you? I mean, surely you have as much to lose as me?'

As threats go, it was veiled, but she had to know what I meant. Yet she merely laughed again without answering, or perhaps the lack of reply was her answer. Either way, I didn't feel supported in this environment.

'You missed my presentation last night,' she said. 'I was very disappointed not to see you there. I discussed my studies of the past year or so.'

'Music,' I said flatly.

'Music and magic. They hold the keys to many of life's mysteries,' she replied. 'Too bad you missed it. I think it would have given you food for thought. '

She still had her finger on the elevator hold. 'In fact, it's really too bad you weren't there. But I think you'll have the opportunity to see my work in action very soon.

Cate was smiling enigmatically as the doors silently closed, leaving me to my fate.

....

'There you are.' Hugh's voice was warm when I walked into our suite. He took me into a large hug. 'Had a good morning sightseeing?'

I huddled into him like a feather duvet on a winter's night. I tried to close my mind to my suspicions of last night, about him and Win. His strong arms gave me the nurturing I so needed right there and then.

How long would it last, though? Once the Covenanters sounded the cry and demanded their sacrifice? I lifted my head away from that shoulder and searched his face. How would his family feel about us, if the worst came to pass? They were close. Family was everything to Hugh. How strong was his love for me? I somehow doubted the Duke would allow his house to be tainted with ties to a traitor to the Kin, even if the charges weren't true, even if Hugh knew they could never be true.

How strong was my love for him, for that matter? I stayed in his embrace for as long as I could. It might be the last one. I might have overstayed my welcome, for after a long moment of my silence, he briskly stepped away.

'Cate's presentation last night,' I began.

'You missed it! Too bad, it was quite fascinating. Music and magic. Imagine the possibilities.'

I shivered, remembering the crystal decorations on the tree she'd brought to his parents' estate for the Ney Year. The beautiful shimmering notes from each ball, and how one had particularly spoken to me. Until Cate touched it and the note turned sour. 'Was she talking about the crystal balls, like she gave to your parents?'

He looked surprised. 'I'd forgotten about those little toys,' he said with a fond smile. 'No, she delved into the deeper philosophy about how music can aid and strengthen personal magic. Very few have worked on this theory before. Amazing ideas, I don't know if anyone has ever examined it from that angle before.'

'I don't see how it could work.'

'It is a little complicated,' he began, hardly pompous at all as he began to mansplain. 'It has to do with vibrations, and the ability to use these to intensify the magic field.'

I nodded impatiently. 'But what's it used for? I can't see any application for this.'

'It would be used for, I don't know, times of war, when one would need to group all one's energies to direct at a foe, quite obviously.'

'So she's creating weapons of mass destruction?'

'What, Cate? Nonsense,' he said. 'You do see the bleak side of life sometimes, don't you? No, Cate would never have such an application in mind. Her work is more theoretical.'

Something was nagging at me, I didn't know what, but I didn't want to let this conversation go. Why could Hugh not see the evil side of Cate? Why did he insist that everything about the woman was above board?

'And how would she use the music for her weapons? Is adamantite involved?' The moment the words came out of my mouth, a light began to dawn inside me, but he didn't give me a chance to explore that thought further.

'Adamantite? I suppose,' he said, cocking his head to one side. He glanced at his wristwatch and gave a start. 'We do have to get ready for the final feast tonight,' he reminded me.

'But we're not leaving tomorrow,' I said. 'Why would the final feast be tonight?' I still had my parka on, the cold which had entered me from the shrine was still in my bones.

'True, but the talks are wrapped up for now. Tomorrow will be just for fun.'

'So, how has it been? Any decisions made? What has it accomplished, this whole delegation?'

'We've made great strides,' he said with satisfaction. 'Beijing has agreed to send out a welcome for all magic practitioners to return, and they will be given full pardons if necessary.'

'And?'

He looked at me quizzically. 'Once the new law gets passed, that is. Things don't move as quickly as we'd like, not when they're on such a big scale.'

A wave of horrified tedium slowly rolled over me. This dullness was to be my future. I sat myself down on the sofa and let his words wash around me.

Hugh took off his shirt and peered into the mirror to examine his teeth. 'They have also agreed to host another delegation in six months' time. Yes, we can be quite proud of the work accomplished this week.'

The future I'd imagined working for the Kin had been one of excitement and magic and overpowering the bad guys like Willem. A future where I would use my power, becoming adept in all things magick, become a hero in my own eyes.

I thought of Margaret, who had foreseen all this and offered me many chances to escape the utter dullness of this future. She'd known me better than I knew myself, yes, but that bridge was burned.

And Rob. That quirky, sort of geeky lawyer, he had his head screwed on right, too. It still stung that he'd dismissed me so; even worse, that I'd deserved his dismissal. I hung my head in shame and admitted to myself that I was responsible for every choice I'd made, yes, even for allowing Cate to manipulate me into 'saving' the day back in St. John's, and being foolish enough to trust her in the first place.

My future yawned ahead endlessly, full of politics and listening to bores yammering on about things which really didn't matter. This was no fun. This was a life sentence.

But perhaps it beat whatever judgement the Covenanters were planning. Right? I turned to look up at Hugh, who was now hanging his shirt back up in the closet.

When I first met this man, he was like a whirlwind of fresh energy, bringing hopes of a new life for me with him, with his talk of the Kin and his exciting work. Once I'd scratched the surface though, he was like any normal guy, like Jack at the Craft Fairs. He was simply a person getting on with his life within the structures he'd been given. A little dull, perhaps, but didn't the Chinese have a curse – may you live in interesting times?

Yeah, I had to admit that Hugh had become dull. Or perhaps it was just that I, and my expectations of life, had grown so much.

My life had been interesting since I'd met him. That meeting had been the turning point of my life, when I found there was hope for a life in magic for me, not just a dreary future in plumbing. Meeting Hugh had been the catalyst, he'd shown me I could be more than just a despised half-blood, that my life had worth.

Everything else that had happened along the way, well, it was all my own fault. My own choices of action. And their consequences.

And now. Now I realized that my relationship with Hugh might be the only way I could be saved, my only hope. Only through my connection with him could I possibly hope to dodge the judgement that should be Margaret's. I hated myself even more now, but I was in survival mode by this time.

I stood up, drew him away from the mirror, and gave him the lovingest, smoochiest kiss I could. At least that wasn't false, and he responded in kind. My future would never be boring, surely?

He drew back with that smile on his face, the smile that used to send thrills right to the deepest part of me. The special smile, just for me.

'We have to get ready,' he whispered, his voice hoarse. He cleared his throat and let go of me, then continued in his normal tone as he turned back to his hair. 'Dress in your finest. We'll be taken to the Forbidden City for a tour. It's going to be a long afternoon, lots of walking, so wear comfortable shoes.'

'You realize you just gave me an impossible instruction? How can I dress in my finest and have comfortable footwear?'

He looked down at the strappy sandals I had in my hands, and laughed at the sight of the height of the heels. 'Didn't you bring something more practical?'

'Yeah, my running shoes,' I mumbled as I looked back into the closet. Of course there was nothing there that would suit the bill.

He came and joined me, staring with me at the sparse offerings of my closet as if to check I hadn't overlooked anything.

'Hmmm.'

'Yeah, I didn't bring a lot of choice. I'm just going to have to wear the sandals and grin and bear it.'

'I'll carry you,' he promised. 'When the going gets rough.'

I bit my lip. If only I could trust that he would be true to his word, because I had a feeling that the going was indeed going to get rough. And not just high-heels on cobblestones rough.

··········

The grand welcome feast was to be held in the heart of the Forbidden City. Despite Hugh's advice for me to hurry, I took the time to rifle through the tourist brochures on the desk of our room. The Emperor's Palace! Even I had heard of the huge compound in the center of Beijing, the former city of China's rulers.

There it was. I gazed at the photo of the huge red building, the golden tiered roofs, the white marble steps. Acres and acres of buildings in the old Chinese fashion, palaces within palaces, indeed a whole city, all for the emperor and his court. The center of the booklet showed the plan. A line of unattached buildings, leading from south to north, and to the west and east houses and more palaces, each built for a specific purpose. The magnitude was stupendous.

Hugh had finished with the shower. I heard him come back into the bedroom, and felt his warmth as he hovered over my shoulders.

'Where is the dinner being held?' I didn't raise my eyes from the map.

He reached his damp arm over my shoulder to trace the procession of palaces and structures leading to the top of the page, the north end of the compound.

'The Hall of Union,' he mused, then his finger found the spot. 'The small one, right there. Between the Palace of Earthly Tranquility and the Palace of Heavenly Purity.'

Those names! I soaked in the delicious foreignness and elegance of them. The map held tiny drawings of each building and the architecture with its many roofs and bright colors. I, Dara Martin de Teilhard, was here in the heart of China. I would be inside the Forbidden City.

'Will we get to explore?' I was almost salivating at the thought.

'Eh,' he replied. 'Probably not much, not tonight. We'll get a bit of a tour of the highlights. You can always go in the daytime tomorrow to see more, but I'll warn you, with eighty thousand visitors every day, it gets a little crowded.'

'Eighty thousand a *day*?' I couldn't even conceive of such a mass of people at once, let alone that many lining up to enter the narrow gate.

'It's a popular tourist attraction now,' he agreed. 'We could always request a private tour after hours. I'll look into it, if you like.'

'Yeah, I would. Can we do that? Is all of it open to the public?' I twisted my head to look up at him.

He drew in a breath as he thought, then shook his head. 'No, parts of it are still closed off. The main palaces are museums. There are almost nine thousand rooms in total, I don't know if they even know how many there actually are. A lot to see.'

CHAPTER 21

I t felt strange to be so dressed up and coiffed so early in the afternoon. By three o'clock, we were waiting in the lobby of the hotel.

Hugh turned to me with a smile lighting his eyes. 'The hotel store!' he said. 'Let's look in there for something for your feet.'

He really was a darling for thinking of me in this way. Alas, the store was more of a tourist shop, with little in the way of comfortable elegant footwear on offer.

'Looks like this is the only thing,' he said, pointing to the cloth shoes on the rack.

Under any other circumstances, I would have thought them attractive enough. Simple black cloth shoes with a single strap, and lots of embroidery. Not something for a fancy dinner and a formal gown, but they would do just fine. I shrugged. What odds, it wasn't like anyone would be looking at me. I slipped the high heel sandals into my purse and put the flats on right there and then. My feet were already a little achy.

Once on the bus, I noted that many other women had done the same thing, so I didn't need to feel out of place at all.

The Forbidden City. Even the name of it was suggestive of deep, mysterious secrets in this ancient realm. The buses carried us the short way down the main roads, pulling up to the huge courtyard, lined with tall red brick walls on three sides. Their very blankness caused the eye to rise above them, and there, towering over everything were visible two layers of golden tiled roofs in the old style, the hip-and-gable which turned up on the ends, and the same, but smaller, at the corners. It was perfect harmony.

I was awestruck, completely speechless. Hugh, not so much.

'This is the Meridian Gate.' He pointed at the three arches in the brick wall facing us. Through the tall open entrance in the middle, I could see white marble steps, and further in the distance, more roofs. I allowed him to take my hand as we followed the crowd up to and through the arch.

'The government closed the Museum to visitors today,' Hugh remarked. 'So this is a great honor.'

He'd been right, there was a lot of walking, because this complex was huge. I'd examined the map of the Forbidden City prior, but it didn't really convey the scale of the place.

From the map, I knew that the site stood on one hundred and seventy acres. The mind reeled to think of that much real estate smack in the middle of overcrowded Beijing. The palace city was built symmetrically, with huge halls running through the center, with houses for the court, servants and concubines on the sides.

The two hundred or so international delegates in our party could not hope to fill the space before us. Far off down the first concreted courtyard, white marble staircases led us up to the first huge building. I couldn't help it, I stood still and gawped like a tourist, way up to the gold tiles, with the intricate eaves all blue and red and more gold. It was beautiful and awe-inspiring.

And romantic. I took Hugh's hand in mine and leaned into him.

We would be okay. We would get through whatever the future held for me. But I had to warn him. It was only fair. And this was a good a place as any for confessions. But before I could speak, we were very rudely interrupted.

'Ah, there you guys are! I missed you on the bus.'

The click of her expensive heels heralding her entrance, Win scurried up to us and stood too close to the other side of Hugh.

'This is really something, isn't it?' There was a proprietary note in her voice, as if she was responsible for this glorious place. She tucked her hand under Hugh's free arm and beamed at us.

The nerve of the creature! She was glamoured to the hilt, yet even in the dim light of this afternoon, her make-up somehow didn't seem too much.

And she was dressed to match the palace buildings. Her red silk Chinese style dress with exquisite gold and silver embroidered flowers running down the length of it echoed the structures before us, and her smooth black hair was in an elaborate up-do, much like the one the Empress had, that first day in Lijiang Alley. Win must have been preparing herself since dawn.

And she was having no difficulty walking in her heels.

I glared at her as I peered around Hugh's bulk. She merely smiled sweetly back at me, then proceeded to take over the conversation with him. He, being the perfect Scottish gentleman that he was, went along with her, charming as ever.

It didn't help that I was feeling a little frumpish in comparison with my flat shoes and lack of makeup. I tried to pull us ahead, to walk faster, anything to discombobulate her, but it was no use. Hugh was a solid weight and matched our steps to her tiny mincing ones.

The two-hour tour of the museum highlights was excruciating. Endless corridors and steps, and the wealth on display was almost sickening in its opulence. Everything was gold and precious stones, and each ancient object held its own story. And there were always more and more steps to climb up and down.

I lost track of which building we were in, the succession of structures was endless with their towering ceilings of gilt and intricate carvings and fine woods. We were led through both sides of the main corridor of buildings, both east and west, and I confess I was quite lost. Win and Hugh seemed to know their way about though, and they didn't stop yammering the whole time.

I couldn't see how she remained so fresh in those heels. My new cloth shoes were hurting my feet, rubbing in unexpected places, and had no arch support whatsoever. But it wasn't just my feet that were burning.

Finally, I had the chance to confront her, when Hugh wandered off to greet an old friend. I sat heavily on a bench and pulled her down with me before she could go prancing off in his wake.

'What the hell are you playing at?' I loomed over her on the bench now she didn't have the advantage of heels.

Her face was a pleasant blank. 'What do you mean, Dara?'

I nodded after my fiancé. 'Hugh. You're chasing him, aren't you?'

She shook her head and laughed with disbelief. 'What's gotten into you? You crazy or something?'

'Don't give me that. You haven't let up on him since you met him the first day here.'

'We have spent a lot of time together on this trip, haven't we?' She leaned her head to one side as if reflecting. 'Maybe he likes my presence more than yours? Perhaps I'm easier to get along with. More pleasant, certainly.'

Her lips pursed in a little smile. 'Besides, I'm just following orders, remember? Seems like you've annoyed Cate in some way.' She leaned closer and lifted up her hand to her mouth, as if we were having a girlie tete-a-tete, and whispered. 'In fact, I'm getting the distinct impression that Cate is making preparations to ditch you. You've really managed to displease her.'

Win giggled even as I reared back from her in horror. 'What the hell, Win? Sounds like you're sucking up big time. Why the change in heart? You were so pissed to be assigned to her unit.'

She smoothed her silk dress along her legs. The expression on her face could only be termed smug as she glanced up at me through the extensions on her eyelashes. 'I'm just taking a leaf from your book, Dara,' she purred. 'I'm hitching my perfect little ass to Cate's rising star. And believe me, she's aiming for the big time.'

....

I actually had Hugh to myself at the dinner. Well, the two of us sat together at the same large table, at any rate, with a mix of other Kin and Chinese delegates. Hugh wasn't important enough to sit with the real bigwigs at the main spot, up on the dais, and that suited me just fine. I looked around, but didn't see Cate anywhere, and that also sat well with me.

I'd managed to shake Win off. I assumed she had disappeared somewhere up Cate's ass, and I wasn't about to go looking for her. I settled in to enjoy the evening.

Except. Win had flat out said that Cate wasn't pleased with me. I was pretty sure she didn't know the whole story, but it was worrying, especially after Cate's own words to me that day. She was getting ready to toss me to the Covenanters as I'd so far failed in my attempts to bring Margaret to her. I hadn't said a word to Hugh about all this. And I couldn't.

I couldn't even tell him the true story about the adamantite stud fixed into my ear last June, or why Cate had placed it there. He thought it was a sign of her affection.

The problem was that Hugh didn't see for himself that Cate's meteoric rise through the ranks of the Kin was suspicious. I couldn't tell him this, not outright, but perhaps I could somehow plant the seeds of suspicion in his mind.

The huge room was lined in red silk, and the chandeliers and all the touches were gold. It was sumptuous, yes, if a bit gaudy. The menu for the evening was two pages long, written in Chinese characters on one page, English on the reverse.

I nudged Hugh with my elbow before the feast began.

'Look at all this food,' I murmured. 'There's forty courses. How are we supposed to eat all that?'

'Yeah, they're really putting on a splash. But don't worry too much, we'll only get a very small amount on each plate, just a tasting really, showing off the best of Chinese cuisine.'

The meal was served during the speeches from both delegations. The translators spoke over the person giving the speech with about a five second delay, and everyone wore mics, so it was difficult to really pick anything out that was being said.

That freed us up to talk as long as we kept our voices low. I wanted to tell him about the afternoon's adventure, but not here. There were too many ears. Instead, we kept the topics light.

'Is Cate up there at the main table?' I asked after a tiny bowl of delicious hot soup was set before us. It was a clear broth, with a single miniature dumpling in the center.

He swiveled his head, and peered over the distance. 'Yes, that's her,' he replied, his voice filled with admiration.

I stabbed at the single tiny dumpling with the sticks provided. I'd never used chopsticks before. I gave up and drank the broth.

'How has she managed this?' I asked him. I searched carefully for the right words. 'I mean, she never used to be involved with international stuff like this. Then suddenly, she's all over the place.'

'Haven't we discussed this before? After your mother returned, and Jon decided to leave Cate, she decided to fully step into her birthright in the Kin. She's doing a marvelous job.'

I nodded. Yes, that was the story she was telling. Not of how she'd tricked me into opening up the leys so she could stick her hand in and steal a direct hit of power, no not that one, but that she'd thrown off the yoke of marriage to come into her own. I tried again.

'But she's up there with all the powerful witches,' I pressed. 'The head of the Euro Kin is at that table, and the President of China. Surely she's not on their level?'

'She's there, so she must have earned her right to be there.'

'But she's the Huxor, right? She only deals with adamantite, not Kin business,' I urged.

'Precisely.' He leaned in closer to me. 'I'll let you in on a secret, Dara. There are many different kinds of power in the political world. The Chinese Kin want to take control of the adamantite. They know that's the route to real power in their world. The Mundane government really doesn't know how to use it, or what it is. Cate is present to direct the best practices of mining and distribution. If they,' he jerked his head up to the front of the room. 'If they can get Cate on board with them, then they'll have the means of controlling the distribution.'

'So it's got nothing to do with her personal magical power?'

He shook his head. 'Doesn't matter. She's their path to controlling the riches. They're sucking up to her big time.

'And you.' His admiration was turned toward me now. 'You have played your cards right, hitching to this rising star.'

I forced myself to smile back at him. This was all going so wrong.

CHAPTER 22

I poked at the rose-scented concoction on the tiny plate with one chopstick. It was a dessert, perhaps made of rice or some other kind of carb, but jellied with glazed flower petals on top of it. It smelled divine, but I'd lost steam by this time, and was merely picking at the wondrous and strange food. Despite my clumsiness with the sticks and the tiny amounts of food offered on the plates, I'd still managed to stuff myself. By this point, too many exotic flavors had passed through my mouth for me to fully appreciate the delicate flavors of this confection.

The translator announced a break at that point so everyone could get up and stretch their legs, and not before time.

'I'm going to try to walk some of this off,' I said to Hugh. Beneath the table, my feet searched for my fancy sandals. I'd removed them the moment we'd sat down, as the long damask tablecloths hid my feet from view.

On second thought, I left them there, and removed the cloth slippers from my purse.

Hugh must be an old hand at the never-ending feasting business, because the pink sweet had mostly disappeared from his plate. How could he find the room? My stomach protested as I watched the last little rose petal drenched in honey enter his mouth. There was too much food here. Too much gold and red on the walls, too much opulence everywhere. My head hurt. The excess was stifling me.

He nodded as he swallowed. 'There's the courtyard just there, if you want to get out of doors for a bit of fresh air,' he said. 'If you don't mind, I'm going to mingle a bit. You think you'll be alright on your own?'

'I'm sure I can take care of myself, Hugh.' Was he joking? There couldn't be a much safer place than here in the Forbidden City in Beijing. Even this evening, even as honored guests with invitations in hand, we'd each been subjected to the full body up and down with the soldier's handheld metal detectors.

The Hall had been steadily growing warmer over the evening with all the bodies packed inside. The noise of all these people talking over the music was giving me a pounding headache. I needed to get outside.

'You're looking rather pale, Dara. The food not agreeing with you?'

Cate. Where had she come from? I hadn't noticed her leaving the main table. I grimaced as I turned to her.

'I just need to get outside for a bit. I'll be fine.'

'You might want to wander in the Imperial Gardens,' she observed. 'If you can find them. I'm sure the greenery will be refreshing and calming after all the noise.'

Hugh drew his brows together. 'I don't think that's permitted, surely?'

'Nonsense, Hugh. What's the harm? We are guests, here, after all.' As she drew him into a deeper conversation of the latest discussions from her table, I took the opportunity to slip away.

A garden would be nice and soothing. Trees, flowers, grass, anything but the constant stone and concrete of Beijing. Greenery and the oxygen unleashed by trees. Yes, that would help my head more than anything.

The moment I walked out the doors of the hall, I took a deep breath of the cooler air. The pain eased slightly almost immediately, yet the ache still pounded through my brain.

This exit led to a narrow balcony at the top of the inevitable staircase leading down to the courtyard below. I peered through the darkness and pulled my shawl tightly around my shoulders against the brisk air. There were a few small groups of people here already, smoking cigarettes and cigars, their voices reaching me in a babel of languages. I needed someplace quieter with less people and their noise.

Gardens. Cate had said there were gardens, but I could see nothing like that around me, only more brick walls and concrete walkways, with the very charming yellow tiled roofs, of course. There was a gateway directly ahead of me, yet it appeared to just lead to more buildings and stone corridors. I'd studied the map, and knew that beyond that gate lay only a labyrinth of quarters for the lesser members of the emperor's court. That wouldn't do. I had no desire to get lost in a maze of buildings.

I slowly picked my way down the white marble steps away from the Hall of Celestial and Terrestrial Union, casting my mind back to the map of the palace grounds. The gardens were at the north end of the compound, so surely the feasting hall had been between the last palace and the garden.

I turned north, to my left, once I'd reached the ground. Yes, there loomed the Palace of Earthly Tranquility directly before me. It was a mirror image of the Palace of Heavenly Purity which we'd walked through to reach the feasting hall, there being no other way to get around the huge structure.

Ah, but closer examination showed that the two palaces weren't exactly the same. The one before me was slightly smaller in scale, which allowed for a narrow corridor between the high stone wall and the palace itself. If my calculations were correct, this should lead me to the gate of the gardens.

This suited me, for feeling so stuffed and logy as I was, I had no desire to mount any more steps in my search for the Imperial Gardens. I glanced behind me. The few groups of people weren't paying any attention to me, so I quietly slipped through between the walls.

There was only darkness and dead silence in the passageway. The stone stretched up above my head, the overhanging roof of the Palace closing me off from the moonlight and the reflected glare of the city. But I felt no fear. There were no supernatural elements here, no ghosts of concubines past. Perhaps it was as Win had said, that all the magick of China had been purged out of everyday life and pushed and squeezed into the cells surrounding the old Buddhist nunneries.

In a place with such a terrible history of abuse and excess and wars, I would have expected to feel more of the past's vibrations echoing, but I didn't give it much thought as I was intent on reaching the fresh garden to breathe oxygen. My headache, although lessened, still remained, and I pushed on through the empty shadows.

And there were the enormous gates leading to the northern-most end of the Forbidden City. And yes, there was the green moistness of the garden was in the air, it was calling to me. I quickly made my way along the path to the towering wall with the gates within.

The tall wooden door, surprisingly, opened easily with a slight push, and I hesitated on the threshold. Was I allowed to enter? The evening's organizers had given the delegates the tour of all the main palaces and museum spaces on our way to the feasting hall, but nothing had been said about us going beyond the prescribed route. So, strictly speaking, we hadn't been forbidden to explore and Cate hadn't seemed to think it was a problem.

On the other hand...

'Are we allowed in there?' The whispered voice cut harshly through the quiet of the space.

Win.

'What are you doing? Following me?' Of course she was. That was her assignment, to keep close tabs on me when not sucking up to Cate and Hugh. She was still following the witch's orders and not letting me out of her sight. How had she snuck up on me wearing those stupid stilettos? 'The gate is open – if they didn't want us in here, they would have locked it, don't you think?'

She drew closer, and looked nervously at the dark opening. Beyond, I could smell the perfume of the flowers, yes, even in January there were blooms lending their fragrance to the air. I could see the whiteness of petals glowing in the pitch black of the gardens within the portal.

'I don't think it's a good idea.'

'Why are you whispering? There's no one around to hear.' I boldly pushed the door open further. It was heavy and designed to close off the interior from the eyes of the court. 'You don't have to come in. I just want a breath of fresh air and some quiet. Go on back to the Hall.'

I stepped through into the garden.

Win made as if to join me, then reached out to grab my arm. 'Don't!'

I shook her off and attempted to close the door, to leave her outside. 'If you don't like it, leave.'

But she followed me on my heels as if she was stuck to me, determined not to let me be alone or give me any peace.

We paused as we stood inside the gate, not even noticing as it silently swung closed behind us. It was pitch black in here, inside the secret walled gardens of the Emperor. And here, here was the supernatural element which had been so absent in the rest of the Palace enclave.

'Do you feel it?' I found myself whispering now, too. My headache was all but forgotten as I smelled the magic amongst the greenness.

Despite the time of year, the garden's air was warm with scents, an almost tropically moist breeze wafted around us. A pathway glowed ahead of us, the white marble pebbles reflecting what little light escaped from the sky, forking off into meandering paths around the groupings of large cedar trees, their branches drooping to the ground from their great heights. There was not a sound in this garden, not even the wind in the branches.

'I think this is a very bad idea.'

Her body shivered beside me. I had an uncomfortable, niggling feeling she might be right, but I would never acknowledge that. Beneath the gorgeousness of the perfumes and the freshness of the over-oxygenated air, there was another tone, a darker tone, an electric magical confluence in the atmosphere of this enclosed garden.

Yes, Win might be right, but I wasn't going to admit it, certainly not to her. Serve her right for following me where she wasn't wanted. The path crunched beneath my flats as I boldly stepped out.

'Like I said, you didn't have to come. I'm going to do a bit of exploring.' I began to wander along the path, letting it take me along the twists and turns until the gate was out of sight. Win's steps behind me were surprisingly subdued, as if she were creeping along, not wishing to disturb any sleeping creatures.

She was muttering under her breath.

'Like I said, you don't have to come along,' I said as I stopped suddenly and whirled around to face her. 'You can –'

My words faltered as a swish of wings of fabric or something sounded overhead, and the faint breeze caused by their passing lifted the hairs on the back of my neck.

CHAPTER 23

'What was that?' Win had jumped onto the path behind me as she shrieked and stood uncomfortably close. Too close. I shook her arm off me.

'Just a bird, an owl or something,' I muttered. I looked up into the sky but all I could see was the reflected lights of the city off the smog cover. There were no stars in this quiet place.

'Or a dragon?' She was whispering now. She moved a little away from me, and stood uncertainly on the path.

We both stood still with our ears open. No birds sounded, no hoots or squawks or even the sweet lonely sound of a nightingale. It was quiet, like the quiet of a crypt. Yet there was still something buzzing in the air, something just out of the range of human ears.

'Do you feel it?'

'What?' I asked reluctantly. I didn't want her to say it out loud.

'The magic. It's all around us.'

'How can that be?' My whisper was low, but furious. 'This is not one of your magick cysts – how can it be? There are thousands of people coming through here every single day. Thousands and thousands of Mundanes.'

'Well, maybe it becomes a magic cell after dark,' she insisted. 'What do you know about it all? I'm telling you there is strong magick here in this garden. Thought you were supposed to be such a powerful witch. You have to be able to feel it.'

I nodded slowly. 'Yeah. Okay, I do, alright?' I lifted my head. I was beginning to regret my obstinance in entering the garden. 'Maybe we should just leave?'

We both stood and looked all around us. We were surrounded by the large cedars whose branches drooped all the way to the ground. I could swear they hadn't been so close a moment ago. I cast my eye to the ground. We were standing at a crossroads of the path, a divergence, where the white marbled pebbles went off in four directions.

'Which way is out?'

'It's got to be behind us. We didn't come very far.' We set off back the way I thought we had come. Win took my arm and this time I let her.

But we hadn't gone ten feet before I could see that this couldn't be the right route. The layout of the trees was wrong, and there was no sign of the portal through which we'd arrived in to the garden.

'Let's try the other direction,' Win urged, still hanging on tight. We retraced our steps, but the crossroads had disappeared. Instead, the path stretched out before us in a single strand of glowing white, curving around the trees.

'That's impossible,' I told her, my voice the barest whisper. 'What's going on here?'

'Oh shit,' she breathed.

'What?'

She heaved the deepest sigh. 'I think we're screwed. We're really up the creek without a paddle.'

'What are you talking about?'

'Do you know what you've landed us in?'

'I? Listen honey, you don't have to follow me everywhere I go. Okay? No one forced you through that gate.'

'Fine. I won't tell you, then.'

'Win.' My voice must have sounded a warning. The skin on my back crawled, itchy with sweat.

'Okay then,' she said after a pause. Her shoulders drooped as if in defeat. 'We're in a vortex. A negative magic vortex.'

I could only stare at her, my mind racing through all of the Venerable Nachtan's lessons on the ancient Greek witches and their philosophies of magic. Nope, nothing came to mind. My shoulders twitched uncomfortably. Negative magic? 'What the hell is that?'

'It's exactly what it sounds like,' she snapped, suddenly flaring back to life. 'And it's your fault!'

Her eyes were burning black as she glowered at me through the darkness. The trees had grown even closer during our exchange, imperceptibly moving when I took my attention off them, like in a game of statues gone horribly wrong. I fought against the pure terror coming to a boil in my gut. I had no idea what Win was talking about, or how we possibly could have caused this situation, but I was seized with the need to make things right because something in the air was very, very wrong.

'Well, whatever,' I said, my teeth clenched against the bile in my throat. My hands were shaking, and it wasn't anger, it was a purely physical reaction, a message from my body to get the hell out of there. Wherever *there* was. 'How do we get out of this?'

'There's one way, and only the one way. I don't see how it can work, not with you.'

'I'm losing my patience here, Win.' And was about to lose that fantastic lengthy feast, too. The honeyed rose petals were not sitting well with the garlic and thyme shrimp. 'What do we have to do?'

She looked up and stared at me. 'We have to drop the negativity.'

'For the love of... Win, never mind our personal politics.' My whole body was breaking out in a sweat.

'See? You're not willing to let it go. We'll never get out of here. And I can't do it by myself because you're here, and you're attracting the vortex!'

'What, do you mean that somehow we've created this... this weirdness that's happening?'

'That's what I've been telling you!'

'It's not just me, Win,' I retorted. My legs were starting shake now. 'It takes two to tango.'

We stared at each other, feeling the pressure of the trees all around us. And then – another swoop of wings, closer to our heads and another. I could have sworn I felt claws lightly catch the loose hairs on my head, yet there was nothing to see. I huddled closer to her.

'Dammit. What do we need to do?'

She turned to face me and took both my hands in hers. 'We have to shut our eyes and disbelieve the negative.'

'The negative magic? The vortex? Which?'

'All of it.' She closed her eyes and drew a deep breath. 'We must not feed the vortex. We must trust each other and loosen the barriers between us.'

After a pause, she opened her eyes again. 'Come on! You need to do this. The vortex is feeding off the negativity.' She'd forced the calmness into her voice, the patience. I could tell it was false.

'But what *is* this thing?' It was a dark force, it was sucking at the very air we breathed, taking the oxygen out of our lungs.

'Christ Dara! Do you want to get out of here or not? We haven't much time left.' She panted as she darted a frenzied glance at the woods all around. The garden had grown perceptibly darker as the reflected light of the city was cut off by the height of the trees now towering over our heads. 'The vortex happens when magick is forced in on itself. There's no presence of the nuns here to temper it, and so when we walked in through the portal, we hit a pocket of magick. You felt it too! And now it's feeding off the feelings between us.'

As if those feelings were all my fault. If she wasn't such a ... If she hadn't ... I opened my mouth to argue with her, but she cut me off.

'It can't end well,' she warned, allowing the fear in her voice again. 'Do you want to end up as a ghost in the Imperial Garden? Because that's what will happen if we don't work together on this!'

I took a deep breath, as much as I could. Whatever. The magick was now building like maggots crawling all over my skin. Perhaps she was right this time. 'Okay. Let's do it.'

'You have to trust me. We will close our eyes and walk. Clear your mind of everything but awareness, be mindful of the bond between us that we are creating.'

'Which direction will we walk?'

'I will lead, if you allow me. Yes? Do you trust me?'

I nodded, then realized she probably couldn't see my action. I swallowed. 'Yes. I trust you Win.' I had to work to shut off the voice which nastily whispered I didn't have any choice in the matter.

'Walk to your left. My right. Slowly.'

We began to move, like a slow dance, one step and pause. Another step and pause. The wind had picked up in that short space of time, like a tornado touching down, then it grew spinning and whirling through the branches of the cedars. I could almost feel those soft arms brushing against me, reaching out to grab us.

'Pay no attention to the things you think you hear and feel.' Win's voice was a soft murmur, a small oasis of peace in the whirlwind around us. I held on to the sound like a lifeline. 'These things are not real. Keep your attention only on the bond between us, the magical bond we are creating. Let Peace be.'

But there was no peace outside our small bubble. The trees, or unseen creatures within them, were murmuring, growing excited, I could picture sharp teeth reaching out to us.

'Stop that flow,' Win said softly, not ten inches from my ear. She understood how difficult this process was. 'Just be aware of you. Nothing can touch you.'

Not even the dragon which swooped yet again, screeching in its defeat. A single claw ripped through my hair as the wings beat all around us. I steadfastly held on to Win and her voice, refusing to allow myself to become a meal for a dragon which wasn't even real.

And then, suddenly, all was silence once again. The wind died as fast as it had begun, the dragon was no more, I could even sense the trees had retreated. I took a grateful gulp of the rich air in the garden. Win stopped her slow crab-walk to the side, but her hands remained in mine.

'Are we there yet?' I breathed. I could no longer feel that terrible vortex of magic, yet the air still wasn't totally mundane and clear.

'You can open your eyes now,' Win replied. Her voice was soft and gentle. She let go of my left hand and moved to my right side.

The night was no longer so dark. The white marble pebbles glowed slightly, but it was a natural glow from the purity of the stone, nothing other-worldly or magical about it. The trees once again kept their distance, spotted here and there about the garden, and the smell of the flowers was not overwhelming, as befitted a garden in winter.

I looked about in wonder that the magical storm had dissipated without a trace. 'You did it.'

'*We* did it,' she reminded me.

Behind me also, all was as it should be. 'How do we get out of this garden now?'

She shrugged. 'Dunno. I totally lost my bearings somewhere there.'

I looked all around me again, full circle this time. There were no landmarks beyond the trees, nothing to show where we were, except a solitary roofline, far above our heads and some distance away.

'Let's head over there,' I suggested. 'Looks like that building is on a rise. There should be a way to climb up and get the lay of the land. It's high enough that we'll be able to see where the Palaces are.'

The path led directly to the structure, and once we cleared the cedars, we were at the bottom of a small hill. It looked artificial, as if a giant child had built a hillock from a load of giant-sized pebbles. We stood at the foot and gazed up.

'Looks like there's a gazebo way up there.'

I nodded in agreement. 'There should be a way up to the top?' I sounded doubtful because I could see no stair way or path through the jumble of rock.'

'Perhaps at the back.'

We set off to circumnavigate the hill. The path, now concreted and well-used with a low barrier fence protecting the hill, led through huge pine trees all around it. We walked all around, yet found no route to the top.

At the front of it again, I held out my hand to stop Win. 'Wait – there, in that shadow. Is that a doorway?'

Curious and curiouser. A doorway set deep into the center of this manmade hill of white marble. This was a terribly strange land.

'It is!' Win jumped over the short barrier to make her way to the wooden door, almost invisible in the shadows.

And it was at that moment that I saw the Chinese lion's head carved out of the white marble. It was terrifically lifelike and fearsome. As was the dragon next to it. Like a large gong sounding in my head, I suddenly knew where we were, and what lay beyond that door.

CHAPTER 24

I recognized it.

'Win! Wait.'

She paused, already over the fence. I didn't know how she was managing these acrobatics while still wearing those Jimmy Choos or whatever her footwear was. 'What?'

'The hill, look at it. Does it remind you of something?'

She drew her head back and looked up at the surface of the wall. The rocks of which it were made were white marble, but had been weathered through the century, picking up smut from the city's pollution, and with lichen growing in the shadows. Time and weather had also played their part in wearing down the details so that the carvings were barely noticeable.

'The walls of Li Minh's cave!' I couldn't wait for her to figure it out for herself.

She stepped back from the low concrete wall in order to take in the larger picture. 'Perhaps there's a resemblance, but —'

"Look.' I jumped over the barrier myself to point out the carvings. My fingers traced the wide mouth and the sharp teeth of the nearest animal. 'The Chinese lion, right? And over here, this is definitely a dragon. Don't tell me you can't see that.'

'Oh. Now I do.' Her brow creased. 'But it can't be. This is a mere coincidence. Do you know how common these motifs are in this land?'

'They're made the same way,' I insisted. 'Marble rocks with carvings on them, all piled together to form walls.'

She shook her head. 'No. Li Minh is in Tibet, or Tajikistan, or somewhere isolated like that. She removed herself from society. This, this must be the Hill of Accumulated Elegance. In the Forbidden City. Dara, we're smack in the middle of Beijing here. Li Minh could not possibly be inside this hill. She would have been discovered long ago.'

I thought of the eighty thousand daily visitors to the Palace complex. A large proportion of them would pass by this hill, each and every day. I looked again at the sturdy iron lock on the shadowed door, then up, up to the gazebo perched on the hill high above. We had walked all around this unnatural structure and hadn't discovered a route to the top. The inside of the Hill of Accumulated Elegance was inaccessible.

'Where is the best place to hide a book?'

'What book?'

'In a library,' I said, not bothering to explain the reference to her. 'Think about it. It makes sense, in a way. Nobody can get in here, right?'

We both looked back up to roof of the pagoda. She nodded in agreement.

'And although the magic has been pushed into cells around the nunneries, that was definitely a cell of magic we walked into just then, right?'

She nodded her head again, much more slowly this time.

'So, it's entirely possible that Li Minh has been hiding out here for years, don't you think?'

Win sighed. 'Well, even if she is, what good does that do us? Should we knock on the door, and shout her name? Do you really think she'd answer?'

'We have to warn her somehow.' Warn her about Margaret Forsythe. My heart still ached when I thought about it, but I pushed that out of my mind in favor of action. 'Help me with this, Win.'

The two of us approached the narrow entrance set deep into the artificial hill. The door was blackened with time, and had no handle to pull. No hinges were visible either, only that solid iron lock with a keyhole. We pushed, but it was a half-hearted attempt for we both knew it wouldn't budge.

'Li Minh?' I whispered into the planks, and lifted my hand up to knock.

'Don't bother.' Win scuffed with the toe of her delicate sandal at the accumulated dirt against the wood. 'This door hasn't been opened in eons. Look at how the leaves have rotted and piled up against it.'

I stared at the door a moment. 'How else would anyone get in? There's no path up the hill – it would even be hard to climb it.'

'Only the birds have access to the pagoda on top,' Win agreed.

'Birds who can fly.'

'Well, that's not us.' Win turned away from the door. 'It's no good, we can't get in there. Even if Li Minh is here, we have no way to reach her.'

I could fly up to the top. Win had no idea of that power of mine. Margaret had taught me that trick in the desperation of the moment on Tomnahurich in Scotland. But this was not the time to admit it. Not even for the possible chance of saving Li Minh from a curse. No.

But. I looked more closely at the keyhole set deep within the door, and I saw that I'd been mistaken. Instead of a regular slot, it was circular in shape. A round indent, with four spokes like a wheel. The thought struck me like a brick wall. 'Jesus, Win,' I said. 'The key.'

'Yeah, we need a key. We'll never get in. Come on, it's time we went back. I'm feeling the magic rise again. I don't want to be stuck in this garden anymore.'

She was right. Like a barometer rising, I could feel the surge of magic building even in the short time we'd been busy trying the door. 'But, the object, that jade thing the Empress gave me for you.'

'That's a circle, a disk, not a key!' But she stopped and slowly turned around again. 'Do you think?'

'Look at it – it's exactly the same shape! It's worth a try. Why else would we have been given it? In all the stories, the heroes are given a magical object for a purpose, it's not just a whim of fate.'

She was so slow to act, I felt I might have to do it for her. 'Do you have it on you?' I urged her.

Win nodded, then withdrew a little silk purse from inside the bodice of her dress. Even in the dusky light I could see the fabric glowing bright red. She undid the flap and lay the small jade circle in the palm of her hand.

'Come on, what are you waiting for?' The wind had been slowly but steadily rising, bringing with it that over-powering scent of blooms which had first heralded the magic storm earlier in this garden. I heard a flap of wings again from a distance.

She took a deep breath, then strode back to the door. I stepped out of her way.

'I still don't think this is a good idea,' she muttered. Her hand hesitated as she reached out with the jade, then she turned to me. 'You do it.'

'Fine.' I snatched it from her. The jade was cool in my hand, and fit perfectly in my palm. I fitted it into the circle, where it rested for a moment, but then a mechanical sound of locks unlocking and gears whirring.

We both stared in awed fascination until the door was quiet again. Then, with the slightest push of my fingers, the portal opened slowly to reveal a pitch black space within.

'Do you think...?'

I nodded. 'It has to be Li Minh's cave,' I said. But I didn't add what was on both of our minds. If the great witch was in here, why was it so dark inside?

Win's gown rustled as she reached into the bodice again. That dress must have an amazing construction, for there were no hints from the outside that anything lay between the silk and her skin.

She blew on whatever it was she'd removed and im-mediately a light glowed from her hand. It was her own slim piece of jadestone, her 'familiar'. The other young witches on Scarp had used wands for this purpose, but Win's was a piece of jade. These tools were used to store the magic in like a battery, so that when called upon, the witch could set it and forget it.

The light was faintly greenish in tone, like her jade, but it shone bright enough to show us the narrow corridor ahead. As with the outside of the hill, the interior walls were created from carved bits of white marble, but with the difference that these had never been exposed to the weathering elements. Each carving gleamed brightly, the faces of the animals jumping out at us in sharp relief through the shadows as Win passed with the light in her hand.

I knew without a doubt what lay ahead of us. The cavern was too quiet, too dark, and the vision Win had conjured in the temple had been too specific.

Neither of us made a sound as we crept through the short corridor. We were both holding our breaths.

And then, there she was, exactly as we'd seen in Win's vision. Her conjuring had been true, with only one exception. Margaret Forsythe was nowhere to be seen. She must have come and gone already, I thought bitterly, not wanting to linger at the scene of her destruction.

I was seized with a sense of déjà vu. This venerable and ancient witch was lying in exactly the same pose as Nachtan had been, flat on her back with her hands folded on her chest as arranged by a mortician in her coffin.

'Is she dead?' Win breathed. She moved closer to the sleeping witch, laying her hand on the soft cheek, the skin so thin we could see the veins through it, even from my distance. Then a sigh of relief. 'No, she's sleeping.'

She turned to me. 'How do we wake her up?'

I shook my head. I'd already tried that route with the Venerable Nachtan, and hadn't been able to get a gig out of him.

'It won't work,' I told her, and could hear the sadness in my own voice. I walked over to her, to offer comfort to those slumped shoulders. An object caught my eye and I stifled a gasp. There in the farthest corner of the floor lay a replica of the globe I'd picked up at Nachtan's. This couldn't be coincidence. I took the three steps to reach it and bent to pick it up.

It lay in my hand, giving off no sensation, no fingerprint of magic, just like the other one. As I studied it, rolling it back and forth in my palm, I thought hard.

This object had something to do with the curse, but what? How? With not a whiff of magic on it, how could this simple glass globe be linked to a spell so powerful it caused the strongest witches in the world to sleep?

I held it up to the light from Win's lamp, in order to study it closer. Like the other glass orb, it was dark, yet reflected light. As I stared into its depths, willing the object to tell its story. I saw a movement in the reflection, a movement that hadn't been there a moment before, creeping silently down the spiral stone staircase which must lead up to the pagoda above.

Our eyes in the tiny reflection with a flash of recognition.

'Margaret!' This burst out of me as I whirled around, as if by saying her name, I could pin her down.

CHAPTER 25

We stared at each other through the dimly lit room

'What have you done, Margaret?' It was only after the words came out that I realized they were a mere whisper of horror, not the shout of anger I'd intended.

The single flame of Win's light danced as she leaped back in fright, away from the staircase and the powerful witch. The shadows jumped, lending animation to the carved animal faces in the walls.

Now the scene was just like in Win's vision, just like that afternoon in the temple off Lijiang Alley. Margaret stood tensely on the stairs, her eyes glittering like broken glass, unable to contain her rage. She lifted a finger to me, I automatically threw up a shield to deflect any shrapnel she might throw my way.

On seeing this action, Margaret gave a disbelieving laugh, but her digit remained pointed directly at me as if in accusation.

'Look at you,' she said. The disgust in her voice made me shiver. 'What have you become?'

I pulled myself up straight. I refused to be cowed by her. 'Look at this,' I tersely threw back at her, moving my arm around the room.

'Sorry to interrupt your *good works*,' she spit. 'You've really gone and drunk the Kin koolaid, haven't you?'

'What are you talking about?' We had caught her red-handed in the act of laying the curse on Li Minh, and she was trying to make *me* look bad? Talk about gaslighting at its finest. 'I've been trying to defend you all this time. And why haven't you answered my calls? Yesterday, you were there on the mountain. Why didn't you speak to me?'

'Trying to trap me, more like,' she muttered. 'I've had my eye on you, and believe me, I'd not fall for your tricks. Why do you think Cate wants you to reach me?'

'It wasn't Cate that wants you,' I said. 'Well, it was, but I wanted to warn you, apart from that, because they were trying to blame you for all this - the Great Zande, Nachtan, and now Li Minh.'

We both looked toward the slumbering witch.

'But my eyes are open now.' The bitterness dripped from every word. 'They were right. I guess Cate knew better than me.'

Margaret narrowed her eyes, shook her head and opened her mouth, probably to spew more of her vicious lies.

'And,' I said, not bearing to hear another word from her. 'This is what you came back for. Not like you to leave something behind.'

I thrust the glass sphere in her direction like a sword. She slowly walked down the remaining steps and looked at it, but I held it firmly in my grasp.

'No, you don't.'

She paused.

'You're very careless, Margaret. It's rather disappointing, I expected better from you.'

Her eyes flashed up at me, but her face was a blank.

'You left the last one too, at Nachtan's cottage.'

'Did I? Hadn't noticed. And where might that one be now?'

'Safe with Cate, where this one is going also.'

She sniffed. I thought at first a putdown was coming my way, but no, she really was trying to grasp the scent of the ball. 'There's nothing on that to tie it to me. Or any witch.'

'Except for the fact of your presence here, which Win and I can both attest to.'

'I came because...' She cut herself off abruptly.

'Yes? What excuse do you have for being here in the Imperial Garden?'

'I came because you were calling me,' she said softly.

My hand squeezed the glass orb so hard I thought it might break. But no, it was made of far sterner stuff than that. 'That's bull, and you know it! I've been calling you for ages, and you never showed up. I certainly didn't request your presence this evening!'

'Those other times, you called for me with deceit on your mind, trying to trap me for the Kin,' she said, her voice level. 'Do you think I'm stupid, that you could fool me in that way?'

I had no answer for this. None at all. 'But I didn't call you this evening,' I protested again, much weaker now.

'No, but I could tell you were in danger.' She smiled. A genuine smile, it looked like. 'You still haven't learned to reign things in, have you?'

Her truth hurt, it cut so cleanly through my self-illusions. 'Were we really in that much danger?'

She laughed. 'You summoned a Wind Dragon and got yourselves wrapped up in a negative vortex! How the hell you made it out of there alive, I have no idea.'

I heard Win gasp behind us. We'd both forgotten she was there.

'Jesus, Dara, how did that happen?' Win asked. Her eyes were unnaturally huge in her pale face, and she had squished herself against the wall, to the point in the room farthest from Margaret.

'I didn't...'

'Yes, you did,' Margaret said, very patiently.

I swallowed. I had? 'I didn't mean it...'

'And that's the worst of it! You chose not to come with me to learn all I could teach you, instead, you've thrown in your lot with the Kin, who want nothing more than to stifle any creativity you have.'

'How... ' Win stuttered. She looked so young and vulnerable and afraid, and it was costing her a lot to speak out. 'How do you know about the Wind Dragon?' This was almost a whisper. She'd aimed the question at me, but it was Margaret who answered.

'She doesn't, it's quite obvious,' she told Win. 'If she did, she would have stayed well clear of it.'

'The Wind Dragon is Chinese,' Win persisted., her voice gaining strength. 'How do *you* know about it? I've studied extensively, and am only now unlocking the secrets.'

Margaret smiled at her, almost kindly. 'I only know of it because while my body was locked in the underground Vaults in Edinburgh for a century, my mind was free to travel and learn. I spent many years in China and

Tibet, watched the history and battles between Kin and Mundane unfold.

'Unlike you,' she continued as she turned toward me, her voice as soft as it was dangerous. 'Whose body is free to go where you wish, to travel where you want, to chase any dream you have, yet you insist on locking your mind away in a box and being prisoner to the ideologies fed to you.'

While my attention was on Win and her reaction to Margaret's words, the older witch walked lightly over to me and plucked the glass orb from my hand. I snatched back at it, but she'd just as quickly stepped out of my reach.

Margaret held it so that it was between her and Win's light, as if trying to peer inside it.

'I didn't do anything to it,' I told her. 'I just picked it up.'

'Do you even know what this is?' She asked me, then sniffed it. Then strangely, she held it to her ear, listening, like one would hold a conch shell at the beach, to hear the ocean.

'Somehow, you've been using these for your spells, your curses,' I said. 'But you're safe. You managed to keep the taint of your magic off it, however you did it.' I turned away from her. I couldn't bear it. I'd worked to clear her name within the Kin. Sought her out and been ignored. After all that, here I had the proof that she was responsible, as Cate had declared.

'But why, Margaret? What's the point?'

'You,' she said slowly. Her tone was flat. 'You have no idea, do you?'

I glanced up at her, trying to catch the meaning of her words from her expression, but her face was a mask. Her wide generous mouth was a grim line and her eyes were duller than I'd ever seen them be.

'What have you done, Margaret?' My question was a whisper again.

'Are you purposefully blind?' Her voice was a rasp.

I was almost happy to see her return to her normal acerbic state, no matter that it hurt.

She shook her head decisively. 'When you're ready to return to the fold, call me,' she said. 'But not until then.'

Margaret passed up the steps again, her dark garments mere shadows in the light. I didn't see her again that night.

'We have her!' The hoarse whisper reached through my thoughts.

I wrenched my head back to Win, still huddled in the corner. I'd forgotten all about her again. She had her phone up to her ear and her eyes were now feverishly bright.

'Yes, inside the Hill of Accumulated Elegance! She escaped up to the pagoda, she has no way of getting away from there.'

I couldn't hear the reply.

'Yes, red-handed. Well, we also found Li Minh.'

Her chest which had been puffed out with pride suddenly deflated. 'Yes, she's asleep. Probably the same thing. No, I haven't, but she ran up the stairs to the pagoda on top of the hill.'

Her face frowned. 'I don't know. Okay. We'll try.'

Win looked up at me as she disconnected the call. 'Cate wants us to go up and disarm Margaret.' Her face grimaced with apprehension.

I heaved a sigh. 'Don't bother. She's long gone.'

'How? You think she's climbing down the sides of the hill?' She shivered. 'No way, that's too steep. Did you see the shoes she had on?' Win steeled herself and faced the spiral staircase, holding her light up to its depths.

'Margaret has flown the coop,' I said. Win had no idea about Margaret's talent for whisking herself long distances in a tiny amount of time, nor even about my own abilities to physically fly. 'Literally. Go on up and see for yourself.'

A wave of exhaustion washed over me. I leaned my back against the wall to let it take my weight, shifting to avoid the sharper bits of carving.

Win placed her foot uncertainly on the first step, then glanced back at me. 'I don't hear her up there. But we have to make sure. I don't want to go up alone.'

'Trust me on this,' I said as I further sank to my haunches.

She must have taken my word for it, for she bravely slipped up the stone steps, taking her light with her as she passed up the spiral. I waited below in the darkness, alone with the sleeping witch.

It only took a moment for light to return down the steps. 'She's gone,' Win said decisively. 'I looked all down the sides too, and can't see her.'

She slid down to sit next to me.

'What do we do now?' She sounded worried, as if there was something we might be able to do to fix the whole situation.

'Nothing,' I told her. 'Cate and the Kin will be here soon enough. They'll kick us out while they examine the place.'

'Why did you let her take that thing? It would have been valuable evidence against her. Not that we need it, because we witnessed her there at the scene.'

'I didn't let her! She grabbed it,' I bit out. I shoved down the suspicion that I could have held more tightly to the orb, or at least held it out of her grasp. No matter, surely. Cate had the other glass orb.

CHAPTER 26

J ust like the last time, the troop of Kin elders rushed
   into the scene. They set up strong lights inside Li
Minh's cave, the better to examine the sleeping witch.
No fewer than five doctors, of varying nationalities but
all of them Kin, poked and prodded and sniffed and
shook their heads.

Hugh stood by me, placing his comforting arm over
my shoulder. Win had no one to offer support, but she
had no need of it now that any threat of danger was over.
Her eyes danced while she peered through the bodies,
devouring every word spoken, and adding detail where
she could. She was in her element, having played a major
role in the night's events.

Hugh listened to this latest episode of the continuing
story of the downfall of great witches. I had told him
everything about my discovery of Nacthan. Everything
except the glass orb, as Cate had requested I keep quiet
about that.

'Pity you couldn't have held her,' he said.

Before I could protest, Cate broke off from the crowd circling the doctors. Her eyes were on me. Win immediately left off her running commentary and attached herself to our small group.

'Do you have something for me?' Cate asked, her voice low amongst the general hubbub. She held her hand out.

'There was another... there was a glass orb at the scene,' I admitted. 'But-'

'But she let Margaret take it back,' Win interjected, pushing herself forward.

'What's this about an orb?' Hugh asked.

Cate ignored his question, and her body tensed like a cat about to spring as she looked between Win and me. 'It's gone, then?'

I raised my head and simply nodded as I met her straight in the eye. I wasn't about to start defending myself against Win's accusations. It wasn't my fault Margaret had snatched the glass ball.

Cate gave a short bark of laughter. 'No matter,' she said. 'We'll find her through that.'

She turned away, drawing Hugh with her.

'I'm sure our job of finding Margaret would be a lot easier if you hadn't given the glass ball to Margaret,' Win muttered, her voice full of spite. The positivity field we'd built up had dissipated. She, too, turned to follow Cate.

'Wait.' I put my arm on Win's. 'Do you realize what Cate just said?'

'She'll have to put a search out for the orb,' Win replied. 'And that's how she'll track down the hag.'

'But-' I couldn't take this thought any further.

'Come on, if you're coming,' Win threw over her shoulder as she set off down the short corridor to the outside.

Cate had said she would find Margaret through the glass orb, *which we didn't have*. The one with no magic imprint on it whatsoever.

So how, then, would she know how to search for it? There was no way. Unless she knew the origins of the orb.

Which meant. I finally had to admit what I'd suspected all along. I had to wrap my head around what it meant because there was only one answer.

So many things crystallized in that split second, as the tumblers clicked into place and the mystery was solved, so easily. I had already known that this conclusion made sense, but I'd avoided it, for it was a terrible logic, a twisted logic of insanity. How Cate always seemed to be in the general vicinity when the curses were laid, making it handy for her to show up at the investigation scene.

Cate's in-depth studies of music and magic. Even the bloody crystals on the tree at Christmas that Cate so thoughtfully brought, so I didn't feel homesick.

And the orbs I found at the scene of the cursing, of course these weren't made from crystal, or glass, but from a glassy metal. Adamantite. The magic metal. She was the world's foremost expert on this substance, being the Huxor.

That moment of awfulness, the moment of realization lasted an age as time fell away in the light of this terrible truth.

This was the woman my father had been married to all those years.

I stumbled outside after the others into the crisp night air. I heard Margaret's name pass through the crowd like flame through a field of dry grass. The whole garden was suddenly crowded with people, a team of official guards laying out the perimeter with yellow scene of crime tape. Another group had wrestled huge spotlights into enclosed space, shining them up into the sky as if hoping to find Margaret lurking in the trees above. The white marble carvings of the hill stood out in sharp relief. Outraged panic squawked in a dozen languages.

How could such a thing happen right under the very noses of the Kin? They questioned and worried, worried and argued. How could a rogue witch have infiltrated their most esteemed witches and caused such a thing to happen?

And then they started braying for Margaret's blood, like hounds at the hunt.

My earring itched again, burning like a wasp sting.

I looked up to see Cate's eyes on me, the insufferable triumph shining through, the madness which perhaps only I could see, now that I knew to look. She saw my knowledge.

'Cate,' I whispered, my voice hoarse with grief for the days to come. 'Why?'

'Who's the most powerful witch of all now?' And she threw back her head and her laugh like broken glass etched its way deep into my spine.

No one witnessed my pain at this terrible burden which had been thrust upon me, the knowledge of the perpetrator of these crimes and at the same time unable to do anything about it, to bring her to justice. Not Hugh, certainly not Win. None save Rob, who as ever was hovering on the edges of the crowd. Our eyes met, and he turned away, then disappeared into the shadows of the night.

....

On the short bus trip back to the hotel, I felt a distinct lack of companionship. Hugh, Cate and Win had taken the first bus out. No one would sit near me, and I could feel eyes on my back the whole time, but they would quickly look away when I turned my head. Everyone, at least of the Kin Britannica, they all knew of my connection with Margaret, and there were enough Kin who believed I was cahoots with her to make me into the pariah.

I went to bed that night, but couldn't sleep. Not until I'd spoken to Hugh. It was late when he got back to the room, after midnight sometime. He sat heavily on the bed and bent to untie his shoes. His face was ashen.

'So.' I sat up and hugged my knees through the blanket.

He nodded as he reluctantly looked at me, his eyes bleary, but he said nothing at all.

'I get the feeling that my name is being linked with Margaret's,' I said softly. Someone had to say it.

After a moment, he nodded as he fiddled with his tie. 'Yes.'

When he looked up again, I couldn't believe the distrust I saw in that shadowed glance, as if he no longer knew who I was.

'Not you, too.'

He denied it too vehemently. 'No,' he said, then took a deep breath. He held it for a moment before dispelling the air from his lungs. 'But I would advise you to stick close to Cate or myself till we leave the country. There are enough witches, enough of the Covenanters, who know of your connection with Margaret, and they're putting two and two together to make five.'

'This is so wrong.'

'Of course,' he replied. 'I spent the past few hours in discussion with Cate, and she has a plan. If all goes right, she'll be able to capture Margaret and at the same time clear your name.'

'Cate!' I spat out before I could stop myself, and I slapped the mattress with both hands. 'Hugh, don't you see this is all a set-up? Cate is behind this whole thing. All of it.'

He stared at me, uncomprehending and amazed.

'She engineered the whole set up,' I pushed on, talking way too fast in my rush to make him understand. 'Don't you understand? Remember the crystal balls at New Years? Her music and magic theory? She's throwing it into the face of the Kin, yet you all refuse to see.'

'Dara,' Hugh said, his voice taking on a dangerous patience. He sat up, his head and body fully turned toward me, holding himself tensely. 'You're not making sense. Cate is the only one on your side. She's the reason you haven't been lynched yet!'

I could only stare at him. My hands dropped limply. Did he even realize what he was saying? If Cate was my only defender, what did that make him?

He stood up abruptly and removed his suit jacket. The back of his shirt was damp with sweat.

'Hugh...'

'Like I said, stay close to Cate or me tomorrow. I don't want any accidents to happen to you. The Covenanters are all riled up. And I trust Cate to come through.' He shot me a bitter look. 'Although I sometimes wonder why she's bothering to save you. You're trying to turn these events on to her? You should be ashamed of yourself. Let go of the ill feelings, the childish resentments. She has done nothing but good for you, despite your past history. She's championed you in the Kin, remember.'

I slowly unwound my limbs from the knot I had tied myself into and, laying aside the covers, stood up. We looked at each other over the vast expanse of the bed.

'Hugh.' I had to try one last time, but I could hardly force the words out of my mouth.

His deep sigh stopped me. He was removing his clothing even as he spoke, and tossing each item on the closest chair. 'This is a real threat. Li Minh was cursed under the very noses of all the most influential, the highest ranking Kin in our world. The nerve of this, the brazenness of such an action cannot go unpunished. You do understand the situation we're in?'

He didn't give me a chance to respond before he went off on another tirade. 'This is devastation. It's no longer some kind of practical joke. Just drop your complaints against Cate, Dara, for your own good. Cate is the only reason Cromwell and the Covenanters haven't strung you up yet.'

'Hugh,' I began yet again, but he threw back the covers I'd just vacated and lay himself down on his own side of the bed. He flicked off the switch of the single lamp.

'Look, it's late, it's been a hell of a day,' he said, already preparing to turn his back on me. 'Can we not discuss this any further? You know where I stand.'

He'd made that abundantly clear, yes. I swallowed whatever I had needed to say. It wouldn't make a lick of difference to us. Not right at this moment.

I closed the bedroom door as I left the room, and paused for a moment outside it, but he didn't call out to me. The sofa in the suite would be comfortable enough for the night, not that I expected I would get much sleep.

Despite Cate's so-called protection, I knew I had to prepare for the worst case scenario.

If the worst came to worst. If the Covenanters succeeded in convincing the majority that Margaret and I were somehow responsible for this crisis, how would I fare? I was innocent, of course, and now I knew for certain that Margaret was too. But would my power be enough to fight off the combined forces of the Kin if they were set to lynch me, physically, metaphorically or magically – it didn't really matter what they chose if they set their minds to it. Because if the worst happened, I was finished anyway. There'd be no future for me anywhere in my world, no, not even in the furthest reaches of mundane society. They would hunt me down.

And if Cate withdrew her so-called protection? I shivered as I huddled into the inadequate single blanket. She could turn them on me as easy as flicking a switch.

And if the worst did come to the worst, where would Hugh stand?

CHAPTER 27

M y path forward wasn't any clearer the next morning. Hugh and I hardly spoke as we readied for the day. It was supposed to be a day of fun and sightseeing, free from the restraints of the endless talks and politics, a last chance to enjoy the wondrous sights that Beijing had to offer. But there wasn't going to be much of that, not with Li Minh down for the count and the Kin running scared.

Before we left the room, though, Hugh drew me into his arms. We stood there like that for a moment, in the warm familiarity of the other.

'Look,' he began. 'This will sort itself out, you'll see.' He gave a half-hearted pat on my back.

He was wrong. Things wouldn't sort themselves out. I had to intervene in order to save myself.

'What do you plan to do today?' A worried frown flitted across his face before he banished it.

'Keep my head down. What do you think?'

He held my shoulders in his two hands and looked directly at me, the first time since last night. 'Tonight,' he began. 'Tonight, Cate has a plan. She's going to draw Margaret in. Your name will be cleared then.'

'How is she going to that, did she tell you?' I didn't hold back on the bitterness which seeped through my voice. Cate would be tracking Margaret through that horrible obsidian glass and adamantite sphere. She could only do that because she herself had created the thing. I could scream with frustration. Why couldn't he see as clearly as I could?

'She doesn't need to tell me her ways,' he said, stepping back with a chill settling on his face. 'Can you not be thankful that she's saving your ass?'

Hugh turned and stiffly held the door open for me.

He switched on a smile and greeted a passing Kin couple. I faintly recognized them. I was pretty sure they were from Belgium. I glanced up at Hugh, his face was still set in a pleasant expression even though I knew he must be roiling inside. Just like me. Yet he was determined to keep up appearances.

Had this been my Dad's life for all those years with Cate? Unable to tell the world that their marriage had broken down irretrievably, keeping up the appearances for the sake of the children, the community and their professional lives?

But for what end, really?

Anyone seeing Hugh enter the conference room would swear he'd had a restful night, that there was nothing on his mind. Shoulders back and relaxed, he was in control. Not weighed down by a significant other who was suspected of driving a cannonball into the Kin.

'What are you doing today?'

Win, her bright red coat in her hands, perky and polished. I watched her watch Hugh disappear into the crowd. I shook my head. I had nothing planned, nothing except to get the hell away for a while to buy me time to think. I turned to go.

She followed me all the way out the main entrance like a shadow. Of Course. That was her job today, even though she would way rather be in the thick of things where all the excitement lay. I stopped, ready to lay into her and tell her to go away, when I realized, what the hell. Let her follow me. She'd do it no matter what I said to her, because it was her assignment for the day. It didn't really matter, anyway.

And it meant I wouldn't be totally alone.

I walked along the busy Beijing streets and she followed. We passed the entrance to the Hutong which held Lijiang Alley, and I looked straight ahead. No way would I return there ever again.

I had thought I might actually like Win, back then, that we could be friends. Not anymore.

Yet, I remembered on that day, our first in this city, when we were recovering from the weirdness of that alley and the jetlag. Win had turned to me, and whispered, no, she'd *mouthed* something right before Cate made her presence known. I stopped walking. She paused at my side.

Win had been uncertain whether she could trust Cate, or at least that's what I thought she had said. We'd been discussing the vision Win had conjured up, the one with Margaret and Li Minh.

I bit my lip, and looked at her from the corner of my eye. Could I even now try to get her on my side? What was the worst that could happen? She could tell Cate, and that didn't matter, Cate was already too aware of the situation she had created. We both began walking again. I waited until we'd passed a busy intersection. Directly ahead of us was a large park. I could see water and trees, a small respite from the hard concrete and metal of the city.

'You know what people are saying about me.'

Win didn't answer, not with words, but I felt her eyes glance at me.

'You were there with me, the whole time,' I added. 'Last night. You didn't leave my side. You know I had nothing to do with Li Minh's curse.'

'Looks that way,' she grudgingly acknowledged after a moment.

I felt the tight bond in my chest loosen, just a little. 'And Margaret. She was just arriving on the scene. Not leaving, as they claim.'

The pause was longer this time before she spoke.

'But she had to have been there before us. We were outside for a long time, there was no other way into the hill.'

'She has the power of flight,' I said softly, almost holding my breath to see Win's reaction to this news.

She stopped and whirled around to look at me. Her eyes were wide under her fringe. 'That's not possible.'

'It is. I know Margaret, and I've seen her do it.' There was no way in hell I was going to share about my own abilities.

'It's unnatural,' Win insisted, although her conviction was faltering even as she spoke.

'Is it? There's lots of legends about witches with the power of flight,' I reminded her. "Those myths don't just arise out of thin air, there's usually some kind of basis to the story.'

'But that would mean...'

I waited.

'That would mean Cate might be wrong,' she whispered. She shoved her hands into her coat pockets.

Our walk continued in silence for a while longer. I wanted her to think seriously about what she'd said, and to know this was a safe place to say it.

We reached the park gates and paused at the ticket office. Win waved her Kin pass and we were allowed into the grounds. Ahead of us, a white walkway led by the side of a lake. There were few people here this early in the morning.

'Do you remember our first day in Beijing? After Lijiang Alley.' I didn't look at her as I spoke.

She didn't reply as we continued along to a bridge. It stretched across the water to an island hill. The mound itself was lined with trees, but further up on the top of the rise stood a tall white pagoda. There were no other people on the bridge. We were quite alone here.

'We were in your room,' I reminded her. 'You tried to say something about Cate. You didn't trust her. But then she was there.'

Win was wavering, unwilling to admit it. I could tell by the way she hunched her shoulders.

'*She's* responsible for the curses,' I continued in a low voice, as quickly as I could. 'I don't know how she's done it, but she has. And tonight, she's going to draw in Margaret and capture her. But Margaret is innocent.'

'But it'll get you off the hook.'

'That's not the point!'

'No,' Win said after a long moment, but her voice was uncertain.

I hurriedly listed off the all my reasons for accusing Cate of setting up this.

'But why? Why would Cate Huxor do such awful things?'

I flashed back to Hogmanay, the pair of us sitting on the oak pew, staring into the mirror across the hall. *Who is the most powerful witch of all?*

'Because she can,' I said simply.

'Just, no. This is not reason enough. She has done a lot for you Dara. You can't act like this.' Win turned to head back in the direction we'd come from, back to the hotel.

She probably couldn't wait to tell Cate my accusations. Dammit, I'd misjudged Win. I should have known better. I followed her back along the route in silence. She left me in the lobby without even turning back to see where I was going.

It was all lost. I had no one on my side, or should I say Margaret's side. Using her own creation that was now in Margaret's hands, Cate would somehow summon the witch to appear into her trap. And the Kin would all be waiting.

Cate knew of Margaret's ability to fly, she would no doubt have all avenues of escape closed.

....

For lack of anywhere better to go, I wandered into the bar. In the daylight, it was as shoddy as hotel bars tend to be without the illusion of glamor lent by night and artificial lights. The long windows looking onto the sidewalk cast a gray light into the room, which only served to highlight the stains on the carpet and the dust on the bottles behind the bar.

I was done. I'd tried my best, but couldn't get anyone on my side. Margaret had no champions with the Kin. The only witch who had known her was lying in the equivalent of Snow White's glass casket, not a mile from where I sat on that fake leather stool.

I had no heart for filling my day with the glorious sights of Beijing. I just wanted to get through the day in one piece.

'Coffee,' I said to the bartender. 'With milk. No sugar.'

I looked into the smoky mirror behind him. The room was fairly empty that early in the day, just me and a guy hiding behind his morning newspaper. I narrowed my eyes and gave him a closer inspection. I recognized that cap.

I drank from my mug, keeping my eyes on that figure behind his newsletter.

Rob. He might refuse to have anything to do with me, but I could always try. He wasn't the first person I would choose to have on my team, but I was in no position to be choosy.

What could he do to help? I swirled the coffee in the half-empty cup, making waves. He was no witch, Hugh said he'd been a poor practitioner, so he wouldn't be of any help in an out-and-out magic battle waged to defend myself, which, pray to the Goddess would never happen.

Rob was a lawyer. Rob despised me, thinking I was just another Kin member seeking out power for my own advantage within the political organization. I couldn't blame him, because really? I had been that, and more.

He was a lawyer who had his client's interests at heart. That was enough for me, because so did I. I swallowed the last of my coffee, then stood up, ready to take him on.

He might be a loser according to the Kin, but, then again, so was I, by anyone's definitions of the term. I smiled at the paper screen he hid behind, and I prepared to pounce.

'Rob.'

The newspaper twitched. I was right, he'd seen me and he was on a mission of avoidance. I sat down opposite him at the round Formica-topped table.

'It's the end of the line for Margaret. The Kin are so sure she's to blame for the cursing, they're laying a trap for her tonight.'

'That's utter tosh.' The newspaper gave a defiant shake.

'What does that even mean?' Tosh. I'd never heard that word before.

'Rubbish. Trumped up charges. They have no evidence she's at fault.' The newspaper twitched again and he peeked out from the side of it. 'Do they?'

Just great. It sounded like even Rob wasn't sure Margaret would have done these awful things.

'They don't much care about evidence. We're talking Cromwell and the Covenanters. They probably won't even bother with a trial if they manage to capture her.'

The *Chronicle* slowly lowered until it lay flat on the table. Rob stared at me through his spectacles. The heavy frames weren't just a fashion accessory. The lenses were thick, making his eyes look like granite pebbles in the harsh morning light.

I'd never, ever known a member of the Kin to need glasses. Mrs. Battersea's spectacles were worn for effect and fashion, while Nachtan's *pince nez* were meant to convey his superiority. Flaws of eyesight were one of the easiest things to fix with magic. Hugh must be right, this guy was a genetic anomaly with little natural power in him. No wonder he'd renounced his place in the community.

He was going to be of no help at all. Still, two minds together had to better than mine alone.

'You haven't heard? Cate has some kind of plan in which she's going to lure Margaret in and somehow capture her and force her to uncurse the great witches.'

'How can Margaret do that when she didn't lay the curses to begin with?'

I darted a glance all around us. The bar was empty save for the bartender fiddling with something unseen behind the counter. I sent out feelers for anything that smelled like a listening device, magic or otherwise, yet there was nothing evident. Still, I couldn't trust the Kin not to be lurking in some capacity.

'Let's go for a walk.'

CHAPTER 28

M y second venture into the outside that morning. Again, we avoided the Hungtos and I kept us on the main street full of bustle and noise. I figured it was safer this way.

As we walked against the wind, I quickly told him everything I knew, or at least what I suspected. As I yet again heard myself reiterate the story, my heart sank lower for the whole thing was sounding more and more outlandish with every retelling.

Rob listened with a straight face, displaying no emotion whatsoever, so I couldn't judge how he was taking it. I just shoved my hands in my pockets and kept pace with him through the crowd.

'Let me get this straight. You believe Cate is using these black magic balls to somehow curse the great witches. She will, again using methods or magic unknown, use the ball that was used to perpetrate the curse on Li Minh to bring Margaret to a predetermined spot this evening, in order to capture her and turn her over to the Covenanters.'

'Yep.' Right. When he put it that way...

'And,' he continued, breaking into my thoughts. 'You suspect these balls are created from adamantite, which, of course, Cate controls.' He broke off and stared into the distance. We were coming upon a body of water, a lake and river system in the center of the city. Not the same artificial lake Win and I had visited that very morning. He leaned against the railing overlooking the river.

'I see.' Rob appeared to be conferring with himself. 'And Margaret is suspected, because?'

'Win had a vision in a temple,' I said. 'We saw Margaret in Li Minh's cave. It appeared that she had just cursed her...'

'But the reality of that vision was that you believe Margaret had just arrived on the scene, like yourselves.'

I nodded.

'And the common factor in each of the cursings, or at least the two we know about, is the dark crystal ball.'

'And me,' I added miserably.

'And Cate,' he pointed out sternly. 'Right then.'

I peered at him from under my bangs, hardly daring to allow hope to rise. 'You believe me?'

'I believe this is all possible.'

I leaned back against the railing. This was a start, a good start. 'I know you can't help, but it's a relief to know that someone else sees reason in all this.'

He peered at me through his thick spectacles. 'Why do you think I can't help?'

'You know, the whole magic thing.'

'Yes, the magic thing.' He was silent for a beat. 'What are you going to do about this? Are you planning to thwart Cate and the Covenanters?'

I laughed bitterly. 'I wish it could be done, but I don't see how,' I replied. 'If Margaret would only show herself, I could warn her.'

He cleared his throat. 'And on the mountain, you said you felt her around you,' he reminded me. 'Do you think it's possible she's keeping an eye out and is aware of everything that's happening?'

I whirled around to face him. 'No!'

He adjusted his cap and looked off down the river, saying nothing.

'No,' I repeated myself, a little less certain this time. 'Because if she did, then, she wouldn't have allowed this to happen. She would have set the Kin straight. Right?'

He shrugged. 'Don't know. I've never met the woman. She didn't bother introducing herself when you released her from the curse.'

'Ah. Yet you still came all the way over here, to try to get me to contact her?'

'I couldn't leave it any longer,' he said. 'The Kin had been sniffing around, which is what caused me to look into her Trust, to see how secure it was.'

'She's hard to pin down,' I agreed.

'So. All this. Are you going to try to contact her?'

'Right now?'

'Will there be a better time?'

'But we're in public,' I objected, throwing my arm out to encompass all the passers-by and the traffic on the road. 'I can't just call out to her here. I need to be, I don't know, on a mountain top, or a holy place.'

'Why?'

'You don't understand magic,' I muttered. The truth of it was that I didn't know why I thought I needed to be in a special place to call her. It just seemed right. After all, you had to treat magic with respect, you couldn't just use it willy-nilly wherever you were. Like by the harbor on a busy Beijing street,

'Won't hurt to try,' he said. 'Unless you're not actually as powerful as everyone says.'

The man was beginning to get on my nerves. 'Fine. I'll just call her, shall I?'

He leaned against the railing, crossed his arms and hooked one leg over the other. The classic waiting pose.

I shut my eyes tight. How had I called her any other time? The dragonfly brooch. That was how. This was useless. A waste of time. I pictured her in my mind, sending out feelers. Nothing, as I'd known. Not even a whiff of her.

I opened my eyes. 'Not working.'

'Hmm,' was all he said.

'Well, anyway,' I said as I pushed myself off the rail. 'I appreciate you listening and believing me.'

'What will you do?'

What could I do? Scenarios raced through my head, visions of me triumphantly rising and exposing Cate for the wicked witch that she was, of being lauded by the Kin and Margaret. Of all the sleeping witches brought back to life, and me being lauded as a hero, instead of vilified. I even threw in some fireworks, while I was at it.

But how could I get to that point? I didn't have a clue, and no flight of imagination could make me believe the Kin would be so easily swayed. There was no way forward that I could see.

'There's nothing I can do, I just have to let the whole thing run its course. Margaret will be captured, I have no doubt Cate has it all planned. I'll be let off once they have their scapegoat, as long as I keep my mouth shut. Cate will go unpunished because no one else believes how evil and self-serving she is.'

'I would advise you to be very careful,' Rob said, his voice quiet. 'There's a distinct possibility that Cate might *not* let you off. You know where the bodies are, so to speak, and she would be best served if you were out of the picture. Permanently.'

....

The night came too soon. Once again, all the Kin gathered inside the Forbidden Palace. I had to hand it to Cate, she sure could pull strings and charm her way into anything she wanted. The flashiest stage for her final showdown, for the performance that would convince the Kin she was their savior, that she was the most powerful witch of all.

If they only knew she'd already proven her power, used her magic and music to trick the most revered witches in the world into succumbing to her musical curse.

Would she ever lift it? I doubted it, for then they would surely tell the world what she had done.

And would she ever let me go? Again, doubtful. Although no one believed me about her, so she didn't really need to bother with the whole earring thing.

Hugh wasn't present that evening. He'd told me he would make it to the palace later, as he had something pressing to do. He couldn't, or wouldn't, tell me what it was. But his absence from the affair didn't auger well for me.

The large red wall loomed before us, and one by one, we all entered the central gate, the Meridian Gate. I could feel the excitement in the air, I could hear it in the voices all around me even if I didn't understand the languages. I pushed myself to follow in the wake of Cate and Win.

I hadn't been invited to the pre-game show, to watch Cate's preparations. Win had taken my place there. Now she proudly walked two steps behind Cate, her head held high, knowing that even her mere presence so close to the older witch had raised her standing in the eyes of the Kin. She could have it as far as I was concerned, but I had no opportunity to tell her this, as she refused to meet my eye.

I'd been excluded from their retinue, yet Cate had insisted I be present and close at hand. My fear was that this meant Cate might be planning to cut all ties with me. That she planned to tie up all the loose ends of the witches who knew about her misuse of power, just as Rob had warned.

If I was her, that's what I would do. Bury all the evidence, preferably six feet under.

I looked around the crowd for a familiar face. My eyes met Rob's. He had his cap pulled low over his forehead, and the glasses were gone in favor of his usual contact lenses. He did not acknowledge me.

It felt as though we walked forever, as we made our way into the heart of the Emperor's City. Up the stairs, down the stairs, through the magnificent halls, each successive room more awe-inspiring than the last. Cate led the procession, Win behind her, and me trailing off to one side, my heart growing heavier with every step.

The two of them were a good match. Both slim, elegantly wearing their silk dresses and their dark hair in elaborate arrangements. And the high heel shoes. Always the damn heels, as if the ability to walk in those things made them special. Me, I wore a dress but with the flat cloth slippers. I had nothing left to prove.

Finally, we arrived at the steps to the Palace of Earthly Tranquility. It wasn't the hall in which we'd feasted the previous night, but the next one on, the last of the great halls before the Emperor's garden.

I wondered if they'd moved Li Minh over to the Palace of Cherishing Essence to join Nachtan in his slumbers, or if they'd left her peacefully in her chosen tower, hidden in plain sight to all the thousands of tourists.

The courtyard was lit all around the perimeter by lampposts, with spotlights on all of the architectural details. Cate climbed the steps alone, just a few of them so she could be seen, and paused when she had reached the place with the best lighting. Her ivory silk gown shone brilliantly in the white light, her dark hair and red lips a foil for the flawless perfection of her skin.

She stood quietly, and slowly the hubbub in the courtyard petered out. In no time, the entire large courtyard was silent, and she smiled down at everyone.

'Thank you,' she said, her voice low pitched but carrying clearly across the space. 'Thank you for coming here tonight. And thank you to the government of China, for allowing us another evening here.' She nodded her head to the group of government Kin officials.

'As you all know, our world has been rocked by the happenings in the past month, by the attacks on our most revered members. And it's not simply one nation that has felt this evil force, but all. Africa. Britain. And now China.' She hung her head sadly, then lifted her hand to quell the murmurings from the crowd below.

All obeyed. It was as if she was casting a spell on them all, but there was no magic involved here. It was pure showmanship as Cate unleashed her charisma.

'We cannot... *I* cannot allow this to go on for any longer,' she continued. 'I have the means to bring the perpetrator here, to bring her to her knees. This very night, before your eyes.'

A troop of soldiers began to climb the shadows of the outer staircases on either side of the main one where she stood. They wore the uniforms of PANEC, the European Kin, and they looked like they meant business.

'I am uniquely able to conquer this witch, although she had unnaturally increased her powers so long ago, and although I am merely the humble guardian of our adamantite sources. It is because I have made such a deep study of this precious metal all my life, that I am able to give this gift to the international Kin. Of course, I ask nothing in return.'

This level of bullshit was making me physically sick. I looked around at the faces of those down below. They nodded and murmured to each other, praising Cate Huxor, elevating her to the status of unselfish savior of the Kin.

Fools! I wanted to scream at them all. They couldn't see, because they didn't know what I knew. They had no idea she herself had drank from the ley lines, had planned it all and risked her very homeland in betting that I could save the day.

Likewise, she had engineered this whole scenario. She'd maneuvered herself into the spotlight, had created the situation, had even learned how to cast a curse on the greatest witches. And now that they were all down for the count, she was poised for glory.

My very bones went cold as I realized the full extent of her plan. I couldn't listen to her anymore as she purred to the crowd and whipped them up into a frenzy against Margaret, for the blinders were falling from my eyes and I could finally see the full extent of her plan.

She had stated she would force Margaret to reveal her secret. But Margaret had done nothing, and the crowd were so riled up right then that they would tear her to pieces without a jury or judge.

The greats would never be released from their spells. Margaret would be dead. No one would ever know the extent of Cate's perfidy except me.

And I wouldn't last long either, I could lay bets on that. And then Cate really would be the most powerful witch of all.

I had to save myself. I quickly searched the crowd. Hugh had still not arrived. And not even he would be able to save me now, not with this crowd. Cate was now speaking of others who had assisted Margaret. At any moment, she would mention my name to the bloodthirsty crowd.

Rob. Our eyes met again through the crowd, and I could see he understood the way things were going. He moved toward me and I toward him, but before I could take another step, I felt a firm grip of iron on my arm.

'Don't go,' Win whispered in my ear. 'She wants you to stay.'

'Are you kidding me?' I turned on her, spitting out my words but keeping my voice low. 'She wants to kill me. You heard her. She said Margaret and her cohorts. Who else would she mean but me?'

Win's mouth gaped. 'No, come off it. Kill you? She just wants to keep you close so you don't mess things up,' she said. After a short pause, she added, 'That's what she told me.'

All of our past conversations were running through her mind, I could see.

'Remember you said you didn't trust her? You were right.'

Win shut her mouth and the grip on my arm loosened. I waited.

'My dearest Win.' Cate's voice crisply cut through the air. 'Please come up to join me. I'll need your help. And bring Dara, also. We'll definitely need to call on her powers for what we are about to accomplish.'

There was no escape now, for all of the hundreds of pairs of eyes were focused on Win and me. I could feel her tremble beneath the blue silk satin of her long-sleeved dress.

'I'll look after you,' she whispered. 'I won't let anything happen to you.'

I shook my head. She might even mean her words, but there would be little she would be able to do against Cate and the wrath of fury she had whipped up in the crowd. We mounted the steps, bright in the spotlights. I stood next to Win, conscious of how I must compare to the other two in their finery.

Then Win picked up the small wooden chest she'd carried into the courtyard. I'd forgotten about it. She held it out for Cate, who undid the clasp and opened it.

Win darted a quick glance at me once the contents of the box were displayed, then just as quickly turned her attention back to Cate. Yes, there were the black orbs, nestled in their red velvet nests within the polished walnut box. Five places. Four spheres. One missing, that would be Li Minh's, the one Margaret had snatched out of my hand.

One for the Great Zande, who slept in Africa. One for the Venerable Nachtan, who likewise slumbered just in the next courtyard over. One for Margaret.

And I knew that the last orb, sparkling darkly in the light of the spotlights, I knew with a certainty deep in my gut right then that the last one had my name on it. Once Margaret was captured, the crowd under Cate's direction would easily overcome me and I too would be damned to sleep.

Then Cate really would be the most powerful witch of all.

CHAPTER 29

D id we need more proof that Cate was the culprit? I didn't. Win, I wasn't so sure about, so snugly was she up Cate's ass. I couldn't trust her, even when she held the undeniable proof right there in her own hands.

Cate lifted her arm to silence the witches waiting below, although they were already rapt with the sight of her and she knew it.

'I have the means to call the evil doer to us this very night.' Her deep tone flowed over the waiting witches like warm, sweet molasses. She had no need to rush, for she had the timing and showmanship down pat. 'Through the magic of song, I shall call her here and she will be unable to resist.'

Jesus. What kind of unearthly magic had Cate created? She must have found how to mix the crystal and adamantine, replicated the target witch's own magic print, then tied the object to her irretrievably. An impossible task, but here she was. Here *we* were, with the evidence before us.

As long as Margaret still held Li Minh's orb in her possession, she would be drawn here against her will. My blood ran cold, as I stared down at the crowd below us. Each and every one of them watched her avidly, their blood lust rising.

With all eyes on her, Cate drew a deep breath. And then the music began. Pitch perfect, a single note started softly at first, then grew as she threw herself and all her magic into it. It spread out over the heads of all below, filling their ears, then rose up past the walls of the courtyard, up and ever up into the night sky. The music sought the echo in the orb Margaret had taken.

Cate was using her full power. I could see the outline of green sparkle and fizzle of expended magic dissipate all around her. Yet still she called to Margaret, willing the fifth orb to return to its nest and bring its carrier with it.

Margaret must have been close at hand, for suddenly the music changed, ever so slightly, not in pitch but in meaning and strength. It reverberated off the stone walls surrounding us and echoed until it was all our minds could comprehend. And then it did change in pitch, becoming ever so slightly discordant, yet still everyone was enraptured.

I could feel Margaret's presence was close. I could almost smell the sea salt crystals in her hair. Did she know what she was being drawn into?

I tore my attention from the sound. I had to act fast. A multitude of thoughts raced in my head while time stood still. The stud in my ear itched, warning me not to make a move, distracting me from the work at hand, but I ignored it. I no longer cared about my reputation within the Kin, no longer cared for my status. Everything I had was falsely gained through Cate's patronage.

None of the crowd of Kin below would question the presence of these spheres, what they were made of or what their purpose was. They couldn't see the contents of the box, only knew that the charismatic Cate was going to pull off something so stupendous, that it would be talked about in the magical world for years to come, and they would be able to tell their grandchildren that they were there that night.

These orbs were inherently, insidiously linked to the curses Cate had laid on the great witches. There must be terrific, awesome power in them. They looked to be made of polished metal, yet I had held them in my hands and they'd weighed little more than glass. Perhaps they were a mix of adamantine with a crystal component and the magic Cate had stolen from the ley line, if such a thing were possible.

If they smashed, would that lift the curses? I didn't know. Crystal could be shattered, I knew from when I had taken down the walls of the Ice King's palace. Taken them down with my voice enhanced with the magic flowing in me.

In order to do that, I would have to know the individual notes which reflected each witch, as Cate did, but there was no time to search them out. I had to act faster than that, if with much less finesse. I took the only option open to me right there and then, and I prayed it would work.

I had only a split second to find my opening. When Cate turned back to the crowd to smile on them magnanimously for the miracle she was about to perform, I took the two steps between me and Win and snatched the box from her hands. With the weight of the wooden chest and the momentum I'd begun, I had no choice but to keep going up the stairs. When I'd reached four steps above Cate, before she had time to react and stop me, I threw the open box down onto the cold marble beneath us.

And that's when the fun began. My mind was so focused that everything that happened next occurred in slow motion and every detail stood out.

The four glassy orbs hovered in the air, remaining where they had been thrown while the heavier chest smashed on the marble, even as Cate turned toward them, her hand reaching out and her voice wavering, wavering, losing its flow.

The orbs slowly gave in to gravity and all four of them began to fall, like an orchestrated juggler's act. First one landed on the step, then bounced high into the air. A second smashed as soon as it contacted the marble, the slivers of dark crystal flying off in all directions. Cate grabbed for the third, but it slipped out of her grasp and, like its fellow, met the same shattering fate on the hard stone of the steps.

Cate frantically snatched at the balls even as her music turned into a scream, like a juggler on a stage. She caught the fourth one inches before it smashed too, and on the rebound deftly grabbed the first out of the air. With a sigh of relief, she held them up to the crowd, victorious.

The collective gasp ran through the bodies below as she turned to me, her vicious smile revealing her small, perfect white teeth. She lifted her right hand and brushed her thumb against its shiny surface, and the thinnest note barely sounded, so thin was the music that it only reached the ears of the two of us standing close to her.

That single note emitted by the crystal orb went straight into my spine like an epidural, and against my will, my brain began to relax into the familiarity of that music. It was the musical equivalent of my magic print, and I could feel my whole wave pattern align, gently winding down.

And something deep inside of me yearned for this peace. I wanted to reach out and take that orb in my own hands, to caress it, and feel the spell like a gentle stream of water running over me, to disappear into the dreams it created in my mind.

This was how it was done, this was how Cate had overcome the most powerful witches of our world. And with this realization, my will to fight back sparked. I had to fight against the spell's magic weaving through my very blood using sheer determination. I gathered what I could of my wits and began my attack. I was fighting for my future. For my life.

I'd never honed my magic fighting skills, but I used what I had in my sparse arsenal. Mustering up ice-balls, I flung them at her but they melted on contact with her raven locks like the most delicate of snowflakes. The note spreading through my veins called to me, telling me to put down my arms, to sleep and to accept.

She spared a second to hand my orb to Win. 'Thrum it strongly,' she ordered. 'Put all your magic into it.'

I dimly felt the changeover, the new hesitancy in the note as Win accepted the sphere. I could even feel her thrill at holding my doom in her hand.

Red outrage fueled me. I pulled together my own magic and I bucked against the music, and against the pain in my ear from the stud. With a roar, I ripped that metal from my ear, tearing its tentacles free of my flesh, and I threw it down on the marble stair like a gauntlet.

My blood streamed down my neck and bodice, but I ignored it, even as it splattered red against the white marble.

I put my whole backbone into this fight for my life. There was no way I would allow Win, Win of all witches, to hold this power over me. I reared up and lifted myself up into the air to get a better fighting angle.

The voices in the crowd hushed, aghast at this evidence of my flight. I was quickly tiring though, and I knew I had to make my last efforts count. From the very depths of my core, I summoned fireballs this time, jagged streaks of flame, not even aiming anymore, but shooting them towards both my opponents.

Win jumped back as one of them found its mark in her lovely shiny hair, and I felt the pull to sleep lessen just the slightest bit as she swatted her head, trying to physically stop the flames from ravaging her hair. I used this moment to up my game even though I was flagging.

I aimed again at Cate, at her weak side, but then she rose to meet me, levitating over the stone stairs. Damnit! And I was the one who'd taught her to fly. My anger spiralled with a vengeance, but I was running out of weapons.

And then I saw from the corner of my eye Margaret, perched on the highest of the stone walls surrounding us, directly across from where we pitched our battle. Her red hair shone in the light from the streetlamps. Unfortunately, Cate followed the direction of my gaze, and with a laugh she held up the other sphere, Margaret's orb, high up above her head, her thumb lightly grazing the surface. The note that sounded was deep, mellifluous, even languid, much like Margaret herself with her lazy magic.

'Close your ears, Margaret! Don't listen to it. Don't let her magic take you over.' I called out, but even I could hear the despair in my voice. Margaret's body wavered slightly on the wall. If she succumbed to the spell, Cate wouldn't need to bring her to false justice, for the fall from that height would crack her skull and no amount of magic would ever heal that much physical damage.

I saw the glint of something falling from her hand to smash into glittering fragments on the concrete far below. Li Minh's orb. But it was too late now. Cate's spell was weaving itself into Margaret's nervous system.

All this while, Cate casually lobbed power balls at me with her free hand, the almost unseen bursts of power that were sensed only from the corner of the eye in the last moment before they hit. The effect was much like being slammed with a series of dodgeballs, not causing a lot of damage yet robbing me of all my breath and dignity.

During this attack, I hadn't noticed that Cate's note of my magic no longer had its grip on me. I glanced toward Win, who had stepped back from the affray, her face pale. She held the globe out as if she was afraid to touch it.

No one in the crowd below rushed forward to assist either Cate or me that I could see. Hugh of course was still not present, Cate had made sure of that.

But there – there was Rob, struggling to break through the crowd. Rob the Unmagickal, the genetically deficient Rob. He couldn't help in this unequal fight, but my heart warmed at the sight of his attempt. I renewed my efforts to dodge Cate's ammunition.

Cromwell held him back with both arms, the two were locked in an embrace but in the struggle he slipped out of his trench coat. He ran and managed to take two of the steps with one long stride before Cate turned her attention to him.

With a vicious sneer, she tossed a power bomb at him, knocking him flat on his back. She also took that moment to send a spiteful stream of burning energy, visible only as a green laser light directed at his chest, intent on burning his heart out. She laughed, the confident laugh of one who was winning the battle without even breaking a sweat.

'Margaret!' The scream ripped out of me. 'She's killing Rob! For fuck's sake, wake up out of it and help him! They'll kill us all.'

That finally got her attention. She slowly opened her eyes to the carnage below and dazedly shook her red hair out of her face. She teetered, but visibly pulled herself together, fighting the call of the music.

My magic began to falter. I could no longer hold myself up in the air, and there was no advantage to that, anyway. My front drenched in blood, I was almost ready to give up, with little in me to continue. I glanced at Win to see what kind of threat she posed and at that exact moment I saw her raise her hand in the air, the one holding my orb, and then she smashed the globe to the ground. The dark slivers lay there harmlessly , shining amidst the splatters of my blood.

We locked eyes and in that moment I saw the determination of her decision. She'd thrown her lot in with me, and in doing so was throwing away her future and all she'd worked to achieve. But then she squeezed her eyes shut. Above us, a dragon took shape in the air. Its fearsome maw snarled as it wove around Cate. It was only an illusion, this dragon, the fiery breath not even singing Cate's hair. But it served to distract her and stop the laser on Rob.

It also gave me the opportunity to take one last shot at the older witch. The final one. Because I had no energy, little magic left in me, and the blood still streamed from the wound in my ear. I hurled an ice ball at her, it took almost everything I had left, but it missed its mark and merely glanced off the side of her head.

It reminded her of my presence. Cate turned to me, red spots of anger in her cheeks starkly contrasting with the paleness of her skin. Her hand rose to swat at me like an annoying mosquito.

Mustering up everything I had, I got another blast of fire off at her. This one smacked her right in her face. She faltered, yet would have easily recovered if not for the sound that rang through the enclosed space.

Right at that moment, the two heavy doors leading into the courtyard smashed open simultaneously, the ancient wood cracking with the force.

Amidst the screams of terror, all heads turned toward the carnage of the splintered doors. A great cloud of dust arose, obscuring the sides of the courtyard. From its swirling depths first stepped one figure, and then another.

Nachtan and Li Minh. With the adamantite orbs smashed, their curses were lifted. The great witches had been awakened, and they were beyond pissed.

Shit was about to get real. I would have cried with joy, if I'd had anything left in me.

CHAPTER 30

Nachtan strode into the courtyard, his normally gray face livid with color for the first time in many years. Dust flew from his robes, swirling in the light of the spotlights as the crowd melted back to form a corridor for his passage. He approached the staircase with rage in his eyes.

Through the smoke, I saw Li Minh framed in the open portal to the Imperial Garden, her simple yellow robe flowing to the ground beneath her feet. She did not move.

Cate recovered quickly, seizing me by my shoulders, thrusting me in front of her.

'This one, Nachtan,' she called through the smoke of the dragon's fire. 'This is the one responsible.'

Of course, he knew the difference, as did Li Minh and Win. But the crowd below didn't. If she threw me down into the Covenanters before Nachtan could muster his old bones up the stairs, I would be finished.

And there was no one to lift a hand to save me. Rob had been securely trussed by Cromwell's cronies.

Yet, there. At the top of the stairs behind us, the Hall door opened. Hugh made his entrance. He stood stunned, looking at everything below him. From his vantage, my struggle with Cate was clear. I didn't know what it looked like to him, whether he thought I was attacking Cate or if he saw the truth, but his hesitation enraged me. No magic was left in me, my stores had been depleted along with the blood flowing from my wound. But I still had spite, and that fueled me.

Without thinking, I reached around and grabbed Cate by her flowing black hair, wrapping the length around my wrist to give me purchase. Hugh's eyes widened in horror at my action. That did it.

Perhaps it was my past as the despised half-blood spurring me on. I'd learned to fight dirty as a kid, learned to defend myself against the Kin kids in any way I could. On pure instinct, I yanked my hardest, angling her before pushing her with all my might, while at the same time letting her hair loose.

She'd been expecting something magical from me but that was how I overcame her. She stumbled over her broken wooden chest and then, in glorious slow motion, tumbled down the marble stairs, the smooth silk of her gown greasing her descent.

Margaret's orb fell with her, smashing to fragments on the way.

The entire courtyard fell silent, even Win's dragon ceased snorting. The smoke cleared and everyone could see Cate as she finally lay, unmoving, at Nachtan's feet. The dragon slowly dissipated into thin air, unnoticed now as it returned to the ether from whence Win had summoned it.

'Dara, what have you done?' Hugh's voice rang through the stone yard. Win gaped up at him in disbelief as I turned to face him.

'*What have I done?*' I repeated, my breath panting as I tried to find sense in his words. I'd just single-handedly taken down the evil witch of the Avalon, that's what I'd done. Had little help from anyone but Win, and Hugh hadn't been around to watch my success. I yelled up the steps to him, 'Where the hell were you?'

He drew himself up stiffly, perhaps affronted at my tone. Or maybe he just then realized my dress was full of drying blood, my hair every which way after my fight, and I definitely whiffed of dragon smoke. No doubt, I was offending him on many levels.

Hugh took a deep breath, and began to walk down the many steps. He looked first at me, then at Margaret still standing in the shadows of the far wall. And then his eyes fixed on Cate. Broken, lifeless Cate.

Below us, Nachtan had already set an unholy glow over Cate's head to keep her unconscious and stable while he directed Cromwell and the Covenanters to strap her to a stretcher.

She wasn't dead then. Maybe that was just as well. I didn't want to be branded as a murderer, and I wanted Cate to be alive to receive her full judgement.

We all watched as the witches scurried to do Nachtan's bidding. Their faces reflected their confusion at what had just happened, puzzled at how Cate had transformed from being the hero of the day to being the subject of the Venerable's great anger. But they obeyed him, nonetheless, for the Kin was a hierarchical organization. While Nachtan had no official title within this organization, for example he wasn't a Grand Master like Johanna, still he had claimed the title 'Venerable' and no one was going to challenge his orders. Much like the army, there was little room for independent thought. Its soldiers were taught to obey.

There was dead silence as Cate was carried out the side portal to the secure hospital wing, the heavy door leaning off its hinges after Nachtan's grand entrance.

He swept his gaze up the stairs, up to where Win and I still stood. He stared at me for what felt like an hour, but it could only have been thirty seconds. But in that short time, I felt he saw right through me.

I began to sweat in the hot spotlights, despite the coolness of the night. I could only imagine what was going through his mind. I had been specially chosen to study under him, the Venerable Nachtan. Look at the situation I'd gotten myself into now. He must be realizing what a wasted effort I'd been for his energies.

It couldn't look good for me. I'd just taken down the hero of the Kin. The witch who had called everyone here this evening, witches from all over the world, and who had promised to expose the evil doer responsible for the terrible deeds done to the revered ones. Was he going to demand that I too be seized? Would he hold that same golden globe over my head to subdue me?

I looked back at him with weary eyes, and I knew, right in the depths of my being, that no matter the outcome, I was finished with the Kin. I wanted nothing more to do with this falseness, with the politics. Power, even magical power, and wealth meant nothing if I couldn't have peace in my life. Peace and freedom to do as I wished. I wanted to be shot of this life, one way or another.

My eyes lifted up to Margaret, still sitting on the opposite wall. All this, I'd done for her, at least I had thought at the time, fighting to keep her from being wrongly accused.

But now I realized that wasn't true, not at all. I'd done it all for me, so that I could live as free as she appeared to be. I wouldn't have a trust fund to buoy up a beachside life of martinis and sun, but that wasn't my goal in life.

I looked back at Nachtan. He had followed my gaze to Margaret, and a soft smile almost lit the cracks of his face, the anger melting completely away.

Of course. He knew I wasn't part of Cate's nefarious schemes. There would be no jail time for me, no being cursed to end my days in the depths of the Edinburgh Vaults. Cate's face had been the last one he'd seen as he fell into his deep slumber.

He wouldn't allow the Covenanters to arrest me. I didn't have to fight to prove my innocence.

I saw in his eyes only kindness toward me now, and understanding, as if he knew more about me than I knew myself. He raised his eyebrows slightly, letting me know that what happened next was in my hands. That my life had always been my own to choose. I may not have made the best decisions all the time in my life, but they'd been my decisions, and they had led me to this very place. To the Imperial Palace in China, yes, but also to this major crossroads of my life.

I smiled back at him, my mind and heart clear and free now. Without further ado, I stepped over to Win and lightly placed my arm around her.

I glanced up behind me. Hugh had paused on his descent. His face was a mass of confusion. I would let him figure it all out on his own time.

'Nachtan, I present to you Win Chen,' I said, loudly and clearly so that all in the enclosed space could hear me. 'Win saved the day. She vanquished Cate, at much risk to herself.'

She started under my embrace, and half turned to me, to deny my words, to give the glory to where it possibly really lay. I squeezed her shoulder. 'Just go along with me,' I whispered.

'But you were the one,' she argued. Her face twisted in puzzlement. She began to shake her head. Her black hair gleamed in the spotlights. 'Why would you give me the credit?'

'Let's just say, this will make both of us happier in the long run.' I smiled at Win even as she stared back in consternation.

'No,' she said. 'I'll tell them the difference, what really happened.' She made to speak out to Nachtan.

I put my hand on her arm, staying her words. 'Wait.'

I looked at her, still looking perfect in her blue silk gown, not a hair out of place from her elaborate updo. Then I looked down at myself. I was bloodied, dirtied and exhausted.

'But it was you who was in danger from Cate.' She wouldn't let it go. 'I... I was prepared to do everything she wanted. I was prepared to hurt you, Dara!'

I could afford to beam at her with forgiveness. 'Doesn't matter. What's done is done. You're planning to stick around with the Kin? Work your way up through the ranks?'

She nodded. 'Of course. It's all I've ever wanted.'

I laughed. 'I used to think that's what I wanted, too. But not anymore.'

It took a moment for my words to filter through to her. 'Wait. You don't hate me for what I did?'

I shook my head. 'Life is too short for that,' I said. 'Let's just say you owe me one, okay?'

'Win Chen,' Nachtan thundered from below. The long sleep must have cleared up his lungs, for his deep voice reached every ear in the courtyard. 'Win, you have done a great service for the international Kin on this night.'

Every single voice there began the chant, softly at first, then growing louder. Well, every voice except mine, and Win's and Margaret's. We were the only ones who'd actually seen what had happened. Win's dragon and its smoke had obscured the sightlines. All they'd seen was the flashy dragon magic and sparks and smoke emanating from the illusion.

The single word which floated up to us, repeated over and over, was 'Win.' Her name echoed amongst the susurrations in every language, starting softly then growing. I took her hand and thrust her arm up into the air, making sure the spotlight remained trained on her while I stepped back into her shadow.

Win. They were buying it. I could bow out. Which I did, gracefully, allowing Win in her gleaming blue silk gown with not a hair out of place to take center stage.

It was better this way. She looked better, too, more like the Kin's idea of how a hero should look. I scratched my neck, the blood had dried and itched like crazy now.

'What happened?' Hugh had come down all the stairs to join us. His eyes searched mine.

'Where the hell were you during all this?' I let go of Win and spread my arm out to encompass the courtyard, although the only evidence of the evening's work was on my physical body, and the slivers of smashed crystal lying on the steps before us.

'I was creating a holding cell for Margaret. Cate tasked me with this,' he said, a smidgeon of pride in his voice. 'But...'

He looked up across the courtyard to where Margaret had sat just moments before. The witch had disappeared. 'But she's still free.' That and so much more.

'I tried to tell you, but you wouldn't listen. It wasn't Margaret behind the cursing. It was Cate all along.'

I took another breath to rail at him, to blame him for his blinkered eyes in refusing to see evil where it had been, but I stopped myself. Why bother? All that I'd thought Hugh was, everything I'd pinned on him, but he was just a human witch. A product of his time and place. Hugh was the heir to a Duchy, and intrinsically linked to the Kin and their politics. He thrived in that atmosphere. He would never, could never renounce this life. It was in his blood.

But it wasn't in mine.

I thought of that horrid ghastly ring of his family's, and I shuddered. This was for the best.

'What, you're turning your back on me?'

I paused from my climb up the stairway and looked at him through my new vision. 'Hugh, actually I think... I'm sorry to do it like this, but I think I'm breaking up with you.'

'You can't do that,' he sputtered. 'Not here. Not like this.'

'I can. I am. But you know I wish you the best. Always.'

CHAPTER 31

I left the courtyard in my soft cloth slippers, not making a sound. I walked out on the Kin, and Hugh, and Nachtan, and in doing so, walked out on my whole life. It was a deliberate choice, although at the time I felt as if I was watching myself from a distance, as if through a glass darkly. One part of my brain cried and grieved for all I had desired, for the recognition within the Kin, for the orderly life, even for the easy paycheck.

But the real part of me knew this was the right thing to do. The only thing to do. I walked through the Palace of Heavenly Purity, hardly seeing the magnificence all around me, the gold glowing in the incandescent light. It was all so beautiful, the palaces of the Forbidden City and the hidden gardens, yes, but the opulence was overwhelming after a while. The accumulation of so much blatant wealth was sickening to look upon.

A nice place to visit, but I wouldn't want to live there.

I walked alone, up and down marble stairs, through the Halls of varying Harmonies. As I exited the last, the

Hall of Supreme Harmony, I felt Margaret fall into step beside me. We crossed the small plaza, and as we started down the steps leading to the gates, she spoke.

'She would never have fooled me, you know.'

I darted a glance at her. Her face was calm and assured. 'Don't be so certain of yourself,' I replied. 'I only understood how the spell worked after she was doing it to me. It was addictive, that music, that single note that was calibrated to each individual, so much so that I wanted to grab the sphere and do the job myself.'

After a pause, she muttered, 'Weak.'

I didn't reply.

'Well, what are you going to now?' she asked plaintively. 'You burned that bridge to nowhere. I don't see you being welcomed into the Duchy now.'

I shook my head. We'd reached the Gate of Supreme Harmony. 'I don't know,' I said slowly. 'I guess I'll have to rely on my own two feet, and see where they lead me.'

Before we exited through the grand gates, we both turned at the sound of running behind us. Rob. We paused and let him catch up.

He stood before us, still huffing a little as he collected his breath. His right eye was bruised, and his thick glasses sat askew.

'Lady Margaret, I presume.'

She inclined her head to him. 'Nephew Robert.'

We all turned and walked through the Gate of Supreme Harmony.

'Your trust fund has issues.'

'So I've heard.'

....

The Thai sun was warm on my legs as I sat half-shaded by the umbrella woven of palm fronds. I lay the icy glass back on the glass-topped table and breathed deeply of the salt tropical breeze off the turquoise ocean. This was, indeed, the life. All compliments of Margaret, for the next little while anyway.

It was the least she could do, considering everything I'd done for her.

I let out my breath, feeling the sun's rays wash away any lingering tension. My phone buzzed by my side. I glanced at it. Mom. Hmm.

She and Dad had received the expurgated version of the China trip and subsequent breakup with Hugh. I was putting off the inevitable scolding and drama. That could wait. I knew I was taking the coward's way out, yes, but I was learning to accept myself as I truly was. And if I was a coward, then so be it.

A shadow crossed my sunbeam, and I squinted up. It was just Rob on his way into the ocean. He'd discovered snorkeling in the balmy waters of the resort, the safe kind which didn't involve going into the water over his head. I smiled despite myself. He was surely the whitest white man ever, lathered as he was in his protective coating of sunscreen. As he picked his way down over the white sand with the flippers on his feet, he resembled some sort of stick insect with his long limbs.

He seemed in no hurry to return home to his law practice.

I closed my eyes again and thought of my week in China and shivered despite my tropical surroundings.

My ear was healed, just about, although Margaret said there might be traces of adamantite left in the scar. Who knew what effect that might have, later on down the road? I preferred not to think about it.

Cate was eventually brought to justice, of a kind. The Kin kind, that is, the sort of justice meted out to those who hold power and position, which is to say not much real justice at all. Her side argued that no one could prove she'd done anything at all.

Yes, all the great witches spoke of being visited by Cate, and being given the gift of the beautiful dark orb which sang so their name sweetly. For Zande, Nachtan and even Li Minh to admit they'd been cursed to sleep by the sound of that crystal, well, then they would have to admit they'd been playing with their personal orb, delighting in the sound of their name etched in crystal. In other words, that they'd each been absorbed by the vanity offered by Cate, instead of recognizing it for the shallowness that it was.

The orbs, having all been smashed in the courtyard that evening, could not be used for evidence. Besides, the adamantite and music mix was a magic understood by no one but Cate, and none of the Kin wanted to admit their personal ignorance by pressing the matter.

So she was basically free to do as she wished, live as she wished, as long as she didn't get involved in Kin politics anymore. With one stipulation - the Venerable Nachtan had insisted she never step foot in Scotland ever again.

Speaking of Scotland, I read in the *Kin Chronicle* that Hugh had moved on. He'd recovered from my abrupt departure quite admirably and had picked up his life as the shining star of the Kin. There was a big photo shoot of him and Win, her flashing the god-awful ugly ring of engagement. They looked happy, so I sent them my blessings from afar.

Margaret sat herself in the lounger next to me, accompanied by the tinkle of ice cubes and the swish of silk. 'It's time we talked. You made your big splashy exit from the Kin. So what's next?'

I shrugged. 'I hadn't been thinking that far ahead at the time. I was too busy saving your sorry butt.'

'Language.' She wrinkled her nose. No matter her power, or her buckets of money, or her love of modern luxury, she was still the grand Edwardian lady at heart.

'Seriously, I have no idea what happens next.' I slowly slurped the last of my drink through the straw, letting the fizz of air float the last few drops of sweet water over my tongue. 'It's been fun living like a Kardashian, and thank you, but I suppose I'll have to move on soon. Go back home.'

That thought landed like a dull thud in my heart. Home. After all I'd lived through, how could I ever fit back in there? I had Alice and Brin's wedding to look forward to, yes, but apart from that...

I loved my parents, even Jon, and couldn't wait to see them again. But to live in their home, I would always be their daughter. I wanted, I needed to be more. There was so much world to see, yet I had no means to travel. I had to flex my wings, but had no job prospects as a magic worker since I'd burned any bridges with the Kin. Unless, of course...

I slid my gaze over to Margaret. Her face was set toward the deep turquoise water. The waves gently lapped the shore, and there wasn't a sign of another human being in sight, save Rob's snorkel bobbing a few feet offshore.

'Yes, well,' she said, finally. 'I'm not planning to stay in Paradise forever, either. I have things to do.'

'Sounds intriguing.' I yawned and stretched, luxuriating in the sun's warmth on my skin, then casually added, 'Perhaps I could tag along.'

She sipped from her straw. Her eyes were hidden behind the huge designer shades. 'I don't know how long I could put up with you.'

I grinned to myself. I was in. That was as good as a declaration of friendship from the likes of Lady Margaret Forsythe. 'I'll try not to get on your nerves too much.'

She removed the sunglasses and lifted her clear green eyes to the cloudless sky above. 'You can't help it. You were always a very irritating witch.'

The end.

....

Dear reader, Thank you for being on this journey. We've come to the end of Dara's story, although, Margaret's last words lead me to suspect we haven't heard the last from her yet. Time will tell.

If you want more of my paranormal stories served with a side of suspense and humor, please visit me at LizGraham.ca.

Why not check out the *Potential Magic* series?

Eve Stratton is fifty-ish and feeling frumpy. Her menopause clashes with the hormones of her teenagers, while her boss wants a younger, hipper vibe for his team. Her mother is needy and Derek, her husband, is going through his own mid-life crisis. She spent her life looking after everyone, yet feels she hasn't even begun to live her potential yet.

Download the series prequel, Draw the Line

But then she meets the Coven, and her true powers are revealed. Join her on her trip through midlife and the discovery of her true self!

Get your copy of the prequel novella ***Draw the Line*** here or at Amazon!

ACKNOWLEDGMENTS

Thank you to cover artist James Helps. Your vision helped capture the essence of Dara's story. I love your patience and your cheeerful words.

Thanks also to Anita Stewart for your critique of this final story. Oh! I love your crisp way with words!

Fellow author Shelley Dorey. You give me the creative community so desperately needed, and your generosity of spirit has encouraged me to take the leap into fulltime author! Watch out world, here I come!

Last but never least, Bob Sirrine, thank you yet again!

And to you dear readers, of course. You know, you already have the magic in you!

ABOUT THE AUTHOR

E M Graham is the Fantasy pen name of Liz Graham. She is an author and artist, working out of her home in St. Johns, Newfoundland. She has a strange affinity for feral cats.